# ALICE SEES GHOSTS

# ALICE SEES GHOSTS

A NOVEL

**DAISY ROCKWELL**

BLOOMSBURY
NEW DELHI • LONDON • OXFORD • NEW YORK • SYDNEY

BLOOMSBURY INDIA
Bloomsbury Publishing India Pvt. Ltd
Second Floor, LSC Building No. 4, DDA Complex, Pocket C – 6 & 7,
Vasant Kunj, New Delhi, 110070

BLOOMSBURY, BLOOMSBURY INDIA and the Diana logo
are trademarks of Bloomsbury Publishing Plc

First published in India 2025



ISBN: HB: 978-93-61317-95-8; eBook: 978-93-61311-07-9

2 4 6 8 10 9 7 5 3 1

Typeset in Fournier MT Manipal Technologies Limited
Printed and bound in India by Thomson Press India Ltd

MIX
Paper | Supporting responsible forestry
FSC® C010615

To find out more about our authors and books visit www.bloomsbury.com and sign up for our newsletters

For sale in the Indian subcontinent only

*For Aaron*

# PART ONE

## GHOSTS

# 1

Nowadays when Alice spoke, she often noted confusion on the faces of her interlocutors. *I must still be speaking written language*, she thought, but was not terribly concerned. *They'll adjust*, she reasoned, and so did not bother to alter her precise diction and elaborate sentence structures. A lengthy spell, now over, of speaking not at all, or only rarely, had inculcated in her a habit of writing down her thoughts, both for her own benefit and to communicate with others. Now that she was back among the speaking, people unoriginally suggested to her that vocal cords must be like any other muscle, that perhaps they needed a workout too. 'Talk more, Alice,' they said. Alice found such observations trite, though she recognized they must feel the need to say something, anything, to address the long silence. And why not? It could be true. It was true that after she was cured of aphasia, her throat had hurt for months whenever she spoke. Her doctor had indicated that the physical pain might be partly psychosomatic, but she routinely discounted his medical opinions now that he shared her bed.

If there was one person who actually seemed to appreciate the way she expressed herself, it was her grandmother, Nanette, who lay dying, slowly, in the dining room of the family house, resplendent in her own grandmother's four-poster canopy bed. She was barely able to form sentences herself now, but this was not for psychological reasons. She had endured a series of strokes which made it difficult for her to move her mouth. Alice felt it less likely she herself had started to speak again due to psychiatric treatment than it was that she'd felt the need to fill the silences created by her grandmother's paralysis. Nanette had had beautiful diction and the loveliest way of saying ordinary things. Even if she was just saying things like 'can opener' or 'refrigerator', one always felt those common household objects take on a magical glow. It was through this alchemy that everything in Nanette's house had been rendered extraordinary, and numerous of her friends and relations had been inexorably drawn to that huge, peculiar, decaying house in the woods, staying on sometimes months, or even years.

When Nanette's ability to produce speech had declined, Alice felt suddenly as though she had been surrounded by harp music all her life without noticing it. Only now, the harpist's hands had dropped from the strings. When Alice first learned Nanette was ill and had taken to bed, it had been a shockingly long time since she'd last visited. Nine months, maybe, or even more than a year. She couldn't remember. As a child, she had spent her summers there, and various other chunks of time after her father had left them. Her mother, Clare, would become overwhelmed from time to time, unable to get out of bed until afternoon, hopeless in the kitchen. Debris would pile up around their small Cambridge apartment, and Alice, who was eight when her father had left, learned to feed herself with whatever was available, burning pots black and creating permanent stains on the small galley kitchen's countertops as she learned how to cook on her own.

'Was she depressed?' Alice's psychiatrist-turned-fiancé Ronit asked when she talked of those days.

'Oh, I don't think it was as simple as that,' responded Alice, always bored by clinical terminology.

When her malaise became unbearable, Clare would get up one day, splash water on her face, run a dusty brush through her tangled hair, and announce it was time to visit Nanette. These visits could extend for months. Clare would call the school and tell them that they had a family emergency. When asked by well-meaning school officials what provisions would be taken for Alice's education, she would reply that Alice was to be homeschooled. Homeschooling, for Clare, entailed occasionally asking what she was reading, and making her write letters once a week to her father, who rarely replied, and certainly not in kind. Alice's letters were long, usually at least four sides of two sheets of stationery, written in her small and perfect longhand (penmanship was one of Nanette's contributions to Alice's homeschooling). Alice was told to write to her father about what she was doing, but as she grew older, this topic seemed increasingly dull, especially since most of her time was spent reading, going to school (when possible) and burning things in the kitchen. At Nanette's she also helped with the sprawling garden and tried her hand at needlepoint, but she didn't think those topics would interest a Man of Business, as she had heard one of her aunts referring to her father.

So instead, Alice's letters were fictional diaries, detailing activities and feelings she herself had never experienced, but which she imagined her father might find worthy of interest. She wrote of girl-scout meetings, tea parties with friends and visits to historical sites. She once wrote to him in great detail about walking the Freedom Trail in Boston on the basis of a pamphlet she had found on the sidewalk near her house. Though the Freedom Trail was near where they lived, it had never occurred to her or Clare to actually go there. Another time she described a camping trip she had taken with her girl-scout troop in which they'd learned to start a fire without matches and how to catch and skin a snake, then roast it over an open fire.

During the sojourns at Nanette's, her letters became more fantastical, due perhaps to the more wide-ranging reading material, some of it inappropriate, most of it dated, that she found crammed in the bookshelves lining the living room, the library and the walls of the upstairs hallway. Did her father doubt, if he did indeed read her letters at all, that at the age of twelve, she and a group of school friends, under the supervision of a Carmelite nun, had taken a cycling tour through Tuscany, visiting the shrines of martyred female saints? The chaperoning nun was described by Alice as fully garbed in her habit, complete with immaculately starched wimple and veil. The heavy wooden crucifix she wore on a long chain about her neck made soft thudding sounds as it knocked against the handlebars of her three-speed bicycle. At any rate, she never got to know whether he'd read all those letters or not, as they received word when she was thirteen that he'd died suddenly, in a skiing accident in Utah, and so the letter-writing part of her education abruptly stopped.

Alice had learned about nuns and Catholicism from books in Nanette's library. She had read almost an entire volume on the lives of women saints before Nanette discovered it lying face down on the cracked and mossy paving stones of the greenhouse, open at a gruesome portrait of Saint Lucia with her eyes plucked out. Nanette had picked it up gingerly, as though it were a dead rodent, and carried it into the kitchen suspended between her thumb and index finger.

'Where did you find this work of paganism, my dear?' she asked Alice sweetly. She held the book before her, brow wrinkled with concern.

'In the library?' responded Alice, wondering if there was a right answer to the question.

'Goodness.' Nanette placed it on a stack of old newspapers in the corner of the kitchen.

Alice was engrossed in making cucumber sandwiches, something she had just read about in a novel from one of the upstairs bedrooms.

'They're never made on that sort of brown bread, you know,' said Nanette, glancing at the sandwich-making as she made her way to the sink to scrub away the contaminants from the book of saints.

'There isn't any other kind,' explained Alice, carefully cutting a large sandwich into four sections. 'This looks wrong,' she added.

'They're to be cut at angles, crosswise.'

'I'll try that with the next one,' said Alice.

'Goodness, darling! How many will you make?' Nanette scolded her gently, for she never raised her voice or resorted to voicing violent sentiments unless the line had truly been crossed into bad taste. Neither did it bother her that her granddaughter laboured doggedly in the kitchen, often nearly destroying perfectly good pots and pans, nor did it occur to her to offer more than passing instruction. In an incident involving a lemon meringue pie, Nanette had subtly suggested that an increase of sugar and a decrease of salt might benefit future incarnations of the recipe, but she did not mention the hardened slick of sugared egg whites that took weeks to scrape off the countertop and part of the stove.

Nowadays, as Alice moved about the house, she looked for the traces of these conversations about cooking and reading. They were everywhere. The kitchen still bore the scars from her experimentation, as did the cooking implements and the pots. She would stand perfectly still, carefully examining a bent whisk in the middle of making an omelette, recalling the time when she'd tried to use it to break up a solid block of brown sugar. Nanette's nurse, brisk and efficient in ways that none of them could begin to comprehend, would swirl into the kitchen with the lunch tray, glance at Alice standing perfectly still among the broken eggshells with a half-grated piece of cheese, and without registering any surprise, make some perfunctory observation about Nanette's eating that day, or the state of the weather. She did not show any surprise at Alice's stiff turns of phrase ('In the course of making this omelette, I came upon a whisk that I damaged many years ago'), and she did not appear at all perturbed by the sight of Clare, who was generally to be found in the living room adjoining the dining room where Nanette lay, stretched out on a chaise longue next to a bottle of wine, full glass in hand, rereading the complete works of Anthony Trollope.

# 2

Alice had been having the most peculiar dreams since she'd returned to Nanette's house. In fact, she was beginning to wonder if she had been hallucinating the last few nights. As she stood in the kitchen eating a piece of stale toast smeared with marmalade, she gazed out the window at the garden sloping below. Her eyes smarted and she blinked. It was either a series of connected dreams or a hallucination. If the former, perhaps it was something she'd eaten, and she might try changing her diet or maybe read a different kind of book before she went to sleep. If the latter, she'd have to inform Ronit, and he would make a fuss and possibly suggest medication, which would be irksome. She finished off the piece of toast, and absent-mindedly wiping the sticky crumbs from her fingers on her nightgown, she wandered into the sunroom and out onto the veranda. She would work with the dream hypothesis first, she decided; there was no need to bother Ronit just yet.

There were long weeds growing between the broken paving stones of the veranda, and Alice had been pulling up a few of these each morning after breakfast, as her contribution to keeping up the family house. She squatted now, her long, pale legs poking out comically from beneath the baby-blue cotton nightgown she'd borrowed from Nanette's drawer when she realized she'd forgotten to pack anything to sleep in. As she pulled up the weeds, she considered her hallucinations – no – dreams. She'd been dreaming vividly of elegant parties. The parties took place in this house, but during an earlier period. She knew it was an earlier period because the house was better kept, Nanette looked younger – perhaps in her thirties – and Clare appeared not yet born. The ages she was easily able to guess because they corresponded to pictures in the photo albums Nanette kept, each picture labelled neatly in her immaculate hand.

Alice paused for a moment, a large chunk of clover clutched in her fist. Dirt poured from the roots of the clover onto the flagstone below. She covered her face with her other hand and closed her eyes. If she'd been sleeping through the night and dreaming about these parties, why did her eyes hurt? That part troubled her. She did feel poorly rested. She was reminded of the fairy tale about the twelve dancing princesses who spent every night dancing in a fairy palace. Every night they wore a fresh pair of silk dancing slippers to the palace, and each morning the slippers were ragged and full of holes. This was how the king had realized they were going somewhere. He then set forth a challenge in which contestants who thought they could discover the mystery were given three nights to figure it out or be beheaded if they failed. Why was it necessary to behead them? Alice wondered if it was possible she too was getting up in the middle of the night and attending parties, and if so, why did she only watch and not interact with anyone? Ronit probably would not buy the idea that she was under a faerie enchantment. She wondered if she should set out a pair of fresh silk slippers each night to see if they were worn to ribbons in the morning. But how was she to find silk slippers? Did people even wear such things anymore?

*Silly girl*, she thought, *you've been eating those questionable cheeses every night after dinner. They probably contain a toxic mould that's giving you indigestion and nightmares with themes drawn from family photo albums*. But her mind kept returning to the parties, and all the different people she had seen there: Nanette and a young Aunty Bix. There were other children, probably her uncles, and adults as well. She did recognize a few friends of Nanette's from around here, and Nanette's sister was there too. Nothing much happened. Alice walked around, feeling wraith-like – she was able to walk and move incorporeally through people and furniture during these dreams – watching people drink cocktails, play croquet on the lawn, act out charades, etc. Her grandfather was not there, but that was reportedly unexceptional since he was away for work much of the time, and into his old age stayed away from Nanette's side of the house. Perhaps even in those days he avoided her parties, or maybe Alice's toxic-cheese-mould-dream-state had written him out of the parties because he was seldom to be found in the photograph albums.

Alice plucked a few more weeds and then stood up, needing to stretch her legs. She yawned and flung the small armload of weeds behind the ornamental hedge that ringed the veranda and walked inside, dusting off her hands. The dirt was now sticking to the marmalade on her fingers, and she considered going in to wash her hands in the kitchen sink, but the nurse was in there scrubbing Nanette's breakfast things. She thought she'd go upstairs and change instead, then go visit Nanette. As she walked up the curving staircase, she thought about last night's party. There had been a nautical theme and a particularly handsome man – tall, red-headed, with a hawkish patrician nose. He looked fit and wore the attire of a sailor. He was too old for it, but then most of the adults had looked a bit foolish in their costumes. Alice stopped on the staircase to straighten a small watercolour of the Place de la Concorde that Nanette had painted as a teenager when she was travelling with her family. What it lacked in artistry was made up for by the exquisite labelling. Alice wondered if she should ask Nanette about the man in the sailor suit.

In her bedroom, a tiny room tucked under the eaves in the former maid's quarters that she'd slept in since she was a child, she looked around carefully to see if there were any signs she might have gotten up and left her bed during the night. What sort of sign would that be, in the absence of fresh dancing slippers? She would have to set a trap for herself this evening. She sat down on the bed, the ancient springs creaking under the weight of her body, and pulled her feet up. They were covered with dirt, so she dusted them off. Maybe if she cleaned her feet very carefully before going to bed, she'd be able to make out telltale signs she'd been out of bed, such as dirt or dried grass. She didn't usually clean her feet, so this would be a good test.

Letting her feet down again, she stood up and set about rummaging through her suitcase for clean clothes. There was a yellow sundress, which she put on after hanging up the nightgown on a hook on the back of the door, and one clean pair of underwear. She went and washed her hands in the tiny, stained sink in the adjoining bathroom. Everything in that bathroom was built on a miniature scale, making her tall, angular form appear exaggeratedly large. The sink was so low she had to lean over to get her hands under the faucet. She brushed her teeth and wiped off her hands and face, then started downstairs to see Nanette. On the landing, she thought she heard a shuffling sound from the direction of her grandfather's old rooms. The rooms were usually shut off from the rest of the upstairs hall by a door, probably to keep the heating bills down, but now it was summer, and someone had opened the door. Who could be down there? Perhaps Clare had gone looking for something else to read besides Trollope?

Alice walked towards the doorway.

'Mother?' she called out. 'Clare?' There was no response. She walked slowly down the hallway and glanced into the bathroom. No one there. The bedroom was empty, as was the dressing room. At the very end of the hall was the study. The door was ajar, and she slowly pushed it open. Next to the fireplace, in his red leather easy chair, a large, leather-bound book spread out on his knees, sat her grandfather, just as she'd always found him when she was a child.

# 3

'Grandfather?' Alice asked, standing in the doorway uncertainly.

Her grandfather seemed to smile, but she noticed he was hazy, the outline of his body jumpy, like an old newsreel.

'Grandfather?' she asked again, taking one step closer.

He smiled slightly, looking straight at her, and brushed his hand over the page of his book in a purposeful gesture. She glanced down at the book. It was an atlas, but she couldn't tell what map he was looking at.

'Are you looking at maps?' she asked.

Again, he brushed his hand over the page. She took another step forward, but as she did so he began to fade. In a moment, he was gone. Alice walked over and felt the seat of his armchair. It was covered with dust. There was no sign of what she had just seen. And this had occurred during waking hours. She feared she would now have to call Ronit, although she supposed it could be a real ghost. Ronit would not be interested in that explanation, she knew.

Alice walked back down the hallway and down the stairs. She passed through the living room. Clare lay asleep on the sofa, a shawl flung over her body. An old hardbound copy of *Phineas Finn* lay open on the floor next to her, alongside an empty bottle of wine and an overturned juice glass. Alice continued on through the great pocket doors that separated the living room and dining room. They were pulled apart just wide enough for a person to pass through.

Nanette lay on an oversized double bed with a metal frame, her head propped up on a pile of lacy pillows. Over her emaciated body were carefully tucked two pink wool blankets and a white damask bedspread with a bouquet of delicately embroidered roses nestled in the centre. The room was panelled in dark mahogany and had never been a cheerful spot. Nanette's forebears scowled from blackly painted oil portraits that picked up the glare of the morning sun's rays shining through the French doors. Their ashen complexions and starched white collars contrasted sharply with the deep maroons, umbers and blacks of their clothing and the backgrounds of the paintings. Alice had removed one particularly dour lady, who was glowering directly at Nanette in her bed, and replaced her with a more colourful still life of fruit she'd always liked. The still life usually hung in the living room, and Nanette had looked upset when Alice made the change, shaking her head vigorously.

*That was my great-grandmother*, she wrote on her notepad, the corner of her mouth twitching with a strong desire to speak.

'I know, Nanette,' said Alice, 'but she seemed stern for a bedroom. I thought the fruit might cheer you more. I know you have always liked the still life.'

*My mother's painting tutor painted it*, she wrote. *When I am gone*, she added, *you must put the portrait back in here, where it belongs.*

'I shall, of course,' said Alice, wondering what, in fact, would happen to everything when Nanette was gone. From one of her uncles, she understood that most of the money might be gone, whatever that meant, and it wasn't clear there was anyone with the interest or cash to take on the monumental task of keeping up the family house, let alone restoring it. She felt, in those days of Nanette's decline, that she was there to say goodbye to the house as much as she was to say goodbye to her grandmother.

Today, Nanette turned her head to look at Alice as she came gliding into the dining room. One side of her mouth turned up in a sort of a smile.

'How are you keeping today?' asked Alice.

Nanette reached her more able hand to her bedside and drew her pad and pencil to her. Her handwriting was no longer what it had been, as she was obliged to write with her left hand since her most recent stroke. It was clear that the bulging, messy letters pained her.

*I enjoy the sunshine today*, she wrote. *You look peaked. Have you been sleeping?*

Alice wondered if she should tell Nanette anything of what she'd seen at night, or of her encounter with her grandfather. She decided to opt for the latter, as it felt more tangible to her. Perhaps Nanette could shed some light on his sudden appearance.

'I've just seen Grandfather,' she began abruptly, 'upstairs, in his study. He was reading an atlas, I think, but then he disappeared.' *Would dematerialized be a better term?* she wondered. Nanette looked at her for a moment, but the thoughts behind her gaze were opaque. She had always been good at keeping her emotions to herself, and with the paralysis, that capability had only increased.

*What could he be wanting now?* she wrote. *It's been so long.*

'I don't know,' replied Alice. 'I was hoping you would.'

Nanette shook her head. She had no interest in topics touching on the person or affairs of her late husband. Any mention of him seemed to awaken in her a mild disdain, and she was quick to dismiss the topic. Alice knew this, but she'd decided to chance it, just in case Nanette had any insights into why he might appear.

'Maybe I was hallucinating,' added Alice, to see how Nanette would react.

*Do you generally see things that aren't there?* she wrote, after a moment's pause.

'Lately, perhaps. I'm not certain. Perhaps it was something I ate.'

*You haven't been drinking?*

'Oh indeed, no,' Alice laughed. 'But I have eaten some cheeses that might have been past their prime.'

*Why on earth do you do that? Is no one cleaning the icebox?*

'Oh no, your nurse is very good about that, but Mother and I had brought some blue cheeses home from the store a few weeks ago and then forgot to eat them. I found them a few days ago and I've been creating a sort of cheese plate for myself after dinner these past few nights.'

*One must take care with moulds.*

There was a lull in their conversation, and Nanette's eyelids fluttered as though she might be falling asleep. Alice went to the French doors and looked out. It would be a beautiful sunny day; perhaps she'd do some more weeding later.

'I've been weeding the terrace,' Alice told Nanette, who nodded approvingly, pleased by the change in topic.

*Have the dahlias bloomed yet?*

'I don't think so,' murmured Alice, as she wasn't entirely sure of the names of all the flowers in the garden. 'I'll check later this morning.'

She looked over as she spoke and realized Nanette had definitely closed her eyes this time. She'd sleep again now, as she did most of the time, and so Alice left the room, quietly pulling the pocket doors shut behind her. Beyond the doors, Clare hadn't moved a muscle and lay just as she had before, mouth open, snoring lightly. Alice walked out of the living room and down the hall to the kitchen, where she stopped in front of the black Bakelite phone mounted on the kitchen wall. She brushed her hand over the curved receiver, trying to decide if she needed to call Ronit.

# 4

Ronit lay on a double bed in Alice's grandmother's house. Alice had agreed to move out of her usual room when Ronit, alarmed by Alice's reports of dreams and hallucinations, had decided to drive out for a quick visit. The bed was in a seldom used guest room on the second floor, down the hall from Nanette's old room. A thin layer of dust coated nearly everything in the room, and in some places it was thick. The room had been shut off, possibly for years, and had a strong smell of damp. The walls were painted a light greenish yellow, which somehow added to the sensation of dampness. Ronit was trying not to move too much, to avoid making the springs in the four-poster bed creak. The noise was agitating, and his nerves were shot after a day at work that had started very early in the morning, followed by the two-hour drive. Then there'd been dinner in the kitchen topped off by some dodgy-looking cheeses.

He hadn't yet had a chance to discuss with Alice her hallucinations, or 'apparitions', as she was now calling them. He wasn't pleased that the first time she'd called him to the house in the past month was for psychiatric reasons, but he also knew that she felt shattered by her grandmother's decline. She wanted to stand perfectly still and have time stand still. He knew she probably hadn't noticed the passage of time, and he thought, as he glanced around the room, she couldn't be blamed for it in a place like this.

Ronit watched Alice as she sat in front of the mirror in a short, tattered pale-blue nightgown, combing her hair, which she had decided to wash after dinner in honour of his arrival. It was twilight, and they hadn't yet switched on the lights. Her skin had a bluish tinge in the waning light, and her long, light-brown hair looked almost grey. Ronit loved to watch her when she was like this, lost in some other world, expressionless, inaccessible. As an impressionable child, he had happened to watch a video cassette of the 1976 Winter Olympics, brought to Kolkata by a cousin from America. Binodini, the cousin, was 'crazy for skating', as she put it, and banished to the ice-skating desert of Kolkata for a prolonged Christmas break, she yearned for any communion with like-minded individuals. At fourteen, she found this exile from her friends and her interests an unusually harsh punishment for she knew not what crime. She was surprised to find a ready convert in her eight-year-old male cousin Ronit, with whom she shared all her stories, scrapbooks and videos.

Binodini and Ronit had watched the video cassette over and over again, sprawled out in front of the television that Binodini's father, an electrical engineer, had jerry-rigged to play movies from their state-of-the-art American Betamax cassette player. They ate bowls and bowls of nimki and drank small cups of tea so numerous that Binodini, unused to such high doses of caffeine, began to shake each afternoon until a grown-up discovered what was happening and told the cook to put an end to the rivers of chai.

Ronit was happy to watch Dorothy Hamill, Binodini's personal heroine, again and again, and quickly became smitten. He was fascinated by these people smiling radiantly while doing inconceivable things in a frigid environment. In his secret fantasies he dubbed Hamill the Ice Princess. Years later, when he was in medical school in Boston, he made a trip out to Denver to see Binodini and meet her husband. Binodini was in her thirties then, a prosperous housewife with three children and a husband who bore a remarkable resemblance to the American skater Scott Hamilton in his commentator days. Ronit had longed to ask his cousin if this was what had attracted her to him, but time, and distance, had erased the closeness of their friendship in those winter days in Kolkata when she used to pour her heart out to Ronit, confessing to him all the secrets of her love life and celebrity crushes.

For his own part, Ronit had not thought much of ice-skating since the 1984 Olympics in Sarajevo, which he had followed on TV with a secret excitement he could reveal to no one at the advanced age of fifteen. All that now remained of his ice-skating craze was a certain latent attraction to ice princesses, an attraction upon which he never once acted throughout medical school in the United States, though he was surrounded now by pale, undemonstrative women. Before he had departed from India, he had been spoken for, unofficially arranged to be married to a family friend's daughter. The relationship slowly unravelled because of the long distance between them. He had been so busy in his medical training that he hadn't bothered with more than an occasional flirtation. Later, when his engagement had officially ended, he'd taken up with a fellow resident at Mass General Hospital, a Sri Lankan woman with whom he shared a need for spicy food, but little else. The relationship, though marked by inertia, somehow grew into a desultory marriage. Forged at a justice of the peace and never announced to the parents of either the bride or groom, it had ended in a surprising burst of flames seven years later, when his wife, Malini, announced that she preferred women, had found a serious lover, and was leaving the psychiatric field to take up ceramics and other traditional crafts.

Thus, it was that in the early days of his private practice, a year or two after the divorce, at the age of thirty-nine, he was a successful single man whose private life was in shreds. It was during this period that he had walked into the waiting room to receive a new patient suffering from aphasia, a referral by a colleague, and seen before him the embodiment of his childhood ideal, his Ice Princess. It was not that Alice Bloodshaw looked anything like Dorothy Hamill, or any other ice skater he could bring to mind, so much as that her bearing and her aura (though he shrank from such new-ageisms, he did find himself using the word in his head) spoke to him of snow and ice.

He had led her into his office, motioned for her to sit in an easy chair placed at a carefully calibrated angle to his, sat down with his clipboard and stared at her, tongue-tied. She sat ramrod straight on the green upholstered chair and stared at him without blinking. Her eyes were blue, but a grey blue that somehow made them lighter than blue. Even her lips seemed drained of blood. She held her hands, long, thin fingers crossed, in her lap. He imagined he could see a fine tracery of veins in her hands, and he wanted to reach out and touch them, just lightly, to see if they were cold.

*I'm done for*, he thought. He'd never considered himself the type to have unprofessional urges. He'd had a number of such colleagues over the course of his career, and they had always disgusted him. That day, he somehow muddled his way through the appointment in a professional manner, wrote her a new prescription for antidepressants, took her medical history (in which she'd written out the answers in a strangely old-fashioned, spidery hand) and arranged for her next visit. Between the two appointments he'd felt jumpy and alarmed. He even called his own therapist and made an appointment.

The next appointment was just as bad. His therapist had suggested he refer Alice to another colleague, but he couldn't bring himself to give her up. After a month of appointments, Alice had walked in one day, sat down and begun to speak out loud, in measured tones, in paragraphs, her phrasings peculiarly stilted. He was never sure what had changed, if she had responded to his treatment, which seemed doubtful, or something else. He'd never seen a case like it, but the strength of his desire for an inappropriate relationship with his patient knew no bounds, and after that meeting, when she had starting speaking again, a line from a bad Woody Allen movie kept running through his head again and again: *I think it's time we terminate our professional relationship, as I have developed feelings for you.*

At the next appointment, their sixth, he resolved to do the right thing. After she walked in and settled down, he said, 'I'm afraid we will need to terminate our professional relationship. I can refer you to another doctor who can treat you more effectively.'

Alice gazed at him steadily with her grey-blue eyes. 'Is there really any need for me to see a psychiatrist any longer?' she asked. 'Now that I have recovered my use of speech, I do not see the necessity, frankly.'

'Well, it's always a good idea to continue treatment for some time, in case there's a relapse.'

'Why would there be a relapse?'

'I ... I don't know, but it happens.'

'It will not happen to me,' said Alice, firmly.

'Perhaps not,' he replied, at a loss, as he watched the conversation escaping his grasp.

'Well then, I imagine we're done here?' she asked, rising from her chair.

'One ... one more thing,' he interjected.

'Yes?'

'It's been a pleasure working with you, and ...'

The well-oiled wheels of social decorum, a system of words and behaviours passed down to her by Nanette for the most part, and at times, Clare, and Aunt Bix, began to whirl in Alice's brain. She stood up, held out her hand to him, and parting her lips in a gracious smile that crinkled the bridge of her nose and the edges of her eyes, she said, 'Thank you so, so very much. I've had a lovely time. I do hope we will meet again sometime.'

A gesture and an utterance that seemed at first to conspire to cut him out of any further discourse with her had suddenly and unexpectedly opened a new window of opportunity.

'The pleasure has been all mine,' he responded, no stranger to social niceties himself, 'Might I add that it would be wonderful to see you again, in a non-clinical setting?'

Alice paused, caught off-guard, her hand still in his. She blinked as she looked at him. Despite her preoccupation with her own mental state and the health of her grandmother, who had just suffered a stroke, she was able to perceive that she was being asked out on some sort of a date. She looked at him appraisingly, as though seeing him for the first time. He was well dressed, clean-cut and reasonably attractive.

'I would be delighted,' she responded evenly, disengaging her hand from his, and reaching for her leather satchel, propped it against her chair. Ronit couldn't believe his luck. He had to think of a time and place fast, before she went away, before she was out of his reach.

'How about tea on Saturday? Would that suit you?'

'Yes, I imagine so.'

'I know a lovely little tea house; I think you might like it.'

'Yes, if you would just note down the address, I shall see you there at four.'

Quickly, he pulled out his pen from his breast pocket and scrambled over to his desk to find a piece of paper. He pulled out his prescription pad, scrawled out the address and handed it to her.

'Thank you very much,' she responded, primly, and with that she was gone.

# 5

Ronit did not know what to make of Alice's latest problem. For one thing, she didn't seem to be convinced that it was a problem. She'd told him on the phone she thought he 'ought to know' that she'd seen her grandfather, dead these twenty years, in his study. She'd also said perhaps he should come out to the house that weekend. There was hesitation in her tone, and he took this to mean she hadn't ruled out the possibility that this could be a hallucination or at least a mental health issue. He'd anxiously asked her all sorts of questions to assess the gravity of the situation, but she hadn't been forthcoming, and her voice began to trail off on the other end of the line.

Now that he'd already been here a few hours, he was yet to have the nerve to broach the subject. Alice moved in a cloud of reproach that rebuffed him whenever the opportunity arose to discuss it. Now that they were truly alone, she seemed unwilling to finish up with her preparations and come to bed, where finally they'd have to talk. At last, he'd had enough of her endless combing, and asked, in as non-psychiatric a tone as he could muster, 'Have you seen him again?'

Alice turned to fix him with a baleful gaze. 'What do you mean "again"?'

'Since the first time that you reported to me on Wednesday.'

'A couple of times, yes.'

'A couple of times? Why didn't you tell me?'

'There was really no difference. They were all similar.'

Ronit felt he was already losing ground. This was often the case, and this, even more than his attraction to her, had perhaps been the most significant indication that he was not up to the task of being her psychiatrist.

'Why don't you tell me more about it?' he asked. 'What did he look like? Did he seem like a real person, or more of a ... a presence?'

'Like an old newsreel,' said Alice, firmly.

'An old newsreel? How so?'

'Jumpy, scratched, maybe a little like a lenticular image.'

'A what?'

'A lenticular image, similar to a hologram, but not the same thing. The image appears to change if you move your head. They use them in children's books and puzzles sometimes. I had one of Sleeping Beauty.'

'I see. And did he communicate with you?'

'Not literally.' She appeared resigned to taking the conversation to its logical conclusion, and laying her comb on the dressing table, she came and lay down on the bed next to him without getting under the covers. He wondered if lying on top of the blanket would make her dusty. He waited for her to finish her thought, but she did not.

'Not literally?' he asked.

'No. No. But he seemed to be smiling at me, and I felt he was indicating something to do with the atlas on his lap.'

'I see. So you feel he was trying to tell you something.'

'Oh yes, I think so. Unless it's not real.'

'Unless it's not real. Do you think it's real?'

Alice lay still and stared at the ceiling. She was wondering how to tell him about the parties.

'There are other things I have seen since coming here. Not exactly the same, but things that feel very real.'

Ronit's heart sank. He wondered if this was something to do with being in this house, so intimately connected with the dysfunction of her childhood, and with her mother camped out in the living room as well. He could see no way of getting her out of here with her grandmother so ill. Would these visions or hallucinations cause a relapse? To whom could he refer her now that she was way out in the country?

'Tell me about them,' he said, trying to maintain a composed, neutral tone. 'What else have you seen?'

'I'm not sure if they were dreams, or things I saw,' responded Alice cautiously.

'What happened in them?'

'There were parties, but in the past. I recognized the people: Nanette, my uncles, family, but from long ago.'

'How long ago?'

'I think perhaps Nanette was in her thirties. My mother wasn't born yet.'

'What makes you think they *weren't* dreams?'

'They are sequential, night after night, and they feel real.'

'They *are* sequential, not *were*? It's still happening?'

'Yes, every night. I feel tired in the morning, like the princesses.'

'The princesses?'

'Yes, in the story, the fairy tale, "The Twelve Dancing Princesses". Do you know it?'

'No, I don't think so.'

Alice recounted the story to him. She grew animated in the telling and propped herself up on one elbow. Sometimes she grew unexpectedly excited like this. It was unpredictable and filled him with desire. He wondered if he might try to kiss her but thought better of it. He had to try to stick to extracting the developing mental health situation first.

'So how does this story remind you of these ... these things you're experiencing?'

'Well, because I don't know!' she said excitedly. 'I don't know if they're real or if they're dreams, or if I'm really there. I feel tired all the time, and I wonder if I have actually been at these parties. Also, I could be hallucinating ...' she examined his face carefully. 'You think I'm hallucinating, don't you?'

'Of course I don't. I mean, I don't know either.'

'So you think I could be travelling back in time?' she asked hopefully.

'Well, no, I think we can rule out that option as improbable,' he said carefully.

'Improbable.' She lay down on her back and glared at the ceiling, her brief bout of animation gone. Ronit felt as though he had popped a beautiful floating bubble. Why did he always need to bring up probability and reality with her? It never came to any good.

'I didn't say impossible,' he said, trying to rekindle her mood.

'But that's what you think. People don't travel through time, and there's no such thing as ghosts.'

'I feel that it's possible to encounter such experiences in a way that *feels* very real. You yourself aren't sure what's happening, isn't that right?'

'Yes, it is right. But with all the disorders I've experienced, there has never been a problem with hallucinations or delusions. Don't you think that's true?' She propped herself up on her elbow again and looked at him hard, as though she could see through his skull, into his brain, and extract the true answer from him regardless of what he said.

'That is true. You've never reported anything like that, to me at any rate.'

'Not to you, nor to anyone else, because this is *new*.' She fell silent for a few moments. They were both lost in thought. 'Supposing,' she resumed, 'supposing that I were to take you with me, to Grandfather's study, every time I go there. Then you will see the same thing I do, when I see it. If I see it, and you don't, that could mean it's a hallucination, and you could give me medication, or ... or one of your friends could, and then we'll be done with it. Let's go now!' She bounced out of bed and onto her feet in an unexpected show of energy.

'Now?' asked Ronit weakly.

'Yes, why not?'

'Don't you usually see him by daylight?'

'Yes, but maybe he's there more by night since that's traditionally when ghosts haunt. Maybe he can materialize more easily after the sun goes down. Come to think of it,' she said thoughtfully, 'perhaps I have been making it more difficult for him to deliver his message to me because I only visit in the daytime.'

By now, Alice was standing by the door, her hand on the knob, waiting for Ronit to get up. It was becoming clear that she preferred to think of these occurrences as actual hauntings. Ronit's attempts to classify them as hallucinations or any other disorder would be received unsympathetically. Why had she called him then? He sat up, put on his glasses, ran his fingers through his thinning hair and swung his feet down on the floor. He didn't like to wander around the house in his boxer shorts and T-shirt, but he knew that she'd be impatient with his impulse to cover up. After all, whom would they likely encounter in the corridor, other than one of the cats, or a wraith? He slipped on his flip-flops and followed her to the door.

# 6

The hallway was pitch-dark.

'Should I turn on the light?' whispered Alice.

'Yes, of course,' said Ronit nervously. 'Why are you whispering?'

'I don't want to scare him away with loud noises. Maybe he doesn't want me to bring visitors,' she hissed.

Ronit felt like going back into the bedroom and crawling under the dusty covers. Between them, he was the one to not believe in ghosts, and yet, he clearly felt more spooked by the situation. Alice turned on a single wall sconce.

'This should be enough,' she said. 'If we keep the door of this corridor open, we should be able to see the light when we get into that corridor. Anyway, when he is there, there is usually a fire going, so the study should be visible.' She took Ronit's hand and led him down to the main hall, where she propped open the door to the corridor. They walked across the hall, and she opened the door to her grandfather's wing. Here too, it was pitch-dark.

'I don't see the fire,' she whispered.

'Maybe we should go back?' suggested Ronit hopefully.

'I will just turn on another wall sconce here,' she said. She switched on the light, a dim bulb with an orange silk shade that cast the expanse of the corridor in a low, rosy glow. Hand in hand, they walked slowly down to the end of the corridor together. Ronit felt increasingly uneasy.

'Oh!' whispered Alice.

'What?'

'The door is shut. I never shut it. Perhaps I should knock.'

Ronit wanted to say *no, don't knock, don't disturb him*, but that would have fuelled the fantasy. Of course she knocked. There was no response.

'I will open it now,' she told him, looking over her shoulder. She slowly turned the creaky knob and opened the door. Inside was also pitch-dark.

'No fire,' she said with disappointment.

'Grandfather,' she said suddenly, in a normal voice, 'I wanted you to meet my fiancé, Ronit Roy. He is a psychiatrist. He is from India.' She stood perfectly still for a moment, then fumbled her hand along the wall near the door until she found a light switch. The switch illuminated a small chandelier set in a surround of gilded ivy leaves in the centre of the ceiling. The room was empty. Ronit was disturbed that this came as a surprise to him. Alice looked disappointed.

'Oh well,' she said. She walked over to her grandfather's chair and ran her hand over the leather seat. 'I always wonder if it will be warm,' she explained. 'But it's usually cold and dusty.' She stood perfectly still and looked all around. She was hoping for a sign, some manifestation of change. She looked carefully at the small revolving bookcase next to the chair. She turned it slowly. None of the books had been touched in the room since his death twenty years ago, except for the ones she had borrowed, but never from this carousel.

'Look, Ronit!' she cried suddenly.

'What?'

'Here's an atlas, and it's been pulled out slightly.' She pointed to a large, well-worn atlas, bound in red leather with embossed gold lettering on the spine. 'It's been pulled out and it's not dusty,' she added, taking it out and blowing on it. 'All these books are full of dust, usually.'

'Is that the atlas he was reading in your … in your encounter with him?'

'Yes, I think so. It looks like it. I must examine this. Thank you, Grandfather,' she called out loudly, as though she were mid-performance on stage, projecting for an audience.

'Do you think it would be hard for him to hear you?'

'Just in case,' she said nonchalantly. 'Let's go look at this now.' She waited until Ronit had stepped out into the hall, then switched off the light. 'Should I close the door?' she asked.

'Leave it,' said Ronit, wanting to be back safely in their room and away from this hideous fantasy. She left the door open, and they walked back down the hallway, crossed the main landing and into their corridor. Ronit quietly shut the door to their corridor and left the wall sconce on. He didn't much care for the idea of fumbling his way towards the bathroom in the darkened hall in the middle of the night.

# 7

Back safely in their room, Alice hopped onto the bed and began to pore over the atlas, legs crossed, hands absent-mindedly braiding her long, lank hair into two pigtails. Ronit pulled out his novel. He felt he needed a breather from the ghost story he suddenly found himself inhabiting. He had imagined a difficult weekend in which he would need to trudge back into the role of Alice's psychiatrist, if only briefly, to help her navigate what needed to be done next. Now, he found himself in some sort of Enid Blyton novel, creeping about a decaying haunted mansion, looking for clues. He hoped that Henry James would prove a reasonable, rational antidote to the madness.

'This is just a standard atlas,' said Alice.

'You sound disappointed.'

'A little. What could he be trying to tell me?'

'Perhaps he's telling you to travel to India,' suggested Ronit.

'Oh, I hardly think that is likely,' said Alice shortly.

Ronit had been trying for the past few months to persuade Alice to travel with him to Kolkata to meet his parents. They had been engaged – at least, nominally engaged – for four months, but Alice became squirrelly at the mention of marriage. Ronit was frustrated with her apparent contentment with this limbo state. Perhaps it was her elusiveness that made him warmer to the topic of marriage all over again than she. This had surprised him. His previous marriage had been such a damp squib that he had never expected to marry again. In those months and years following Malini's sudden departure, a deep queasiness about the entire institution had enveloped him. Nothing could have surprised him more than his sudden realization within a month of his first kiss with Alice that he was entertaining wedding fantasies. He imagined introducing her to his parents, wondering if they would have a simple ceremony or one of those colossal 'event weddings' his friends were having these days, where the couple choose a resort-like setting and insist on all their friends and family flying in for a long weekend of multicultural events and festivities. By then, of course, he knew Alice better than to ever imagine her participating in any such thing. There would likely never be a www.alicewedsronit.com website for friends to visit.

In fact, he could sense about her a force field that repelled all mention of marriage. This was no doubt why she was single when he met her. By the second month of their relationship, determined to propose to her while they were picnicking on the banks of the Charles, he had somehow made a hash of a long prelude about how much she meant to him. She misunderstood his intent, and in the end, it seemed that what she thought was being proposed was that they move in together. She accepted.

After they had cohabited in a two-bedroom condo in Cambridge for over a month, Ronit decided that he could wait no longer, though he still could not identify the source of his urgency. He purchased a sapphire ring with a small stone and an understated setting, made reservations at an expensive French restaurant, and urged her to dress up for the occasion. Any other woman would have smelled a proposal in the air, but Alice had seemed genuinely taken aback when he finally brought it up.

'Marry you?' she asked, looking searchingly at his face, as though trying to discover some hidden meaning. 'You want me to marry you?'

'Nothing would make me happier,' he had added, nervously bunching his napkin in the hand that wasn't proffering the ring.

'Nothing?' she asked, still uncomprehending.

'No, nothing, Alice, I want to spend my life with you.'

'This is very unexpected,' she said, thoughtfully, 'but I suppose we could get married if you wish.'

It was not the sort of acceptance that an ardent petitioner would hope for, but he was willing to take it. He had ordered champagne, and after two glasses and a caramel coffee torte, Alice was suddenly buoyant and cheerfully toasted their engagement several times. She pulled her purse onto the table, a small, silver-beaded clutch, slightly bald in places, and after fishing around in the recesses, she triumphantly pulled out a tube of orange-red lipstick which she proceeded to apply evenly enough without taking recourse to a hand mirror.

'Now that I am a fiancée, I must wear make-up!' she crowed and lifted her glass for another toast. 'To *la condition humaine*!' she cried.

It had been a glorious success of an evening after all. They stayed out all night, going to bars, strolling through the streets hand in hand. And yet, after that night, Alice had clammed up about the wedding. She never wore her ring, and when he had asked her if it was improperly sized, she replied that it was too heavy. When Ronit suggested dates for the wedding, she changed the subject. Nervous, he asked her if he might tell his parents of the engagement, and she asked *why not*.

'Because you don't seem to want to talk about it. Perhaps you're having second thoughts.' He hated to say those words, but he was feeling increasingly anxious that she might be entertaining doubts.

'Well, there's no need to rush, is there? Being engaged is fine.'

Once he told his parents, of course they were eager to have him bring her to meet them. They'd never even known about the first marriage, and by now they'd entirely given up hope of him ever marrying or producing grandchildren. Instead, they had turned their sights on his younger sister, an installation artist in New York City, who showed even fewer signs than he of finding a mate and producing offspring. The news of his engagement to Alice filled his mother with fresh enthusiasm and she started a steady drumbeat of emails and phone calls demanding a firm date for their visit. When Ronit raised the issue with Alice, she showed little interest. This was because, he finally learned, she'd taken a trip to India in her early twenties to visit a yoga ashram and it had gone poorly.

She'd been going through a period of depression, and a friend who was a yoga enthusiast had convinced her to come on a retreat sponsored by her yoga studio. She had promised Alice the trip would be beneficial to her mental and physical health and fill her with uplifting and joyous emotions.

Instead, Alice had contracted amoebic dysentery from Ganga water she had accidentally ingested during a puja ceremony, and head lice from the Scandinavian seekers with whom they had shared a room. After Alice had lain writhing on her cot for several days, her friend had finally had the bright idea of having their group leader call for a doctor. The doctor had come, blanched at her state, and bundled her off to a tony infirmary in New Delhi that was frequented by the diplomatic community. There, after a gut-wrenching few weeks, she was cured of her twin ailments and promptly dispatched back from whence she came via the kind offices of US consular officials.

This was at least the reason that Alice had given for her reluctance to visit, but Ronit could not help but wonder if it were an excuse to avoid the actual commitment of marriage. Her evasiveness around the topic rankled with him, and he experienced her refusal to travel to Kolkata as a rejection.

'Why don't you look at the India page?' Ronit suggested acerbically. 'You never know, he may have put a bookmark or a Post-it there.'

Alice glowered at him and returned to flipping through the pages, occasionally remarking on a set of boundaries no longer current, or a changed country name. Suddenly she let out a shriek and gripped the edges of the book.

'What!' Ronit asked with alarm. Had she seen a rat, or a ghost? Would she start having seizures now?

'You were right!' she cried.

'About what?'

'Look!' She brought the open page over to him and looked at him expectantly. He saw a map of a section of the Himalayan Mountains just north-east of New Delhi.

'The Himalayas?'

'Yes, don't you see?'

'See what?'

'The page, it's folded at the corner.' She pointed to the right-hand corner above the map, which was folded down in a tiny triangle. Ronit examined the fold carefully, and lifted it gingerly, patting it down again. To him it looked as though it had been folded long ago, but he also saw in this perceived supernatural occurrence an opening.

'That is unusual,' he ventured.

'I think this is the same region where I was before,' she said excitedly. 'I was in Rishikesh; do you see it there?'

Ronit looked carefully. 'Yes, it's right here, it's spelled with an H – Hrishikesh, here.' He pointed to the city.

'Yes, yes, there it is! What could he be telling me?'

'I don't know. Did your grandfather's business have anything to do with India?'

'I don't know, I don't know!' Alice was excited. 'Maybe I should go and look in his files now!'

'Not now, darling,' Ronit said in a soothing tone. 'It's late. Let's get some sleep.'

Alice looked at him thoughtfully, surprised to see him going along with the idea of her grandfather as a ghost. It made her suspicious but relieved. She had dreaded another discussion about medications and psychotherapy.

'You are right,' she said, closing the book carefully. She placed it on her dresser ceremoniously, as though it were a holy book. 'In the morning, I can also try asking Nanette and Mother.'

'Yes, that's right,' said Ronit doubtfully, imagining the unhelpful reactions that might emanate from those quarters. 'We'll find out more in the morning.'

# 8

Alice sat in the living room watching her mother stir the cup of coffee she had brought her. Clare reclined odalisque-like on the gold and purple paisley chaise longue in a full-length blue kimono loosely tied about an old pink satin nightgown, both of which had been pilfered from Nanette's bureau upstairs. Her skin could easily be described as alabaster, aided by the fact that she rarely went outside and ate very few vegetables. Despite her drinking habits, the wrinkles on her face were fine and difficult to discern in the perpetual twilight of the living room, with its sombre, mauve-patterned wallpaper and heavy mahogany display cases and bookshelves. Clare's dark hair was streaked with white at the roots. This was the first time Alice had ever noticed any white or grey in her hair. She had not realized that she dyed it. She had not imagined that her mother's vanity would provide her with enough impetus to acquire a bottle of hair dye and then go to the trouble of applying it to her head. Apparently whatever preconditions were needed to enable her to colour her hair in the first place no longer pertained in this house. It wasn't likely she had even brushed it in days.

When she finished stirring the coffee and placed the spoon at the edge of the saucer, she looked up at Alice questioningly, then shielded her eyes from a shaft of light that suddenly fell across her face. The sun had appeared momentarily from behind a cloud. She waved her other hand towards the drapes, and Alice got up, slowly, and walked over to the French doors. She glanced at the shaft of light, then adjusted the drapes so they would block the sun falling on Clare, while allowing the objects in the room to remain visible. She sat down again.

'Did you sleep well?' asked Alice, unnaturally, for they rarely discussed such things.

'I would still be asleep if you hadn't brought me this coffee,' observed Clare evenly.

'Yes, of course, but I thought with Ronit here you might wish to wake up earlier.'

'What, is he coming in here as well?' asked Clare, displeased.

'No, no, but I thought we might all lunch together. Maybe even in the village.'

'Oh, good heavens, I should think not,' laughed Clare irritably. 'Are you going to start acting like the purser on a cruise ship now that your *fiancé* is here?' She always uttered the word 'fiancé' as though it were a fake word, a term invented by the greeting card industry, perhaps. Her disdainful tone evoked for Alice the kind of cards that one can buy in the supermarket and send to recently engaged couples. She thought of the silhouette of a man and a woman holding hands, walking on the beach, bathed in the tawny light of sunset, and then in golden script, a wordy, meaningless poem about the beauty of sharing one's life's journey. Now that she actually found herself affianced, she could not shake the shame of that word and tried to avoid it at all costs. Perhaps this was why she could not bring herself to wear the lovely ring Ronit had given her. The weight she had complained of was not contained in the actual object but in the heft of that undesirable word.

'No, of course not,' said Alice, determined not to be deterred from her goal by the sarcasm. 'It was just a thought,' she added. She waited for Clare to take a few sips of the coffee, hoping it would clear the cobwebs from her mind for long enough to ask her a question.

Clare sipped silently. After a moment, Alice said, 'I have a question.'

'Do you?' Clare put her cup down and looked her in the eye, as though daring her to ask. With the drapes blocking the sun from her face, her sharp features were shadowed menacingly.

'Yes,' said Alice, firmly. 'My question is this: Did Grandfather ever visit India, or have business concerns or friends there?'

Clare looked at her curiously and tapped a drop of coffee off the spoon back into the cup. 'Who told you that?' she asked.

'No one,' said Alice, truthfully. 'But I ... I found a book relating to India in his study and I wondered. Ronit asked, as well.'

'Did he now?' She took a long sip from her cup and placed it back on the saucer carefully. 'Are there any cookies or crackers in the house? Anything to nibble on?' she asked. Alice felt as though she was being held hostage. Sensing her real desire for a meaningful answer, Clare planned to drag the process out as long as possible. Alice felt fairly certain that she would have to agree to buy her more wine in the village by the end of the conversation.

'I think so,' said Alice, rising.

'Cookies would be my preference,' added Clare.

Since her early childhood, Alice had always disappointed her mother with her steadfast self-sufficiency. 'She's like a goddamned independent nation state,' she had once overheard Clare complaining to someone at a party. This independence of Alice's had seemed a further affront to Clare after her husband had left her. He had not needed her, and neither had her daughter, her supposed dependant. Clare desired to be needed by someone, or to be needed for something, but her corrosive wit and apparent disdain for her fellow man made true intimacy nearly impossible.

In addition, she had always felt herself above work of any kind and had not received any education or training beyond secondary school, for which she'd had a rudimentary finishing-school education. Rather than training her mind or teaching her skills, her education had simply provided a thin veneer which had hardened and grown brittle over time. It was this brittleness which contributed to Alice's independence. She had always sensed that if she asked too much of her mother, she might crack, and then she would be left with no one to sign permission forms, and no one to enrol her in school, when she went.

As Alice grew older and more independent, Clare felt increasingly hostile towards her, seeing her every action as a personal insult. It infuriated her that Alice refused to fight back, and she contrived to get a rise out of her by any means necessary. Of course, whenever she did manage to upset

Alice's equilibrium, Alice would shut down completely. She'd stop talking altogether, which was even more maddening. Now that she was back to talking again, the cycle could recommence. Clare was ready for it.

At times like this, when Alice did need her mother, or needed something from her, Clare quickly became greedy, almost triumphant, the experience of being depended upon creating in her an outsized, and temporary, sense of self-worth. As a canny child, Alice would have happily supplied her mother with a steady supply of perceived dependence, but she had learned from experience that the emotion was unsustainable, quickly breaking down and creating havoc for both of them. On one occasion, when Alice was ten, she had asked her mother for help with her French homework, knowing that this was one area in which Clare had received an adequate education. Clare became excited. She uncharacteristically cleared off the dining room table with great energy so as to turn it into a laboratory for their French tutorial. She made tea and set the table with the best china, and asked Alice to make some cinnamon toast for them to share as they worked. Every time Clare was about to sit down at the table, she would think of some other atmospheric touch that would enhance their educational experience. Suddenly, she lay down on the sofa, hugging her bony elbows to her body, tears in her eyes, and asked Alice to bring her a drink. 'Scotch and soda,' she had said in a quavering voice.

Alice, unsurprised, had gone and fixed the drink and set it on the side table near her elbow.

'We'll do the French later,' said Clare, her eyes staring hollowly at the ceiling.

'That's fine,' said Alice quietly. 'I'll give it a try now, and let you know if there are questions later.'

'Yes, later would be best,' said Clare, closing her eyes. 'Can you please turn off the lights in here, and that music? It's so loud, so bright.'

# 9

Alice returned to the living room, a small plate of shortbread cookies in her hand. No doubt they were stale, but she didn't imagine Clare would actually eat them; she only wanted to drag out Alice's moment of need. A child must by necessity be tolerant, but Alice, as an adult, had less patience for these scenes. She decided to push back against her mother's brief bubble of self-importance.

'I will also ask Nanette,' she said. 'But I thought I would ask you first.'

'Nanette does not discuss that subject,' said Clare, her eyes shining with this small triumph. 'You're better off with me, darling.' She sat up, reached for a cookie and nibbled at it. 'When did we get these? Are they fresh?'

'I don't know, but I doubt it,' responded Alice, unconcerned.

'A bit stale, but edible,' said Clare, replacing the cookie on the plate after taking a tiny bite. 'India, then.'

'Yes, India. Did he go there?'

'Oh yes, oh yes, he did. He went often. When I was a child, he spent a month there every year. He went for longer stretches after he retired. When we were children, he always sent us each a postcard. A letter for Nanette.'

'Did he have business there?'

'He said he did.' She smiled enigmatically.

'You don't think so?'

'He never said what he did there. And the trips displeased Nanette. Of course, they rarely spoke anyway, but she was particularly icy about the India trips in that way that only Nanette can be.'

Alice looked at Clare thoughtfully. She had always considered Nanette an emotional refuge, but she wondered if her ability to freeze opposition with a chilly stare of disapproval could have helped to shape the person her mother had become.

'Do you know where he went?'

'I have no idea. He sent postcards, so there was no return address. That is something Nanette would know, if she's willing to tell you.'

'Perhaps I could learn something from his files.'

'Good God, are they still up there? I'll never understand why she didn't just send all his things to the dump when he died. It's a bloody Egyptian tomb up there. I'm sure even his clothes are still hanging in the closets.'

Alice hadn't considered the matter in that light. Grandfather's things remaining just as they always had been was a state of affairs in keeping with the way the house was run. No one and nothing was ever erased or discarded. The layers of family just continued to build, accretions of artifacts, dust and distorted memories. She did realize that her grandparents' marriage had not been a happy one, but she had never questioned it. What marriage had been happy? She couldn't think of any offhand.

'Why did she dislike him?' Alice asked suddenly.

'Who?'

'Grandfather. Why did Nanette dislike Grandfather so much?'

'Who knows. He was kind enough, though he kept his distance from her. Perhaps they weren't suited. So few people are.' Clare lay back against the sofa cushions. She looked deflated, as though the energy she had had for their conversation had been spent.

'Did you say you were going into the village?' she asked faintly.

'I might show Ronit around.'

'Yes, of course. I'm sure he'll find it remarkably quaint.'

'Perhaps.'

'If you go, please buy more wine.'

'I will,' said Alice, getting up. There was no point, she had learned, in completely cutting off the supply. Things only got worse. Luckily, Ronit would have enough money with him to buy a case so she wouldn't have to go back to the liquor store for a while.

'I am going to go and talk to Nanette now,' she said.

Clare did not respond. She was looking around on the floor for her novel, which had got tangled up in a shawl.

# 10

Alice pushed open the pocket doors to the dining room wide enough to slip through. Nanette was eating her breakfast: Melba toast, a soft-boiled egg, tea with cream and sugar; just as it had always been. Nowadays it was the nurse who crumbled up the toast and dropped it into the large end of the egg cup with the mashed egg, but otherwise, Nanette's breakfast was unchanged from when Alice had been a child. Nanette looked up and smiled graciously when she entered. She looked alert, more so than usual.

'Good morning, Nanette,' said Alice, loudly, to make sure she heard. 'It's so lovely to see you.'

Nanette nodded and reached for her pen and pad. It was too far to stretch with the tray across her lap. Alice hurried over and gave the pen and pad to her.

Nanette wrote: *It's a lovely day. Is your mother up?*

'Yes, she is. I made her coffee.'

*How thoughtful. And how is Roman keeping today? Did he sleep well?*

Her handwriting had become more quavery. Alice sighed at the distortion of Ronit's name. She knew that in better days this would have been substituted with an exaggerated mispronunciation that gave both the sense that one was trying *very hard* with a foreign name, but that it was frankly unpronounceable.

'Ronit is well. He's looking at the books in the library.'

*How nice to have a man of learning in the house. The books must be terribly happy.*

Alice smiled. Her grandmother had always adored having male guests in the house, the only exception being her own husband. But then, he wasn't a guest.

Alice sat down near the bed and prepared to ask her question. She crossed her hands in her lap and took a deep breath.

'Nanette, I'd like to ask you a question, one that you may not wish to answer.'

Nanette looked at her expectantly, her delicate brow furrowed.

'I was wondering if you could tell me where Grandfather went on his trips to India.'

Nanette closed her notebook and carefully placed it and the pen on the bedside. She folded her hands across her stomach and stared fixedly out the window, away from Alice. This meant the conversation had been terminated. Alice, not entirely surprised after her mother's warning, stood up.

'I'll talk to you later, Nanette,' she said, and smiled, though Nanette refused to look in her direction.

Back in the living room, her mother was reading again.

'Did she tell you?' she asked, looking up.

'No.'

Her mother gave a satisfied chuckle and went back to her book.

# 11

Ronit was not in the library after all. She found him on the terrace. He was sitting on a metal lawn chair, rusted in spots, drinking a cup of coffee and reading an old, hard-covered book from the library. She stood in the doorway and looked at him. The morning sun brought a slight shine to the top of his balding head. He had on his black flip-flops, a pair of neatly pressed cargo shorts and a very new-looking grey T-shirt. He was sitting hunched over the book, reading intently. She wasn't sure if he did this because he needed new glasses, or if reading made him lost to the world in such a way that he was no longer conscious of back pain. All the same, he looked handsome, she thought. Very distinguished. She was glad she was engaged to him, and not his patient anymore. He really was very nice.

'What are you reading?' she asked.

He looked up, startled. 'I found a 1920s travelogue of Eastern Europe,' he said, closing the book with his finger still marking his place. 'It's got a whole chapter on the Romani. Fascinating stuff.'

Alice smiled.

'What did you learn?' he asked.

'I learned that Grandfather used to go to India every year for a month, and more after he retired. I also learned that Nanette refuses to discuss the matter.'

'Your mother told you the other part?'

'Yes. And she wants more wine for her trouble.'

'Are we going into the village?'

'Yes, but later we must start to look at his files. Then we can find where he went.'

Ronit had in the past ten hours completely changed his approach to the matter of Alice's hallucinations, or visions, or hauntings, or whatever they were. Until the India entry in the atlas had been found to be significant, he had been beside himself with worry about her mental status. But when he saw how her attitude towards the country had changed when linked to the ghostly apparition of her grandfather instead of an unfortunate gastrointestinal ailment, he had suddenly found himself in a different camp. The ghost had accomplished what he had been unable to for months. He was now willing to help it, or him, however he could. He would worry about mental illness later, he reasoned, feeling only mildly uneasy about the decision.

*

After a delightfully fresh meal in the village, Alice and Ronit returned to the house with the Sunday newspaper, bags of groceries and a case of cheap white wine from the region of Alsace.

Ronit sat down to flip through the Sunday paper, but it was just more of the same sabre-rattling about Iraq's alleged weapons of mass destruction.

'What a sham,' he announced, dropping the paper on the table in disgust.

'What is?' asked Alice.

'All these characters, Donald Rumsfeld and so on, trying to find an excuse to invade Iraq. Outrageous!'

Alice always avoided the news if she could. Ever since the Twin Towers had fallen, she made sure to close her eyes and hum softly to herself as they drove through the toll plazas draped in flags and 'UNITED WE STAND' banners.

'Why don't you put away the wine,' she suggested quickly.

'In the fridge?' asked Ronit.

'Oh no,' said Alice, 'we put it on the cellar stairs. It's very cool down there.' Alice showed him the door to the cellar and went to put away the groceries, relieved she had avoided the conversation. Later she would fish out the magazine section and do the crossword, which was all she wanted from the Sunday paper.

With some trepidation, Ronit opened the door to the cellar and felt about on the damp wall for a light switch. Once this was accomplished, he was alarmed to see a number of bare wires hanging out of the switch and wondered if he had narrowly escaped an electric shock. The stairs seemed too narrow for an entire case of wine, so he decided to take it down to the bottom. There was some rubble and a pile of crumbling bricks at the foot of the stair. Bits of insulation lay strewn about, as though rodents had been nesting nearby. The rest of the cellar was cloaked in darkness, as the dim light from the poorly wired switch at the top of the stairs did not reach much further than this. He looked around for another switch and found a long string hanging from a bare bulb, which he pulled.

The cellar now illuminated, he looked about him. Though the space showed signs of disuse, it had apparently housed a substantial wine collection at one time. No doubt this had been slowly wiped out by Clare, or other heavy-drinking members of Alice's clan. Ronit picked up the wine case and set it on a shelf close to the stairs. As he was turning to leave, he suddenly noticed another light on at the other end of the cellar. Though the cellar made him uneasy – subterranean spaces were something he knew of mainly from mystery stories – he felt oddly drawn to it, so he walked over to take a look. There was a small hallway lined with numerous bottles of wine. He found this curious – how had this collection escaped the attention of the tipplers upstairs? He reached out and pulled a bottle from the shelf. It was French, from 1945. He wondered if wine could really keep that long.

During his residency, some friends had begun to take an interest in fine wines in anticipation of being properly compensated for their work at some point in the future. They had taken courses on wine appreciation. One had even dropped out of the residency and become a sommelier, pointing out that after all, it was really the same work he had been doing as a psychiatrist, but he would be better paid, more appreciated, and sleep in late every morning. Ronit had never paid much attention to the details of their wine education, other than enjoying whatever they had selected.

He pulled another bottle off the shelf. This one was from 1952, a rioja from Spain. He noticed that the bottles were shiny, not dusty, unlike most things in the house. Was it too damp for dust down here? But then there should be mildew. He looked around. There were no cobwebs either; in fact, the whole area looked tidy. He wondered if he should bring a bottle up to show Alice. They'd have to keep this a secret from Clare, who could not be trusted and would happily polish off what might be a valuable collection. He looked around, wondering which bottle to bring up. Suddenly he noticed a nice bottle of champagne, standing upright on a shelf, on a silver tray. Maybe this would suit. Alice was fond of champagne. He examined the label: 1967 Chateau LaFitte. That sounded nice. He looked around for a switch but could see none and imagined it was connected with the switch at the foot of the stairs. Returning to the stairs, he pulled the string and walked gingerly back up. He found the kitchen empty when he emerged from the cellar, so he decided to chill the bottle and surprise her later. The fridge was crammed with food, much of it of an uncertain provenance. Ronit placed the bottle in the door, but then, thinking better of it, wrapped it in a dishcloth and stowed it way in the back behind some ancient bottles of preserves.

# 12

Alice was upstairs in her grandfather's study when Ronit came looking for her. She was seated cross-legged, her posture perfectly erect, as always, flipping through a file folder marked 'investments'.

'Where have you been?' she asked, looking up.

'I just went to put the case of wine in the cellar,' said Ronit.

'You've been gone for ages; I thought you must have gone spelunking down there.'

'I did wander around a bit.'

'It's quite creepy. I wouldn't have thought you would like spending time down there. I always run back upstairs as quickly as I can.'

'Actually,' said Ronit, 'I made a rather surprising discovery.'

Alice looked up, her interest piqued. She was always interested in talking about the house's surprises, which were infinite, she felt.

'What did you see?'

'There's a small hallway, almost a butler's pantry, beyond the main room of the cellar. The light came on when I turned on the main light. It's full of old and possibly valuable bottles of wine.'

'That can't be,' said Alice flatly, and then asked, 'how can that be?'

'It's there, I swear it. I brought something up for dinner. I don't know if it will be any good, it's so old.'

'Where did you put it?'

'I wrapped it in a dishcloth and stowed it in the back of the refrigerator, behind the jams.'

'Good. But did you put some bottles from the case in the fridge?'

'You told me not to.'

'But she will always look there first. What if she finds the bottle wrapped in the cloth?'

'Oh dear, perhaps I'd better go back down.'

'But hang on a second, look at this.' Alice handed him some old manila envelopes marked 'India Holdings'. 'I've found some things. He had investments there, I think, though it's hard for me to make sense of this sort of thing.'

Ronit opened the first envelope carefully and pulled out some sheets of paper. They looked like financial reports for a company called Harkey Dune, LLC. The name sounded vaguely familiar, though it was odd. Of course, he could not make head nor tail of the documents either. Even the memoranda, not all finance sheets, were confusing.

'What do you think?' asked Alice.

'I'm not really sure. It's a bit hard to understand. Foreign investment was restricted in India after Independence, so maybe he owned shares in an Indian business.'

'Maybe that's it. But what we need mostly is an address or something like that,' said Alice with determination. 'You'd better put some of those other bottles in the fridge,' she added. Ronit sighed and got up off the bed. Slipping on his flip-flops he went downstairs again.

Drawing up his courage, he returned to the cellar door, switched on the light at the top of the stairs, and descended with a purposeful step. At the bottom, he again pulled the string switch, illuminating the room. This time the little hall on the other side did not light up. It was curious, but he had no desire to linger, so he walked quickly to the case and pulled out two bottles of the Alsatian wine, and then a third one.

Returning upstairs, he placed them conspicuously in the front regions of the refrigerator, inside the rack along the door, and on the top shelf, in front of some of the newer groceries, so as to catch the eye of the seeker immediately. He was about to shut the door of the fridge when he thought he might just check on the status of the champagne. He reached back behind the old bottles of blackcurrant jam and grape jelly but found nothing. Unwilling to believe that it had already been removed, he began to pull out bottles and small plates of dried-out leftovers and place them on the floor to get a clear view of the back of the shelf where he had placed the bottle of Chateau LaFitte, but there was nothing there. Could she have already found it? He was surprised that the items on the shelf did not look more disturbed in that case. He sighed and gingerly began to replace the items one by one, wondering if it would be considered unsporting of him to pitch out some of the more egregious ones that were taking up so much space.

# 13

At teatime, Alice came downstairs from a lengthy nap, looking for Ronit. She found him on the terrace again, hunched over the travelogue, his chair dragged a few feet across the flagstones to the only remaining patch of direct sunlight. Even midsummer in New England was chilly for him, and he had fled the damp of the house for what sun he could find. Alice thought of him as an iguana at times like these. When he became dispirited by the lack of sunlight in winter, she would have him sit under a blanket by the sunniest window in their apartment or suggest that they go have tea in the winter garden at a local hotel. Ronit looked up when he heard her approach.

'Did you sleep well?'

'Yes, sort of, but there was another party.'

'Ah, and I wasn't there to see if you put on your dancing slippers.' He smiled.

Alice frowned. 'I think I'm meant to notice a certain person at the parties,' she said. 'A man.'

'Do you know who he is?'

'No. I've seen him in photographs. He's tall. Handsome.'

'Then he must not be difficult to notice.' Ronit found himself feeling jealous.

'No, he's not. But he's not someone I've seen in the photograph albums. Most of the parties seem to be taking place before my mother and aunt were born, so I don't know if there's any sense in asking Clare about him.'

'You could ask your grandmother?'

'I don't know. She did not take kindly to my questions this morning. Oh, and the nurse says Nanette would like to see you after teatime.'

'Oh,' said Ronit. 'Should I tidy myself up?'

'Yes, I think so. Not too much, but she likes men to be a little formal.'

Alice didn't want to say so, but she also knew that Nanette would think better of Ronit if he were dressed up. The only other time they had met, Ronit had worn a sports jacket. She thought that might be a good idea again. She wasn't sure if she thought of Nanette as racist as such, but still, he was a dark-skinned foreigner, something that Nanette might find interesting, and a little suspect. Maybe that was racist. In any case, she didn't want to think about it too hard.

'I will get tea together,' said Alice. 'Maybe you can wear a blazer or something, if you brought one.' Ronit, who generally preferred to be more formally attired than most of the American men he knew, had indeed brought a blazer and even a suit, in case the need should arise.

In the kitchen, Alice busied herself with the tea. She prepared a tray with some of the new cookies they'd bought in the market and brought it to the library. Then she prepared a cup for her mother, took it into the living room and set it down on the coffee table next to her, where she was reading the Sunday paper. A bottle of champagne, half empty, stood on the floor next to her. Clare caught Alice looking at it.

'Looking for weapons of mass destruction?' she asked slyly. 'So thoughtful of you and your gentleman friend, your *financier*, to bring me champagne,' she purred, her words slurred.

'That was meant for after dinner,' said Alice shortly. She leaned down and fished through the pile of discarded sections of newspaper, looking for the magazine section.

'There's still some left,' said Clare, lifting it up and shaking it to show that the bottle was not empty. She chuckled. 'I should have known. I thought it was a new direction in psychoanalysis for me from your Indian prince. Oh, and if you're looking for the crossword, I started it for you.' She handed her the crossword, already half-filled in with a pink felt-tip pen.

'He's a psychiatrist, and you may finish it, if you wish. The champagne and the crossword.' Alice turned and walked out of the room. She found Ronit in the library. He looked every inch a country gentleman, wearing a flax-coloured linen jacket, a white shirt with a pale-green tie and khaki trousers. She knew Nanette would be pleased. She went up to him and kissed him on the cheek and ran her hand over the tie.

'You look just right,' she said. 'My mother has drunk most of the champagne,' she added. 'And she's taken the newspaper, so it's likely to end up in the bathtub.'

'I was afraid of that,' said Ronit. 'The champagne, I mean. It was gone from my hiding place when I went to put the other wine in the door of the fridge.'

'She's clever that way,' she said, as she mixed milk and sugar into his tea and handed it to him.

'Most alcoholics are.'

Alice sniffed. She did not like to think of her mother in those terms. In fact, the terms in which she thought of her were far more damning. In her head she used the word *harpy*, or sometimes even *harridan*. The language of fairy tales and fantasy came more easily to her than that of addiction.

'Do you really think that? That that's the main thing?' asked Alice.

'That what's the main thing? Her addiction?'

'I just don't know if she does it because she feels compelled to. Sometimes I think she just does it to taunt us, or even to taunt herself.'

'Well, that could be.'

Alice never asked Ronit to make a psychiatric assessment of Clare, partially because she didn't want to hear her condition, or her illness, or whatever it was, discussed in clinical terms, but partly because she knew he would not give one if she asked, and she was grateful for that. He was already painfully aware of the line he had crossed to be romantically involved with Alice, and he wasn't about to cross back over it for her mother. He did of course feel a blurring of categories when it came to Alice herself. As her boyfriend, or her fiancé, he felt protective of her, and this included her mental health, which was in a precarious position at the moment.

'Shall we go to Nanette now?' asked Alice when Ronit had finished his cup of tea.

'Yes, let's go.' He stood up and brushed his jacket and tie in case some crumbs had fallen from the cookies. Being led into Nanette's chamber was like being brought before the queen. He needed to look his best.

# 14

As they walked through the living room to Nanette's bedroom, Clare scowled at them from behind *The Eustace Diamonds*. Ronit noticed that the bottle of champagne was two-thirds gone now. Clare caught his eye as he looked up from the bottle and smirked but said nothing. They proceeded through the pocket doors, where they found Nanette just finishing her tea. The nurse was seated in the corner, knitting a tiny candy-pink acrylic sweater on a circular needle. Alice hoped that Nanette, who was violently opposed to all synthetic fabrics and wools, was too ill to notice the yarn.

'Good afternoon, Nanette,' said Alice, as she leaned down and kissed her on the forehead. Nanette held her hand and looked her in the eye as though she wanted to say something. She looked sad. Then she noticed Ronit standing behind Alice. Alice saw her assessing his appearance, perhaps trying to remember him. She had only met him once before, a year previously. Her memories of recent events were not always sharp. She looked pleased and smiled. Alice stood to one side so Ronit could address her.

'Good afternoon, Mrs Ramsey,' he said, his voice pitched loud from years of practice treating elderly demented patients. Nanette held out her quavering hand, and he took it in his and smiled. 'You are looking well,' he said. 'And your new bedroom is very grand,' he added, gesturing to the walls of the dining room. Nanette indicated that she'd like her pad, and Alice handed it to her.

*We all must die*, she wrote.

Alice was surprised. Nanette rarely spoke of her condition at all. She felt a sudden queasiness in the pit of her stomach and sat down in a chair by the window.

'Indeed,' said Ronit, unfazed. 'It is the human condition.'

*I've waited for you*, she wrote. *I'd like to give my blessing to you both, for a long and happy marriage.* Her hand shook as she wrote, not from emotion, but because it was getting increasingly difficult for her to handle a pen. Alice was again surprised, this time by her expression of a sentiment that sounded almost religious.

'We are grateful to you for your blessings,' said Ronit, smiling, and took her hand again. Nanette nodded approvingly, the paralysed side of her mouth twitching, as though she wished to smile. She held up both her hands and waved Alice and Ronit towards her. Alice stood, awkwardly, not sure what was expected. Ronit held out his hand to Alice and guided her to his side so that they were both quite close to Nanette. She nodded again and held a hand over each of their heads as they bent down. *It was sort of like communion*, thought Alice, who had partaken of that sacrament only rarely in her life. Nanette's eyes were closed, as if in prayer. The two of them stood obediently, heads down until she withdrew her hands. She reached for her pad again.

*Take good care of Alice*, she wrote.

'Of course,' replied Ronit.

*Alice*, she wrote, *there is a small box in the drawer of this nightstand. Please take it out.*

Alice pulled open the drawer as she was told and sorted through a variety of small items: nail scissors, eye drops, lozenges, a sewing kit, such things as Nanette had always kept by her bed. She remembered sorting through them when she was young and being scolded for it, until Nanette had realized Alice had merely been setting them out in rows, not trying to consume or destroy anything. In the back, she found a small jewellery box covered in blue velvet, a bit worn. She held it up for Nanette to see and she nodded. Alice opened it carefully. Inside was a gold ring, set all around with tiny pearls. The ring was very small. Alice pulled it out and tried it on her ring finger. It was a little tight, even on her lean fingers, but she managed to pull it on.

'I've never seen this,' she said. 'It's beautiful.'

*It is a special ring. For your wedding*, she wrote.

Alice felt herself beginning to sob, and dropped to her knees suddenly, her fingers covering her face. She felt utterly unprepared to part with Nanette, even when so much of her had already gone. She had been leaving for quite some time, but Alice had fooled herself into believing that if she stayed in the house, if she stayed close by, they could not be separated the way distance had separated them in the past. In giving her the ring and blessing her union with Ronit, she knew Nanette was giving her away to the groom, as the father traditionally does at a wedding. She could not bear the sudden flow of grief she felt, and she hugged her legs to her body, burying her head in her knees. Outside her grief she could hear Ronit talking to Nanette. She didn't know what he said. Nanette must be responding. Ronit had never seen her experience such tremendous emotion. It had literally toppled her off her feet. Still, he was calm, unruffled. Eventually, she felt his hands on her shoulders. He was crouching down in front of her, trying to hold her still. She realized she had been rocking back and forth and now felt foolish. Ronit put his arms around her and whispered into her ear, 'shhhhh, shhhhh. Everything will be fine, you'll see. I love you; I love you. Alice. Alice. Try to stand up. Come with me.'

Slowly, she stood and wiped her eyes with the back of her hand. Ronit handed her a tissue and she blew her nose, loudly. She wiped her face again and turned towards Nanette. Nanette lay back against her pillow, her silvery bob thin and wispy against the white pillow. Her beautiful face was gaunt and expressionless, but her eyes were open, following Alice's movements. Alice went to the bed and leaned over and kissed her on the cheek, clutching her narrow shoulders. Nanette closed her eyes for a moment.

'Thank you, Nanette. It means so much to me, thank you.' She felt the tears begin again, and choked them back, sniffing inelegantly and holding the soggy tissue to her face. Ronit still had his arm around her shoulder, she realized.

'We'll come see you after supper,' whispered Alice, and Nanette nodded slightly and closed her eyes, as though the flood of Alice's emotions had exhausted her. Ronit led Alice out of the room slowly. She glanced at the nurse as they walked by. She sat and knitted, her needles silent, plastic, her eyes buried in the pink synthetic yarn. Outside the door Clare looked up at them with interest. *She must have heard me crying*, thought Alice, resentfully. She felt terribly exposed and walked through the living room as quickly as possible, feeling her mother's cyes raking her back as she went. Ronit led her slowly through the hall and up the stairs. On the landing she turned to look at her grandfather's room momentarily. She saw way at the end of the hall the light was on. She saw his slipper protruding.

'I can't see him now,' she muttered to herself, as she shuffled down the hall to their room.

# 15

Alice did not come down for dinner that night. Which meant there was no dinner since Alice was the cook. Clare was left to forage in the kitchen, and the night nurse, Rhoda, made Nanette a cheese sandwich and a small cup of tomato soup. Upstairs, Ronit convinced Alice to take a hot bath and change into her nightgown. While she was bathing, he took a small broom and engaged in some covert dusting of the bedspread and the area around the bed. When she came out, she lay down limply on her side of the bed. In the dusk, her light-brown hair, her pale skin and her baby-blue nightgown all seemed roughly the same shade of bluish grey. She looked as though she were drowning, he thought, his Ophelia.

'Let's switch on a light,' he suggested. Alice did not respond, so he switched on the two bedside lamps, which bathed the room in a rosy glow. 'Would you like a book?'

'I don't know,' whispered Alice.

He looked at the pile of books on her nightstand and brought out a new novel by a woman author he had heard of. 'How about this one?'

'Finished.'

'Ah, how about these short stories?'

Alice turned and looked at them. 'Okay.'

'Are you hungry? Would you like something to eat?'

Alice held the book against her chest and stared at the ceiling without responding.

'Why don't I go down and put together a plate with the cheese and crackers we bought and maybe some wine?'

'No wine,' said Alice firmly. 'Anything but wine.'

'Is there anything else?'

'I think there's gin,' she said.

'Your mother doesn't drink gin?'

'Just wine these days.'

'How do you want the gin?'

'Lemon, sugar, soda.'

'Like a gimlet?'

'Yes.'

In the kitchen, Rhoda, the night nurse, was washing up Nanette's dishes. She was much chattier than the day nurse. When she learned that Ronit was a psychiatrist, she was thrilled.

'It's so fantastic, Doctor, to have a physician in the house!' Her tone was mildly flirtatious. She threw back her head and laughed as she dried the dishes, leaning an ample hip against the counter. She was a large, fleshy woman with curly blonde hair and bright blue eyeshadow. Ronit was disconcerted, both by her evident interest in him, and her garish aesthetic, which was incongruous in this decaying manse. He supposed, though, when he thought about it, that he was also out of place here. Perhaps her boldness towards him was motivated by a sense that they were both outsiders. Ronit carefully arranged the crackers on a white plate ringed with bluebirds and placed the cheese on another plate of the same pattern. Rhoda helped him find a tray, as she told him in detail about the challenges she had faced as a single mother undergoing her nursing certification training. It was a tale not unfamiliar to him, and he expressed appropriate sympathy along the way. But his responses were distracted, and he realized as he stirred Alice's gimlet that Rhoda had just said something he was expected to respond to.

'I'm sorry,' he said apologetically. 'I missed what you just said. It's been a difficult day.'

Rhoda tut-tutted sympathetically. 'It's hard for them, isn't it? Mrs Ramsey is such a lovely lady.'

'She is,' he said. 'She means a great deal to Alice.'

This remark, with its touching concern for the well-being of his fiancée, had the desirable effect of discouraging Rhoda, who suddenly withdrew into a more professional demeanour, and set about efficiently finishing the tidying up.

As she was about to leave the kitchen, Ronit asked suddenly, 'Will she be up to seeing any visitors this evening, do you think? Mrs Ramsey, I mean.'

'Oh, I don't know, Doctor. She seems a bit weakly; but if you'd like, I'll check with her.'

'If you could, I would appreciate it. Alice had spoken of visiting her again in the evening.'

Rhoda smiled pleasantly and set out briskly for the dining room. Ronit set the cocktails on the tray and waited for her return. Moments later, he heard a door slam and footsteps racing towards the kitchen. Rhoda entered breathlessly, her large body straining from these vigorous movements.

'It's Mrs Ramsey,' she said. 'I believe she's passed.'

Ronit hurried past her and rushed through the living room, past the now upright figure of Clare, who despite her sedation, sensed something was awry. In the dining room, Nanette lay motionless, her eyes wide open, her face ashen against the pillow. Ronit rushed to her side, felt her pulse and held his hand over her mouth. She was gone.

'Will you declare her?' asked Rhoda quietly.

'Of course,' he said.

# 16

No one but Aunt Bix had come to stay in the house before or after the funeral, and even she had only come the night before, to help with the arrangements for the reception. Alice had not seen her three uncles, now in their late sixties, since she was a teenager. There was a gap of ten years between Roger, Lewis and Stormton, and Bix. Clare was the youngest of the five, two years younger than Bix. She had always been the baby. The uncles had come directly to the church, arriving about half an hour before the ceremony. She had seen Stormton first, and recognized him not for his resemblance to himself, but for his uncanny similarity to her grandfather. He had grown portly, his hair was white, and he sported a bushy moustache that completely covered his upper lip. His navy blue suit had been tailored for his body at a slimmer stage, although he had never been a slender man. He breathed heavily as he climbed the stairs to the front door of the church, where Alice stood awaiting the guests in a black sheath she had found in Nanette's closet.

'Uncle Stormy,' she said quietly, and held out her hands to him. He took them lightly and kissed her cheek. He smelled of pipe tobacco, just as his father had done. 'Have you come alone?' she asked.

'No, no,' he replied, 'the rest are parking the car. You look lovely, my dear, so like her.' He stopped himself, not wishing to continue with a remark that would remind him of his mother, and of grief, an uncomfortable sentiment.

Coming up the path, she saw her uncles Roger and Lewis, and behind them their wives, and some of their children. Roger and Lewis, each a replica of their father, walked uncomfortably, their suits clearly over-warm for their bodies on this summer day. Roger walked with a cane now, as did his wife, who came behind him. Alice kissed each of her relations, and led them into the church, pointing the way to the pew where Bix and Clare, whom they all called Trixie, were seated. As Alice stood in the rear of the church, she thought how funny it was that each of the men should resemble their father so precisely, while Bix and Clare looked exactly like Nanette. She watched the two of them standing in the pew, backs ramrod straight. As they turned their heads towards the aisle to greet their brothers, she could see their identical profiles in silhouette, a pair of cranes at water's edge.

Ronit, who had been helping with the placement of the flowers, came to her side, and she pointed out the row of uncles, aunts and cousins. He was amazed at her clear-headedness following Nanette's death. After her collapse at Nanette's bedside, he had expected the worst when he'd gone to bring her the news. But she had risen quietly from the bed, walked deliberately down the stairs, through the living room, where the couch was now empty, and into the dining room, where she found her mother weeping on the floor in the corner.

'Come,' she said, holding out both hands to Clare, who took hold of her, staring up with a tear-stained face. Alice pulled her up off the floor, embraced her, kissed her on both cheeks and then said, 'Mama, let's say goodbye now.'

Ronit stood in the doorway and watched as Alice led Clare over to the bed. She lifted Nanette's limp, white hand, and joined it with Clare's and her own.

'Do you want to say anything to her?' Alice asked Clare.

'I can't.' She stood still as a statue, staring at Nanette. Then, hesitantly, she murmured, 'Goodbye, Mother.'

'Goodbye, Nanette,' said Alice evenly. 'Please visit us. We will always need you.'

With this, Clare broke down again, and Alice led her gently away, brought her to the kitchen and seated her in a wooden chair. She placed the cheese and crackers, earlier abandoned by Ronit, in front of her. 'Eat, Mother,' she said. She poured her a glass of milk as well. 'Drink this,' she said, setting the milk before her on the table. Clare obeyed her and the wet redness of her face was slowly replaced by an exhausted pallor.

'She needs to sleep,' observed Alice to Ronit, and together they led her upstairs to the room that had always been hers, where she had been meant to sleep on this trip but had rarely entered. Alice pulled back the sheets and helped Clare in. Checking back half an hour later, she had seen that her eyes were closed and her breathing even, so she switched off the lights.

# 17

The church was about half-full. Nanette had been very popular in local society, but she was eighty-six when she died and few of her friends remained. When everyone stood for the recessional, Alice turned to look at the crowd. The mourners were grouped together, mostly towards the front. She noticed a man standing alone in one of the rearmost pews. He was elderly, but tall and trim. His silvery hair was neatly cut, and he was dressed in a crumpled black suit. Alice did not know him from the village, but he looked familiar somehow. She heard whispering down the pew and turned to see that her uncles had seen him too. They were whispering among themselves in a tone of urgency.

There was no need for pall-bearers as Nanette had stipulated in her funeral plan that she be cremated. As they processed from the church, Alice looked to her left, towards the pew where the man had stood, but he was no longer there. She saw him outside, standing beneath the ash tree in front of the church. He looked a bit lonely, and she considered introducing herself to him, when she saw two of her uncles hastening towards him. She was stopped and offered condolences by a lovely old woman, a contemporary of Nanette's, from the village, and while she tried her best to offer the woman her full attention, she could not help but be distracted by the rising voices coming from the direction of the ash tree. The woman noticed that Alice's attention was being divided, and she turned and looked in the direction of the commotion.

'Ah, one had not expected to see *him* here,' she observed softly, nodding towards the man beneath the tree. When her head moved, the feathers sprouting from her black straw hat bobbed in unison. The feathers blocked Alice's view and she shifted slightly to one side.

'Who is he?' she asked, curious.

'Oh, have you never met him? Of course not, of course not. He was long before your time.' She smiled. Alice saw Bix and her mother standing at a slight remove from their brothers, speaking in whispers as they watched the scene.

'His name is Jim Smith. He was a great friend of Nanette's at one time. Quite a poetic figure.'

'My uncles do not seem happy to see him here. Why is that?' asked Alice, fixing the woman with an intense gaze. She knew it would be difficult to get anything like the truth from her relations, who all ignored incisive questions about family history or responded with sarcastic ripostes that tended to lead one ever further from the truth.

The woman looked at her kindly, her soft blue eyes filled with compassion. 'It was said at one time,' she replied with a smile, 'that he was her lover.'

In the scene beneath the tree, the unwanted visitor was turning to go. Alice thanked the woman and walked purposefully towards the arguing group. Just as she got near, a tiny woman, all dressed in black with a small hat draped in netting walked nimbly over to her and caught her by the arm.

'Such a tragedy,' she said, in a gravelly voice shaped by years of heavy smoking. 'Your grandmother meant the *world* to me,' she drew out the word 'world' in a drawl, her yellowed teeth locked together. 'You must be *devastated*,' she added. Alice craned her neck to follow the swiftly vanishing figure of Jim Smith. Her uncles were returning to the groups in front of the church. Alice shook the hand of the mourner with the netted hat and murmured her thanks. She wanted to cry, not with sorrow, but with frustration. She knew why she recognized Mr Smith. He had been the man in her vivid dancing dreams.

# 18

In the week that preceded their trip to Kolkata, Alice sat on the living room floor of the apartment she shared with Ronit, surrounded by boxes of files she had collected from Nanette's house that she thought might be related to her grandfather's travels to India. She had removed the files surreptitiously, before the will was read to the family, in case their ownership might pass to someone unfriendly to her cause. She did not necessarily regard any of Nanette's children as 'enemies' – not even her mother, who was not likely to notice the absence of boxes of files – but she did not wish to take any chances. In the middle of this week, before their departure, the will would be read to the children of the deceased by the executor, Nanette's lawyer and distant cousin, Lawrence Drawbridge. By the time its contents were unsealed, Alice would probably have the information she needed, so if someone happened to notice the great holes in the file cabinets, she could always return them. However, this outcome seemed unlikely. At the funeral, the apathy of Nanette's offspring for the family house, for the treasures it contained, had been dispiriting.

The will, she knew, was mainly of interest for the possibility of money. From what she understood of snatches of conversation overheard between her uncles, the trust bequeathed by her grandfather would liquidate at the time of Nanette's death. It was up to Nanette, in her will, to decide how to distribute the capital, or to reincorporate it into a new trust. She had been exceedingly tight-lipped about her intentions at the end of her life, and no one knew what she had planned. Most of her five children were in need of funds, some more than others. The existing trust had doled out to each of them a small annuity that was considered a supplemental income by those who had done well, and a subsistence income by those who had not, particularly Clare. These annuities would now come to an end with Nanette's death and there was much tension between the siblings as to who might benefit. No one was even sure how much money was left, with so many of them living off it, and that large house could have been draining the trust too, for all they knew.

There was some suspicion, for example, towards Clare, whom everyone knew to have been camped outside her mother's room for months before her death. Alice found the notion absurd that Clare, in her inebriated haze, could have moved anyone to make major changes to a legal document, much less someone like Nanette. Nanette had stipulated that the will be read out a month after her death, in Boston, some three hours distant from the family home. It was speculated that the location had been chosen as it was more convenient for the homes of her children, but when the announcement was made, there was much consternation and even anger at the one-month waiting period. The uncles had attempted to get the date moved up, but Lawrence Drawbridge had remained unmoved and scheduled the meeting at his office in the city.

That meeting was now two days hence, and Alice was trying to avoid contact with the family until it was over. She could no longer tolerate her mother's tearful late-night phone calls alleging conspiracies between her various siblings to do her out of her inheritance, and email notes from her uncles and aunt angling for information she might have gathered during Nanette's last days. Instead, Alice turned off her ringer and sat among the files, trying to make sense of terse financial notes written in her grandfather's crabbed handwriting.

So far, she had learned that her grandfather had had business interests in a city called Muzaffarnagar. He had been in his father's textile business, which mostly manufactured the fabrics used to upholster furniture as well as heavy drapes. Presumably much of the fabric was imported through this Muzaffarnagar connection. She had been aided in this discovery by a conversation between Ronit and her uncle Lewis, who, feeling at a loss as to what to say to an Indian person, had told him that their father's business had handled imports from India. Ronit, seeing an opening for more information about Alice's grandfather's travels there, had asked if he, Uncle Lewis, had ever travelled with his father.

'Oh no,' was the testy answer. 'I should say not. Of course,' he added, realizing his response might sound insulting to Ronit's homeland, 'we were never asked. It was strictly business, you know.'

'Aha. Do you know where these business interests were located?'

'That, I'm afraid I don't know. Roger may know. He worked at the company for a time, before it was sold off.' He tapped his brother on the back, who had grown rosy-cheeked from his third whiskey sour.

'What's that?' asked Roger.

'Where did Father travel when he went to India, do you know? Alice's fiancé, here, uh, Row-*meet*, is keen to know.'

Ronit smiled and held out his hand. 'Ronit,' he said.

'Pleased to meet you,' said Roger, shaking his hand vigorously. The third brother, Stormy, had also turned towards them, and another introduction was effected. The three men were heavy of body, but also immensely tall. Ronit felt as though he were trapped in a tableau of Botero sculptures.

'Do you remember then? Rodge? Where Father went in India?'

'Oh, yes, of course. On the tip of my tongue. Long name, starting with M ...' he looked hopefully at Ronit, as if this might be all the information that was needed for him to guess the right city.

'Was it in the north?'

'I believe yes, or it could also have been the south,' said Roger thoughtfully.

'I remember there were plenty of Zs in it,' contributed Stormy, also in his cups.

'You are absolutely right,' cried Lewis. 'Now I remember that! Starting with M, plenty of Zs. Quite, quite long.'

Ronit rattled off a few names like this, one of which was Muzaffarnagar. Everyone had agreed that it was one of those.

'The thing is,' ventured Ronit, 'Alice and I are planning a trip to India to see my family. She would like to know more about the family connection.'

'Alice is going to India!'

'How intrepid! Wasn't she terribly ill there at one time?'

'Yes, but –'

'An adventurous girl, that.' Stormy and Lewis both slapped him on the back and suddenly all three brothers seemed to dematerialize, no mean feat, he thought, considering their size. He wondered, as he watched them moving nimbly through the crowd towards the bar, how many of them suffered from gout and heart disease.

Since bringing the files home, Alice had indeed discovered records of correspondence with Muzaffarnagar. Of course, these were not Grandfather's business files. Those would have long ago been transferred with the rest of the company's files when it had been sold to a larger conglomerate in the seventies. But she had also discovered another M place, called Mussoorie. This had shown up on postmarks of letters to Nanette in her files. The letters themselves were curt and businesslike. He always asked after his children, but the absence of any personal relationship between the two of them was more than evident. On a few of these envelopes, she had also found an address, which she had noted down.

Ronit had promised they would visit one or both of these places when they went to India, although the thought of trying to squeeze in such side trips to another part of the country when he had so many family members to visit made him anxious. Already his mother, ecstatic at the prospect of meeting her future daughter-in-law, had planned numerous gatherings and outings. How he was going to fit all this in on his three-week vacation he did not know. Alice had suggested she go to Muzaffarnagar and Mussoorie on her own, after he returned to the United States, and he had tried to explain to her that his family would never allow her to travel on her own and would most definitely send a proxy in his place if he were to leave. Thus far, she had been unable to process this level of protectiveness and was ignoring the problem entirely.

# 19

On the morning the will was to be read, Alice saw she had missed a message from an unknown caller. When she checked, she found it was from Lawrence Drawbridge, asking her to attend the meeting. How odd, she thought. He said in the message that he had tried to call her a few times before but had found the number he was calling was incorrect. He explained that Nanette had specified that Alice should be present when the will was unsealed. Alice could think of nowhere she'd less like to be, but it was Nanette's wish, so she must obey it.

With a heavy heart, Alice boarded a train and travelled to the address she had been given. Arriving a little early, she found herself in front of a large, new brick office building. It was an impersonal spot. The choice felt ominous to her. She stood in front of the building in her light-green checked sundress, wondering if she should go in early or not. Soon she saw the lumbering figures of two of her uncles climbing out of a large car, and decided she would retreat into the interior of the building rather than running the risk of having to stand in an elevator with them. She pulled open one of the large glass doors and walked over to the elevators. There was a directory of offices, and finding that the office she sought was on the ninth floor, she stepped into the elevator and pressed the button. As the doors slid shut, she saw Uncle Lewis and Uncle Roger coming in through the front door. *Just in time*, she thought.

On the ninth floor she walked down a thickly carpeted corridor and found the law office advertised with a brass plate on an orange door. The door pulled open noiselessly, and inside she was greeted by a pleasant receptionist.

'Are you here for the Ramsey will?' she asked.

'Yes,' said Alice, looking around. 'Is no one else here?'

'Not yet,' said the receptionist, 'But I will tell Mr Drawbridge that you are here,' she said, pressing a button on her desk.

'Thank you,' said Alice.

Moments later, Lawrence Drawbridge emerged from an office and came out and shook Alice's hand.

'Alice! Lovely to see you,' he said. 'I don't know if you remember me. We met a number of times when you were a child.'

'Yes, I saw you at the funeral,' said Alice.

'Of course, of course. I'm very sorry for your loss. It's everyone's loss, really. Nanette was a lovely, lovely woman.' He led her by the elbow down a small hallway and into a sterile-looking conference room furnished with a large laminate table surrounded by orange plastic chairs with stainless steel arms and legs. 'Do make yourself comfortable in here,' he said. 'There's a buffet lunch, as you can see,' he said, waving his hand towards a side table. 'Coffee, tea, juices, some sandwiches and such.'

Alice looked at him suspiciously. She didn't like the idea of sharing a catered lunch with her mother and her mother's siblings. She suddenly began to feel oppressed by the recirculated air in the building. Why did he need *her* to be here at all? The idea that she was a beneficiary in the will had crossed her mind, and she didn't like it. If Nanette's children had reason to resent her, she would prefer to be as physically distant from them as possible. She wished that she and Ronit had booked an earlier flight to Kolkata. She would already be halfway around the world, and she would simply not look at her email for a few months until everyone's energies had dissipated.

She sat down on a chair in a far corner and hugged her canvas bag to her chest. She shivered in her thin sundress in the full-bore air conditioning. Just then her uncles Lewis and Roger entered the room, talking in low voices. They both looked surprised to see her there and their conversation dropped off.

'Alice!' said Roger, recovering. 'Hadn't expected to see you here!'

'I only learned I was to come today,' she said quietly. 'Look, there is a buffet.' She pointed. The mention of the buffet proved an adequate distraction for the two men, who pushed their way past a row of chairs to survey the offerings. Lewis gave Roger a plate and they both began to load their dishes with sandwiches, potato chips and pickles. By now Uncle Stormy had entered the room. Uncle Stormy was an art historian, and though he was not as well off as Uncle Roger, he was also not as impecunious as his brother Lewis, who had a bad habit of making dodgy investments. Of all her uncles, Alice was decidedly the fondest of Stormy. Stormy greeted his brothers, who pointed out the buffet, and said hello to Alice in a kindly tone. He looked a bit worn and she wondered if this was related to the ongoing legal battle relating to his son Daniel's felony assault charges. She wondered if the legal fees made him a more anxious stakeholder in the will than he might otherwise have been.

Stormy was followed by Aunt Bix, who kissed each of her brothers and came around the table to plant a kiss on Alice's cheek as well.

'So lovely to see you again, dear,' she said. If she had not expected to see Alice here, she certainly did not betray that emotion. Alice thought of all her cousins, maybe ten in all? And wondered why they were not there. Of course, none of them had spent as much time with Nanette as she, but with her aunt and uncles in the room she felt singled out.

Lawrence Drawbridge returned to the room. He entered with a smile plastered across his face, and clapping his hands together, he announced, 'Well, we're almost all here! Just waiting for Clare; I'm sure she'll be here soon.' There was a general rolling of eyes. No one really believed this.

'I'll tell you what, Lawrence,' interjected Roger, 'I think we might as well get started. There's no knowing when Clare will arrive.'

Alice sat perfectly still, her lips pursed, gazing at her hands as they clutched her bag. She could feel everyone's eyes on her, asking, silently, when – or if – her mother would arrive. She offered no information as she had none.

'Perhaps we could wait just a few more minutes,' suggested Bix, softly.

Alice was trying to imagine her mother in a room like this. She almost felt that if her mother came to the front door of this building, she would turn back. She would be repelled by the sterility and the newness. It might not even be possible for her to enter. Everyone was milling about, quietly making small talk, preparing to sit down. Bix sat near Alice, a miniature muffin on a paper napkin before her and a Styrofoam cup of tea in her hand. Her hair was perfectly styled, an even shade of auburn. She must dye her hair as well, thought Alice. She wore a spotless white silk sleeveless shirt and a salmon linen skirt. Around her neck was a small string of pearls. She fingered her pearls nervously with one hand, but then turned to smile at Alice, the expression of calm on her face contradicting the rapid movement of her fingers as they clicked the pearls together.

'Your mother tells me you're off to India,' she said brightly. Alice tried to imagine the source of Bix's anxiety. She had understood that Bix's husband had left her well off and she wondered if she actually needed money. Perhaps it was simply the state of not knowing, or the anxiety of being in the room with her siblings. Or a desire for closure.

'Well,' said Lawrence Drawbridge, seating himself at the head of the table. He placed a large file folder on the table from which he withdrew a sealed manila envelope. 'Perhaps we'd better get started. If Clare shows up, I can go over the details with her afterwards.' He adjusted his lemon and navy striped tie and put on his reading glasses. Everyone fell quiet and sat down. Mr Drawbridge looked over his glasses.

'Nanette wrote her final will with me about a year ago, following her stroke. There had been earlier versions, but this was the last.' He carefully unsealed the envelope with a letter opener. 'She asked me to read out a letter to you all, after which I am to summarize the details of the will.' He pulled the documents from the envelope and lifted a sheet of paper from the top of the pile. As he cleared his throat, about to read, the door opened suddenly, and Clare came bursting in, hair dishevelled, eyes red. She wore an emerald-green cocktail dress of Nanette's and carried Nanette's black alligator clutch. From her ears hung large yellow wooden hoop earrings, incongruous with the rest of the ensemble. The earrings swung wildly as though she'd flown into the conference room instead of walking. Dark sweat stains marked the armpits of the dress, which was made of a silk too heavy for August.

'Ah, Clare,' said Lawrence Drawbridge, looking faintly alarmed. 'We were just starting, please take a seat.'

Clare ignored him and lurched over towards the buffet table, where she proceeded to fill a large plate with one of every item. She grabbed a bottle of juice and a sparkling water with her free hand. The clutch lay abandoned at the edge of the buffet. Satisfied that she had taken everything on offer, she turned and gazed at everyone with shining eyes. She was about to sit down near the door when she saw Alice. She seemed stunned, and in the moments that followed, everyone held their breath, wondering if she would explode. Instead, she manoeuvred clumsily towards the corner where Alice had tried to hide herself and threw herself into the seat between Bix and Alice.

'I knew you would come to support me, darling,' she said to Alice in a stage whisper. She squeezed Alice's bicep so hard she winced, and then, just as suddenly, turned away from her and began to greedily consume a turkey sandwich.

Lawrence Drawbridge cleared his throat, looked around and resumed, 'As I mentioned a few moments ago, Nanette asked me to read out this letter to all of you before sharing the particulars of the will with the group. Ah, here we are,' he said, and held up the letter and began to read:

*My Dear Children,*

*I have asked you to gather on this day in a place far from our home, in order to remind you all that it has been many years since any of you have called Lilac Hill your home. It is with this in mind that I have arranged the will in the manner I have chosen, and I ask that each of you respect my last wish to take the necessary steps to keep the house and its legacy maintained in the best manner possible after I am gone.*

*Your loving mother,*
*Nanette*

The room was silent when Mr Drawbridge had finished reading the letter. The discomfort on the part of Nanette's children was palpable. Her message had been clear: *your lack of interest in the house will cost you all in some way*. The silence was interrupted only by Clare chewing a handful of potato chips. Alice was not sure when she had last seen her mother eat a full meal. There was something macabre about watching a bone-thin woman consume handfuls of potato chips. She was in fact so thin that Nanette's slender tailored dress hung on her body like sacking cloth. Alice looked down at her hands again and shuddered.

Mr Drawbridge coughed slightly and shuffled the papers around. 'In pursuance of the spirit of your mother's letter, the broad outlines of the will are as follows: Nanette has reincorporated the trust, which is to be inherited by Alice Bloodshaw. Each of Nanette's children has been left a sum of five thousand dollars. All current annuities will cease. Ms Bloodshaw is also given discretionary power to withdraw funds from the principal of the trust for the purposes of maintaining the family property, Lilac Hill.' There was a gasp, from Bix, and angry snorts from some of the uncles. Mr Drawbridge continued, 'This brings me to the next item, which is that Ms Bloodshaw is to inherit Lilac Hill, as well as all the contents of the property, including Mrs Ramsey's personal effects. She is to allow Mrs Ramsey's children to remove a small number of keepsakes, as long as said removal does not detract from the overall character and value of the house, as determined by Ms Bloodshaw in conjunction with the executor of the estate, Mr Lawrence C. Drawbridge, or his designated successor, upon his decease.' Mr Drawbridge turned the page and glanced over the top of his glasses. 'I think that gives you the general outline of the will,' he said. 'The rest of the specifics I can go over with Alice.' He took off his glasses, folded them and placed them in his breast pocket.

'So that's it, then?' asked Lewis, somewhat shaken. 'Alice gets everything?'

'Yes, that's correct.'

'So she's left it all to Alice,' said Roger. 'What in God's name ...'

'Are you sure this is the final will?' interrupted Bix, timidly, trying to avoid looking at Alice.

'Hold on!' cried Clare suddenly, dropping a half-eaten roast beef sandwich onto her plate. 'Hold on – did you just say she left everything to *Alice*?'

Alice shrank within herself. She had chosen the wrong seat. There was nowhere to go, and she was trapped. Clare stood up, suddenly, and screamed, a high-pitched keening sort of a scream. She threw her plate of food across the table towards Mr Drawbridge, who flinched. Her aim was poor, and it ended up on the floor. She then began to pant. She leaned over the chair next to hers and vomited onto the carpet. Her siblings looked on in horror. Alice jumped up and rushed to her side, but Clare grabbed her by the shoulders and dug her fingernails into her flesh, shaking her. 'You harpy! You bitch! You stole all our money!' she screamed at the top of her lungs. Uncle Stormy lunged over and pulled Clare off Alice.

'Mother, I did nothing, I didn't know,' cried Alice, frantic and confused.

Clare kept chanting 'Harpy! Bitch!' and began to lean over and knock her head against the table. Lewis and Stormy managed to restrain her while Lawrence Drawbridge called the police. Once the authorities had arrived, Alice's uncles and aunt left the scene as quickly as possible, muttering darkly about legal action and contesting the will. Clare was taken off to Mass General, where the staff maintained a thick file of her visits. Alice alone remained behind with Mr Drawbridge, which had been his intention, after all, although he had not meant to effect the thing in precisely that manner.

Amidst the detritus of the buffet lunch, Mr Drawbridge sat down again, brushed off the legal documents, put on his glasses and turned to Alice, who still stood, frozen, on the other side of the room.

'Are you ready to sign the documents?' he asked.

# PART TWO

## VOYAGE

# 20

Alice lay on her side on a narrow wooden cot, reading a novel by Bankimchandra Chatterjee Ronit's father had lent her. Through the open window across the room, she could see the air was thick with rain. Monsoon rain, she had realized, was not made of drops. It was solid. The streets were awash with floodwaters right now and there was no point in trying to go anywhere. After the stress of the previous months, and all the unpleasantness Ronit had faced going through security before their flight when he was subjected to a 'random search' – thanks to Bush's 'War on Terror' – and then the long, claustrophobic plane ride, Alice found this isolation comforting. Ronit's family's house was not in any immediate danger of being flooded itself, and there was enough food and water to last a week. Nonetheless, everyone fretted over the rising waters and the men went out periodically to inspect the damage, returning each time drenched to the bone, their umbrellas useless in the deluge. Alice embraced her seclusion. Internet service was spotty to non-existent, with power frequently knocked out and phone lines down. No one could reach her. She was on an island, and while on the island, she resolved to make the most of Ronit's father's collection of literature, which was extensive, and to drink tea as long as supplies lasted.

Because they were not married, Alice had been given the guest room in the flat, and Ronit had to sleep in the living room. Alice had been surprised by the arrangement, as Ronit had forgotten to warn her this would happen. It was all self-evident to him. To Alice, this added a new dimension to the idea of marriage, an institution that, to her mind, had always seemed extraneous to the fabric of society. She now saw that marriage could be a means of crossing a barrier, a way for two people to be alone together. On the other hand, she did not actually mind having her own room and rather liked it. It completed her isolation.

What she had not budgeted for was that while this separate sleeping arrangement banished Ronit from her bedroom, it did not banish anyone else. The guest quarters doubled as a storage room for clothing and many other household items. It proved to be a high-traffic area. The family's servants, a woman who did the cooking and cleaning, and a boy who helped with errands and heavy chores, were surprised whenever they found the door not only closed but bolted from the inside. On such occasions they would shake the handle and push at the door, assuming that there was some malfunction in the knob or hinges. When Alice got up to unfasten the latch for them, she was greeted by looks of consternation and surprise. The ensuing conversations had to go through several layers of interpretation, from which Alice learned that they were worried that something was amiss with her. She had resigned herself now to simply leave the door wide open unless she was changing her clothes.

She heard a soft knock and looked up. Ronit stood in the doorway, smiling at her.

'How is the book?' he asked.

'Excellent,' she said. 'I don't think their marriage will work out,' she added. 'I'm not even sure if the heroine is human. And now a woman he married as a child has shown up.'

'I don't think I've read that one,' he said. 'Everyone loves Bankim, though.'

'I can see why. It's a page-turner. Your father says he has more in English.'

'He has everything,' laughed Ronit. Ronit's father, I.P. Roy, was a professor of English literature at Jadavpur University and a distinguished critic. The book Alice now held in her hand had been edited by him, and it was from the blurb on the back that she had learned he was a distinguished critic. Though he'd lent her this book, he was a man of few words, and she had only so far heard him discourse on the rainfall, and even that quite infrequently. Small and lean with a thick thatch of white hair and a neatly trimmed moustache, he mostly sat in a woven easy chair and read the news, first in Bangla and then in English, using a large, spherical magnifying glass that resembled a crystal ball. Every now and then he put his reading material aside, and grasping the arms of his chair, hoisted himself up to go in search of his rain boots. Alice wondered if he would tell her distinguished things about literature after the rains had stopped.

'My mother would like to know if you want a cocktail,' said Ronit.

'Yes, please.'

'What would you like?'

'I don't know what the choices are. We've been having beer, but I'd prefer something else.'

'There's Scotch, gin and rum. You could have a gimlet, or a rum and Coke or plain Scotch. That's what my parents drink.'

'I'll have a rum and Coke,' said Alice. 'Should I come in?'

'Yes, if you'd like.'

Alice stood up, yawned and stretched, somehow exhausted from a day of reading and napping. Or maybe it was the jet lag. She was wearing a pale-blue kurta of Ronit's, and a white pyjama that had been produced from a drawer in the room where she was sleeping. She had packed light, intending to buy appropriate clothing after she arrived, but the flooding had rendered shopping unnavigable, so she had to make do with what was available.

In the living room was seated Ronit's mother, Debashree, reclining on her chaise, a glass of Scotch in her hand. She was dressed in a white sari with a yellow blouse and wore heavy gold earrings and a few gold bangles on her wrists. Her hair was cut in a short, wavy bob, shot through with streaks of white that looked quite glamorous. *She does not dye her hair*, thought Alice.

'Alice!' cried out Debashree when she saw her come in. She waved her hand languidly towards the armchair next to her. 'Come sit, my dear,' she said, patting Alice on the arm. Her fingernails were short, but heavily lacquered with dark-red polish, and Alice was intrigued by the fact that she had rings on almost every finger, some set with large and unfamiliar stones. Alice wondered if it would be a faux pas to ask about the rings.

'How are you keeping, my dear?' asked Debashree. 'I've not seen you all day. I was afraid you'd been taken ill because you've been in bed so much. People often fall ill during monsoon, you know. I asked Ronu if you were unwell, and he said you were still jet-lagged.'

Debashree had herself been lying in bed, or on her chaise, for much of the day, but because she thought of the guest room as a storeroom, she found it troubling that someone would want to lie in it if they had other choices. Ronit had been meaning to suggest to Alice that she move into the living room during the day, knowing his mother would find it peculiar, but he had been planning to let her rest another day.

'I'm fine. Thank you,' Alice smiled.

'Now listen,' said Debashree, 'there's something I've been very curious about. Is it true that one must remove one's shoes now to fly in the States because of a man who had turned his boots into little bombs?'

'Well …' Alice hesitated, worried she might be drawn into a conversation about current events and come up short since she tried to avoid the news as much as possible. 'There was a shoe-bomber, yes, but one only has to remove one's shoes to go through security. Then we can put them back on.'

'Oh, that's a relief!' cried Debashree. 'I had been imagining everyone getting back their shoes with their luggage!' She laughed warmly.

Debashree was a poetess, as well as a mainstay of artistic society in Kolkata. Alice had never known anyone with such a fast-moving mind. In her poise and good taste, she reminded Alice of Nanette, but her brain seemed to whizz about the room at top speed, like a bee, always searching for new ideas or impressions. Alice liked to watch her speak and wave her sparkling fingers in the air; she made everything she discussed sound exciting.

Debashree, for her part, had decided she was pleased with her future daughter-in-law. She hadn't known what to expect, as Ronit was typically unforthcoming about his bride-to-be. 'All I know is that she's White,' she complained to her husband after one particularly unsatisfying phone conversation with Ronit. 'Why is he so damned cagey? Is it his profession?'

'Could be,' responded Professor Roy, without glancing up from his lecture notes on the nineteenth-century British novel. 'He lacks facility with descriptive language,' he added after a moment.

'I'm afraid you are right,' replied Debashree ruefully. 'I just want to know what she does, what she looks like, the usual things. He doesn't need to impress me, but he knows that, I'm sure.'

'Perhaps he doesn't know how to describe a foreign woman to us,' suggested Professor Roy, carefully jotting an asterisk next to a passage on *Our Mutual Friend* and then inserting a corresponding notation on the bottom of the page where he wrote: *cf. queer theory.* He liked to surprise his students with cutting-edge theory. Despite the fact that he never used a computer and was only vaguely aware of the existence of email, he managed, through a bookseller friend, to stay thoroughly current with his field. He was imagining delightedly the looks of shock on his students' faces, always sleepy in the afternoon seminar, when he would suddenly suggest, *pace* the American theorist Eve Kosofsky Sedgwick, that the relationship between the schoolmaster Bradley Headstone and the dilettantish barrister Eugene Wrayburn might have homosexual undertones.

'That could be so, something lost in translation, perhaps,' mused Debashree. 'I only wish he would bring her here so we could see for ourselves. I promise not to judge her unfavourably.'

True to her word, Debashree had not judged Alice unfavourably, and, on the whole, rather liked her. Alice was quiet, tall and pale, and she seemed to waft rather than walk about the house. She did not appear to have any fashion sense at all, and when the floodwaters receded, she would need a bit of dressing up before she could be brought out among their friends. But overall, she thought she would make a favourable impression. Debashree wondered why her son had not gone for someone more intellectual. He was himself highly educated and had grown up in a literary household. From what she gathered, Alice had not even completed college. Ronit had mentioned some time at a women's college, followed by a brief stint at Harvard. Was it within the purview of a mother-in-law/daughter-in-law relationship to coax her towards finishing her degree? She seemed bright enough, if a little hazy. She had mooted the idea to her husband the night before as they were reading in bed.

'Perhaps you could help her enrol in Jadavpur and then Ronit could practise here for a time,' she suggested hopefully.

Professor Roy smiled but did not look up from his new book of critical theory by Slavoj Žižek.

'Well, you could at least persuade her to finish her degree at Harvard, couldn't you? As I understand it, she's inherited a bit of money, and between that and Ronit's salary, I'm sure they could afford it.'

She sighed and placed her book of Bangla poetry across her bosom. 'I don't much care whether or not they give me more grandchildren, because Charu has given us plenty; I just don't like to think of Ronit in an intellectually arid environment.'

Professor Roy smiled again and underlined a particularly thought-provoking sentence with the mechanical pencil he kept by his bedside.

'Well, at any rate, she's reading Bankim now, thanks to you, so that's a start,' she remarked with resignation, and picked up her book again. She decided, as she read, that she would have to figure out what Alice's intellectual strengths were and go from there. So far, they knew next to nothing about her, and if Ronit was not going to explain what he saw in her, she would have to figure it out herself.

# 21

When Ronit returned with the drinks on a small tray, his mother was asking Alice about Nanette's funeral. Alice seemed to like his mother so far, but he worried that she would not take kindly to all her questions. There was much about Alice that was a mystery to him as well, and he was anxious that one or the other of them might take offence during these interrogations.

'And your mother, then, has she adjusted?'

'Adjusted?'

'To the loss of her mother – such a difficult passage in life – when my own mother died, I lay in bed for weeks! I was inconsolable and Poshu was beside himself.'

Professor Roy, whom Debashree referred to as Poshu for reasons known to nobody but themselves, raised an eyebrow. He was engrossed in the letters to the editor complaining about municipal responses to the flooding.

'My mother did not react well,' suggested Alice hesitantly.

Ronit jumped in, 'Her mother was very upset, but she is recovering.'

'Poor thing!' cried Debashree. 'I imagine time will heal the wounds.'

'Yes, and the programme Ronit found for her,' added Alice with a smile, for she had found it very funny that Ronit, in conjunction with a psychiatrist at Mass General, had managed to talk Clare into enrolling in the kind of tony rehab programme she had always ridiculed in the past.

'What sort of programme was that?' asked Debashree, glancing sharply from Alice to Ronit.

Ronit hesitated, so Alice clarified, 'A rehabilitation programme, for drinking.'

'Oh dear!' cried Debashree, clapping her hand over her mouth. 'The poor thing, the poor, poor thing! I must say, I'm sure I had more than my share of cocktails when Mummy died, but thankfully no one thought to lock one up for that in those days.'

'Alice's mother was not well even before her mother passed away,' said Ronit, awkwardly, not knowing how to gloss over the fact that his fiancée's mother was, in his view, a flagrant alcoholic.

'And then the arrangements for the funeral and so forth must have been absolutely too much for her. So sad! It reminds me of my childhood friend, Minnie ...' And Debashree proceeded to narrate in detail an account of a friend's descent into madness at the loss of a child. Ronit marvelled at his mother's ability to absorb shocking information and render it less shocking than something else she had heard. This had the effect of making her interlocutor feel that whatever they had shared was really quite ordinary in comparison to something someone else had had the ill fate to experience. It also made them share more, and this, of course, was one of Debashree's many ingenious tools for extracting information from people who might be less than forthcoming.

'And your grandfather, your mother's father, he was deceased many years before, isn't it?' asked Debashree, moving in gently to extract more of the story.

'Yes, Grandfather died twenty years ago, when I was around ten years old.'

'Ah, so she – Nanette – was all alone then for all that time. How very trying for her.'

'Oh, I don't think so, not really,' replied Alice, thoughtfully. 'They were not close.'

'Not close? How difficult! But they remained married, did they not?'

'Oh yes, they never divorced, but they lived in separate parts of the house. Grandfather had his wing, and Nanette had the rest of the house; it was hers, you see.'

'A family house? How lovely.'

'... but Grandfather travelled a great deal for business, so when they were younger, I believe he was often away. I learned recently,' added Alice, hesitantly, 'that Grandfather travelled frequently to India until he became too ill to do so.'

'Oh my! How interesting! Did he have friends here, or was there a business connection?'

'There was a business connection, in Muza– Ronit, what was the name?'

'Muzaffarnagar. He had a textile business that imported fabrics via an office in Muzaffarnagar.'

'... but he also spent time in a town called Mussoorie.' Alice took pains to pronounce the name correctly, as Ronit had taught her, so that it didn't sound like Missouri.

'But Mussoorie is a delightful place! I used to visit a friend there in the summers. Lovely mountain walks and such views! You can see the snow mountains in autumn.'

'I would like to go – I hope to go there soon,' said Alice, avoiding eye contact with Ronit. 'I have the address, the address from which he wrote to Nanette and his children, my mother and her siblings.'

'How interesting,' said Debashree, glancing over at Ronit. She noted the pained expression on his face. She decided she had better tread lightly here, not knowing what was bothering her son. She wondered if Alice had given any thought to what she might find at the address in Mussoorie. Subtly changing the direction of the conversation, she asked, 'And when did you come to learn of your grandfather's visits to India? It sounds as though this was a recent discovery.' She saw that Ronit now looked aghast, but it was too late to put the genie back into the bottle, so she smiled pleasantly and took a sip of her Scotch.

Alice was silent for a moment, and then she said, 'I'm not sure how it happened, but I had a premonition, or ...' she glanced up at Ronit, who was now staring intently at his sandals as though he was unsure of the fit. She didn't want to annoy him, but the urge to discuss her favourite topic was too great, and she sensed an ally in Debashree. '... or I felt ... I felt I saw his ghost,' finished Alice with a sudden air of finality.

'A ghost?' asked Debashree with surprise. 'His?' She had expected an accidental discovery among the personal papers and effects of her grandmother. This was something altogether different. Professor Roy looked up from his newspaper.

'In what form did he manifest?' he asked, in a tone so matter-of-fact one might have thought he was talking about the weather again.

Now that his father had given the ghost conversation the imprimatur of his serious attention, there was no going back. Ronit rued his decision to go along with the ghost story when it had suited his goal of persuading Alice to travel to India. It was too late now. He stood up and asked if anyone would like another drink, but they all demurred, so he went into the kitchen to pour himself a double peg of the duty-free Scotch he had purchased for his parents at the airport.

'I saw him in his study,' said Alice, warming to her topic now that she felt she had a sympathetic audience for the first time. 'He was sitting in his armchair. The light was on. He smiled at me. There was a large book in his lap –'

'Aha,' said Professor Roy with satisfaction. 'Here is the clue. Tell us what the book was.'

'Well, it was an atlas, but he faded from view the few times I saw him, so I couldn't tell what map he was looking at.'

'How interesting!' said Debashree.

'Yes! Then when Ronit came to visit, I took him to Grandfather's study to see if he would … if he would ... manifest, as you say – and he didn't, but I saw a particular book pulled out on his reading carousel ...' She noticed a perplexed look on Professor Roy's face. 'It's a small rotating bookcase one keeps by one's reading chair. I think it's called a reading carousel.'

'Ah yes, I know what you mean. Go on: the book?'

'So, one book in particular was pulled out slightly, and I didn't think it had been before.'

Debashree hugged her arms and shivered with delight. 'How exciting, a ghost story! I can't stand the suspense.'

'... and the book was the atlas. It was an atlas of the world.'

'A world atlas!' cried Debashree. 'And he had picked out the India page for you, hadn't he?'

Ronit stood in the doorway to the kitchen, swirling his drink. The cook was frying and chopping vigorously in the tiny space, but he found her activity soothing in comparison to the disastrous conversation taking place in the living room.

'That's exactly it!' said Alice. 'The page with the map of India, of northern India, was folded over! I took the atlas back to our – my room – and I was flipping through it, and I was beginning to feel I was on a wild goose chase, when suddenly there it was, and I showed it to Ronit, and Ronit had not shown much faith in my story up until then, but after that he agreed to help me solve the mystery.'

Debashree smiled to herself. So that was it. Her son, the sceptic, had been appalled by his fiancée's ghost story until he had seen an advantage to it.

'And of what vintage was the atlas?' asked Professor Roy thoughtfully.

'The copyright was from the sixties. So it was older.'

'Ah, that is good. If it had been more antique, the borders would have been all different, and we might need to worry about the content of the message. But this one sounds reasonably up to date.'

'Yes, I suppose so,' said Alice.

'And your grandfather,' he continued, 'when you saw him, how corporeal was he? Did he look solid, like a real person?'

'No, a little blurry, like an old film. Sort of jumpy.'

'Sort of jumpy,' Professor Roy repeated and stroked his chin, lost in thought for a moment. 'When I saw my father's ghost, in the old house, he produced a similar effect. He was translucent.'

'Yes, that's exactly it!' said Alice. 'He was translucent. But you saw your father? Did he speak to you? I did hope that Grandfather would speak, but he just seemed to smile.'

'Oh yes, he did speak,' said Professor Roy.

'What did he say?'

'He told me to dig up a tin box in the backyard of the family house where we were still residing at the time. He said that the box contained the documents necessary for me to win our protracted legal battle over the ownership of the house.'

'Was it there?'

'It was indeed. And we eventually did win our case, although the byzantine procedures of our legal system put Dickens's descriptions of the Chancery courts in *Bleak House* to shame. We had to move out of the house, and the case was not resolved until fifteen years later.'

'Oh my! Did you ever see your father again?'

'I did not. He was not a man for loose chatter. He had something to tell me, he said his piece and he dematerialized.'

'*Poof!*' cried Debashree, with a smile, throwing her hands in the air.

This was all news to Ronit. He had never heard of his long-deceased grandfather's role in his parents' legal battle over the Roy family home.

'When did this happen?' he asked.

'The visitation?'

'Yes, I don't think you ever told me that.'

'We didn't want to disturb you in your studies. You were in medical school in the States already.'

Ronit grimaced. Now he was surrounded by ghost people. Next, they would probably hold a séance or commence table-tipping. The pressure cooker whistled merrily behind him, releasing plumes of steam, so he was forced to step away from the kitchen and return to the living room.

'You don't like ghosts, beta, do you?' asked Debashree, with an indulgent smile. Ronit was trapped. He could not risk offending both his father and his fiancée in one go. He sipped his drink and didn't respond.

'He's the most scientific member of our immediate family,' explained Debashree to Alice, grasping her wrist with a bejewelled hand. 'This strain of scientific rationality was passed from Poshu's mother, who was a science teacher, very unusual and impressive in her day, and then it can be found in Poshu's younger brother, Ronit's uncle Binoy, who is an electrical engineer, and then it made its way to Ronit. The rest of us are hopeless: hopeless poets and romantics.'

Ronit had heard this genealogical history hundreds of times before. It was always perfectly clear what was considered the better genetic inheritance out of the choice between rational scientist and hopeless romantic, and he had drawn the short straw. Alice, however, was not particularly interested in who was rational and who was not, and she wished to return to their shared visions of ghostly apparitions.

'I wonder if these types of ghosts – or what did you say? Manifestations – I wonder if they are common?'

'I should think so,' mused Professor Roy, 'though from what I have heard and read, the manifestations are different to different people, that is, the form they take.'

'A dear friend of ours – you know her, Ronit, Rosa – she once encountered her mother in the form of a bird that came to her windowsill.'

'A bird? Did it speak?'

'No, but it tapped out some seeds in the form of a circle, and a cross, and days later she learned that she was pregnant and was due to deliver on Christmas day, which she did do. She's Christian, you see.'

'How did she know it was her mother?' asked Alice, wondering if her visitation had been inadequately imaginative.

'She was quite sure of it,' said Debashree. 'I think most people have a sense, you know, a tingling, like Spiderman.'

Alice laughed, and Ronit was struck by the fact that it had been a long time since he'd seen her do that. The cook leaned out of the kitchen to announce that dinner was ready, and as everyone stood to move over to the dining table, Debashree added, 'Well, how lovely of your grandfather to have entered your life in this way. We must do whatever we can to help you go to Mussoorie. But not,' she cautioned, 'before the rain stops and not before we have gone shopping and introduced you around, and attended Nikhil and Shrila's wedding, and ... oh, there's so much to do.'

# 22

Sure enough, as the floodwaters receded, their social engagements increased. Alice had a whole new wardrobe and took to wearing saris even when they weren't going out. There was much less time to read and lie in the storeroom, but Alice enjoyed meeting Ronit's extended family and friends. Her ghost story was now known far and wide among their circle of acquaintances and many people had their own encounters to report. Ronit cringed at each of these conversations, but he had long since lost control of the narrative. On evenings when they weren't dining out at someone's home, which were few, they often went to the Club, where Ronit's sister Charulata, her husband and four children and her parents-in-law also joined them.

Ronit and Alice had precious little time alone during these days and oddly, it was at the Club that they had the greatest chance of separating themselves from the perpetual crowd. In his youth, Ronit had spent a good deal of time in the upstairs table-tennis room which had been immensely popular in those days. Now the room seemed to have fallen on hard times. A single fluorescent bulb hung in a corner of the room, making it difficult to see over the table, and when the power was on, it blinked at unpredictable intervals. The room felt dank in the monsoon weather, the fan rattled, and the table listed to one side, making it impossible to set spare balls down. There were, however, two reasonably comfortable armchairs in the corner farthest from the lamp, and Ronit was able to make a convincing case to his family that he was filled with nostalgia for those days in his early teens when he had spent hours with his friends in that room playing endless tournaments fraught with tense competition.

The first time Ronit had announced that he and Alice wanted to go and play during cocktail time, Alice was greatly surprised but gamely went along with it although she had no idea how to play table tennis, or any other sport involving a ball, for that matter. Ronit was thankful that she had kept her reservations to herself until after they had left the veranda and were making their way up the grand staircase to the mezzanine.

'I don't want to play table tennis,' whispered Ronit. 'I want to talk to you alone.'

'We can't do that without table tennis?'

'It wouldn't be considered proper, when we're here for such a short time and there are so many people to see.'

'Is three weeks a short time?'

'Yes.'

After the first time, it became a matter of course that the two of them would take their drinks upstairs and return half an hour later when the first seating for dinner began. At first, Ronit made a few attempts to teach Alice the game, just for the sake of form, but he soon saw the futility of this, as Alice's eyes never seemed to focus on the ball, and her first instinct when she saw something flying through the air towards her was to duck. At any rate, it was impossible to balance one's drink on the table, so they took to sitting in the armchairs, drinks in one hand, paddles in the other, to give the impression that they'd just sat down for a rest.

These moments felt deeply romantic to Ronit, and he wondered if Alice felt the same. To have his fiancée, his treasure, all to himself in this space that was, truthfully, so redolent with nostalgia, seemed a gift, despite the fact that they inhabited the same condominium on the other side of the world. Alice's affect was impenetrable here, as always, and her grey eyes seemed focused at some point far off in the future, or at least across the room.

On one such occasion, he tried to gauge her feelings at that moment, sharing his own fulsomely. 'Alice,' he said. 'I can't believe my luck, to be alone here with you. My love,' he added. And then, 'I love you.'

Alice smiled faintly and her eyes scanned his face, looking for some sort of sign. 'We're not exactly alone, though, are we?'

'Well, it's so hard to find a moment alone while we're here. I think this counts.'

'I suppose so.'

Just then a line of Charu's children, mixed in with some other children of unknown provenance, came racing through the room and danced round the ping-pong table, after which they exited through the side door, unleashing a series of high-pitched screams as they went. Most of them were wearing capes.

'I don't think that counts,' he added, feeling slightly foolish.

'Why don't you stay longer?' asked Alice suddenly.

'Longer? But how? My practice ...'

'Yes, but how am I to get to Muzaffarnagar and Mussoorie? No one will let me go alone.'

'They'll send someone with you, I'm sure.'

'But I don't want to go with *someone*.'

'Do you mean you want me to go? You want to go with *me*?'

'I would prefer it.'

Ronit realized he should not be surprised that the woman who had agreed to spend her life with him, at least in theory, desired his company on a trip that was important to her, but he was, nonetheless. It was rare for Alice to express a need directly in that manner. Perhaps, he thought, she did feel the romance of the moment, of sitting together in the wood-panelled room in the blinking light of the bulb in the corner, sipping cocktails.

'If you want me to come, I will arrange for coverage,' he said, taking hold of her hand. 'I would do anything for you, Alice,' he added, and then felt foolish.

She smiled wryly. 'Well, I wouldn't go *that* far.' Alice chuckled. 'But it would be nice,' she added.

And so, it was decided. At dinner, Ronit announced his intention to accompany Alice on her journey. His parents were relieved and delighted he would stay in India longer. His mother promised to find friends for them to stay with on their journey but Ronit somehow managed to scuttle that idea. He had in truth been looking forward to being alone with Alice in a hotel, even if it was one of those seedy hill-station hotels that were frequented by honeymooners from the plains.

# 23

Two weeks later, Alice and Ronit flew to New Delhi; they took the train to Muzaffarnagar. As they stepped out of the train they were drenched in a sudden downpour – a late monsoon shower – and scurried under the awning of a nearby roadside dhaba to get out of the rain. The steaming hot chhole and freshly fried bhature looked delightfully tempting to Alice and she suggested they stop there for lunch.

'No, no,' said Ronit. 'One mustn't eat at these places – you, in particular – you're bound to get giardia or worse.'

'I thought that was street food?' asked Alice, disappointed. 'Your mother said not to eat street food.'

'How is this not street food?' asked Ronit. 'We are literally standing in a street,' he added, pointing to the muddy rivulets just beyond the overhang of the awning in which swam all sizes and manner of vehicles.

'But it's a restaurant,' pleaded Alice. 'It's not a food stand.'

'It's not worth the risk.'

'Please? What else can we do? We're stuck here. Just a little bit?'

Ronit sighed and rolled his eyes. 'What do you want?'

'That stuff?' she said, pointing to the chhole.

'The chhole-bhature?'

'Yes?'

Ronit despondently ordered two chhole-bhature for them and then demanded that the waiter thoroughly wipe down the available table and seats.

'What a dirty rag he had,' Ronit muttered with disgust. He pulled a bottle of hand sanitizer and a handkerchief from his backpack, with which he scrubbed the table again, then his hands, then handed the bottle to Alice. Alice held it in her hand and glanced at it dubiously.

'I hate this smell,' she said with a grimace.

'Please use it,' implored Ronit.

Alice put a small drop in her palms and rubbed them together, then sniffed them. 'Yuck,' she said, as she sat down.

The waiter soon brought two amazingly puffy bhature with stainless steel dishes filled with rich, creamy chhole, each topped with a rapidly melting dollop of ghee. Alice cried out with delight and fell upon the meal with enthusiasm.

'This is amazing!' she cried. 'Why don't we eat this every day?'

'Because we'd need an industrial-sized deep fryer, and we'd get heart disease and die an early death?'

Ronit had to admit the food was delicious, but such things always were, and he was convinced this indulgence would come to no good. By the time they had polished off their meals and Alice was greedily licking her fingers, the rain had stopped. A small clot of boys stood about two feet away watching with great interest the spectacle of the tall White woman who licked her fingers like a tiny child.

'Which country?' asked one little boy.

'Have you any stamps?' asked another.

Alice looked up at them, puzzled. 'Why do they want stamps?' she asked Ronit.

'They probably collect them,' he suggested.

'For collection, ma'am,' said the little boy with an interest in stamps. He was polite and wore a spotless school uniform.

'Ah, you mean American stamps?' asked Alice.

'Yes, ma'am.'

'New?'

'Used is okay,' he said.

She rifled around in her bag until she found an envelope with an unread letter from the lawyer. She slit it open and took out the letter, which she stuffed back in the bag, avoiding reading any of the words as best she could. Then she handed it to the boy.

'Thank you, ma'am,' he grinned, and the boys scampered off.

'They were sweet,' said Alice.

'Let's get going and find the address,' said Ronit. He worried that Alice's remarkable appearance was going to slow down their journey in this muddy city, where, as they say in old-fashioned travel guides, there was nothing much that need detain the traveller. Perhaps if they could hurry, they would make it back to the bus stand in an hour, with enough time to catch the last bus to Mussoorie. Then they could avoid staying in whatever hotels were on offer here, which Ronit was sure would be the stuff of nightmarish back-page newspaper stories: bug-infested, not built to code, liable to collapse at any moment, and full to the brim with corrupt, low-level government officials on tour to collect bribes from around their provincial constituencies.

Alice pulled her notebook from her bag and looked up the address.

'306 ½ Vakil Rd (behind temple),' she said.

After asking the proprietor of the dhaba for directions, they set out on their way. As Ronit had feared, they were stopped by numerous curious pedestrians who wanted to know where Alice was from (in English) and sometimes had more profane questions to ask of Ronit (in Hindi). Ronit was thankful that Alice, at least, could not understand the latter queries and hurried her along the narrow, muddy streets as quickly as possible.

The directions proved to be wrong (*of course*, thought Ronit), and they had to correct their route several times along the way. After thirty minutes, they at last arrived where 306 ½ Vakil Road should be but found nothing there. Ronit inquired about the address of a few passers-by who claimed ignorance, before finally resorting to knocking on the doors of 306 and 307, at the second of which, the door was finally opened by an elderly woman, who looked irate, and asked him in Hindi what he meant by creating such a racket during nap time.

In his broken, middle-school Hindi mixed with Bangla, Ronit explained that they were looking for 306 ½, and asked if she knew where this address could be found.

'It can't,' she snapped shortly. Then, noticing Alice for the first time, she asked, 'Is that foreign woman with you?'

'My wife,' said Ronit.

'She's very tall,' remarked the woman with interest. 'Skinny. Come in for tea,' she added suddenly, in a tone that brooked no argument.

'What is she saying?' asked Alice impatiently.

'She says there is no 306 ½ and she has invited us in for tea,' explained Ronit, his patience well and truly wearing thin with the whole experiment as he glanced down at his mud-covered sandals and then at his watch and saw the possibilities of leaving Muzaffarnagar by nightfall quickly slipping away.

'Oh yes, please,' said Alice to the woman, nodding vigorously.

'But the train? If we want to leave tonight ...'

'But we need to find out what happened to 306 ½,' said Alice, glancing at him reproachfully.

The old woman nodded in affirmation. '306 ½, I will explain,' she said to Ronit. 'Come in now, I will make tea.' She motioned at them to come, and he felt as though he were being scolded for some lapse in etiquette when only moments ago, she had seemed intent on driving them away.

'Are you sure?' he asked Alice, pleadingly, but she was already following the woman into the house.

# 24

Later that night they lay side by side on a wide bed that was rather hard and lumpy. They were both naked save for the magenta, floral-patterned polyester sheet that covered their bodies. Alice had a novel in her hand which she was not reading. Ronit held a folded-up newspaper across his chest. The room was lit by a blinking fluorescent bulb that cast a bluish tinge over the enormous, lightly furnished room. The air conditioning was not working, and the humidity was overwhelming, though the slowly circling ceiling fan overhead offered some comfort.

'Why are there so many men in this hotel?' asked Alice. 'It's strange.'

'This isn't the sort of city that families travel to on vacation,' explained Ronit, staring at the revolving blades.

'What does that mean? Families? I was asking why there were no women.'

'Around here women don't travel alone. That's why I'm here, right? If women were staying here, they would be with their families.'

'Well then, why are there no families here?'

'Because it's not a tourist destination. Not a vacation spot. This hotel is probably for business travellers and politicians.'

Ronit felt deeply pained to be spending the night at this hotel. Alice was attracting far too much attention, though of course she was oblivious to it all. When they had realized they would miss the bus, he had called a friend in Delhi and asked him to look on the internet for the most expensive and elite hotel in the city, hoping there might be such a place, and that it would be a marginally suitable destination for Alice. His friend had come up with this place, the Ambassador Regency Hotel, and perhaps it was the fanciest hotel in town, but it still had broken air conditioning, no families and a suspicious-looking restaurant. Thankfully, besides the preponderantly male clientele, Alice seemed oblivious to its many failings.

'I wonder why I expected the office to still be here, somehow … intact,' said Alice.

'Well, there was always a chance that something remained.'

'Yes, but they sold the business so long ago. It's just depressing the building was torn down.'

'Well, maybe they didn't like the mess created by that ½ in the address.' Ronit laughed at his joke, but Alice ignored it.

'It was nice she remembered Grandfather, though,' said Alice, referring to their teatime conversation with the woman at 307 Vakil Rd.

'Yes,' said Ronit, 'that does give us a confirmation that he spent time here.'

'I hope the other address is not torn down as well.'

'Maybe not, if it's residential,' said Ronit, not sure if he hoped that the ghost-chase would simply end this way, in two demolished buildings, or if, more charitably, he hoped that Alice would find something of what she was looking for.

'My stomach feels a bit off,' said Alice, lightly massaging her belly through the slippery sheet. 'I knew I would get sick again.'

'You make it sound like it's simply a question of fate,' snapped Ronit. 'Like you had no control over whether or not you ate chhole-bhature at a muddy dhaba.'

'It could be from something else,' suggested Alice. 'Like the tea and biscuits.'

'Very doubtful. Tea is boiled; biscuits are packaged.'

'Or it could be air-borne?'

Ronit turned away from her in annoyance and flipped the page of his newspaper with a damp crackle.

'What? You don't think it could be air-borne?'

'Of course not,' he muttered.

'But the buses are crowded, like planes ...'

'One cannot catch a gastrointestinal bug from the air,' snapped Ronit.

'Oh,' said Alice.

Ronit turned back. 'You sound disappointed.'

'I just thought it was much more uncertain.'

'No, it really isn't.' Ronit sighed. He realized he had been wrong to snap. Alice's education was spotty, especially in the area of the sciences, and she had been raised by people who delighted in formulating their own eccentric explanations for medical complaints and phenomena in the natural world.

'So, when I was sick in India before, it was because of something I ate?' mused Alice.

'... or drank?' added Ronit. 'You know this about drinking the water and so on. Why do you seem surprised?'

'I don't know,' said Alice. 'To me that sickness seemed related to the retreat, to the annoying Europeans there. To the lecherous guru my friend slept with. I was so disgusted, so filled with loathing for the whole thing, it felt like that was the reason I got sick.'

'Well, you can't rule out the impact of your psychological state in making you susceptible, but you probably ate or drank something that was contaminated.'

Alice smiled. 'So, it *was* psychological. I knew it!' She leaned over and kissed Ronit, then settled down with her cheek on her pillow and closed her eyes.

# 25

Alice covered her face with a blue muslin dupatta and hugged her knees as the bus from Dehradun to Mussoorie lurched back and forth following the sharp switchbacks up the mountains. Her body bounced lightly between the yellow-tinted window and Ronit, who braced his body with his hand against the seat in front of him so they wouldn't both end up in the aisle. The rest of the passengers seemed unaffected. A group of schoolboys sang songs and excitedly talked and laughed, jumping about in the rear of the bus as though they were taking an amusement park ride and not riding to their doom in a death trap. Ahead of them were a few families, some honeymooners and some White tourists. Even the tourists seemed unaffected.

'Are you all right?' asked Ronit. 'Ten more kilometres.'

'Is that a lot?' asked Alice in a whisper.

'Not generally, but we are going pretty slowly.'

'It feels fast,' said Alice, who was sure she was close to vomiting. She held her hands over her mouth and felt the gas from her stomach bubbling upwards. She had eaten only toast and tea that morning, but she could taste both in her mouth.

'Soon,' said Ronit, reassuringly, 'we'll be there soon.' He put his arm around her and squeezed. Alice shrank even further into a ball.

At the bus depot they were surrounded by touts and coolies, but Ronit managed somehow to dispatch them and hired a taxi to take them farther up the hill to their hotel, the Honeymoon Lodge.

'More driving?' asked Alice, weakly, as she clutched her stomach.

'Do you think you could walk it?'

'No.'

'Then get in, it's a short ride.'

Alice managed to hold in the meagre contents of her stomach all the way up the hill but promptly lost them as she stepped from the cab. The driver seemed pleased she hadn't vomited inside the taxi and cheerfully suggested a number of home remedies for morning sickness, out of the mistaken belief that Alice must be newly pregnant.

'Congratulations, brother,' he said in Hindi and warmly shook Ronit's hand with both of his.

Ronit smiled weakly and thanked him, not wishing to prolong the time they stood at the edge of the steep, narrow road with Alice swaying weakly, in danger of becoming sick again at any moment.

Inside, they checked in and were given more congratulations, winks and nods for their supposed newly-wed and already conceived status. Alice understood not a word, and her sickness made her oblivious to the body language that might have alerted her to the topic at hand. They were taken upstairs to the Honeymooner Suite with Snow Mountain View. The former grandeur of the room was evident from the numerous mirrors and chipped gold bedstead. The room smelled of damp from the rains and the white carpet had seen better days. There was indeed a silhouetted lining of the snow mountains, but since it was a foggy day, they were not actually visible.

Alice lay down across the bed and held her stomach.

'Why don't you get some rest?' asked Ronit. 'Do you want a bath first?'

'Do you have the address?' asked Alice.

'For what?'

'For the house, for finding the address.'

'Of course, darling, when you're feeling a bit better, we'll go see.'

Alice sat up and looked at him angrily. Ronit hadn't known she had the energy in her to sit up in a rage.

'We've come all this way. You're not going to stop me now!'

Ronit stared at her in disbelief. Did she have a fever? He leaned over to feel her forehead and she smacked his hand away.

'Don't patronize me!' she yelled, and getting up unsteadily, she went to the bathroom where she remained for quite a long time. After a while came the sound of the toilet flushing and then running water. Alice re-emerged, her bangs damp. She looked so fragile he was sure she might teeter over.

'I'm ready,' she said.

# 26

The house they sought, Cosmos Cottage, was two kilometres up a very steep set of switchbacks, they were told by the hotel manager.

'Or you could take the shortcut,' she said brightly. 'This is what we always do.'

Ronit struggled slightly to understand her Hindi, which was locally accented, as were her hill-climbing habits.

'How steep is the shortcut?' asked Ronit, sceptically, as he glanced out of the corner of his eye at Alice, who was slumped over in a shiny black vinyl armchair on the other side of the lobby.

'It's straight up,' she replied. 'Takes no time. Do you prefer a taxi?'

'Do you want a taxi, Alice?' Ronit called out across the room.

Alice glared at him. He went over to her side, leaned down and gingerly touched her back.

'A taxi might be easiest,' he said softly.

Alice raised her eyes and gazed at him balefully. Her skin had turned sallow, and her eyes were ringed in purple.

'This is a pilgrimage,' she said slowly, in a low voice. 'On pilgrimages you walk. Your mother told me so.'

Ronit sighed, exasperated at this sudden turn towards assimilation. There were so many ways in which Alice seemed utterly oblivious to cultural differences. Why must she follow the rules for visiting pilgrimage sites now?

'The infirm are allowed to travel in automobiles,' he suggested, trying to keep his voice even and calm.

'We'll walk.'

Outside, they walked to the point where the possible paths forked and Ronit indicated the choices of straight up or zigzag. Despite being close to delirium, Alice recognized that straight up would be beyond the pale for her. Slowly, they began the ascent along the zigzag, Alice stopping, short of breath, frequently, and sitting on the stone guard rail. A light drizzle began. Ronit attempted to give her an umbrella, but she shrugged him off. By this point, he was finding her almost impossible to communicate with. She seemed to be floating up, operating under some kind of adrenaline rush that was propelling her those last steps up the mountainside to her destination.

At one section of stone guard rail, a group of langurs sat snacking on blue hydrangeas they'd pulled from a nearby garden. Alice started to walk slowly towards them as if she planned to sit in their midst and rest.

'No,' hissed Ronit, pulling her back.

Alice looked at him uncomprehendingly.

'I'll just sit a moment,' she said, conversationally.

'You can't sit with the monkeys,' he said, holding onto her arm firmly. 'It's not safe.'

'Why?' Alice asked the question as a child might, confirming Ronit's impression that she was no longer playing with a full deck. He hoped she was merely foggy from illness and that she had not contracted some horrible brain disease. As he tried to reply to her in a way she'd understand, the other part of his mind was racing through possible worst-case scenarios of this kind. Meningitis? He had been weak in infectious diseases, and it had been so long ago. *Lazy, lazy,* he thought. *And now I'll pay for it.*

'Monkeys are wild animals,' he said. 'Not our friends. I will help you walk a little farther, like this,' and he steered her by the elbow, his arm firmly around her, 'until there's a spot where it's safe for you to sit down.'

A few yards up the road, the langurs safely out of view, he pointed to a moss-covered rock by the side of the road. 'There,' he said, 'you can sit there.'

Alice, now suddenly obedient, dropped down on the rock and hugged her knees, turning her cheek sideways to rest against them. The hillside above them was thick with now-wild cosmos. The magentas and lavenders of their petals perfectly matched the lavender cotton sari Alice was wearing, and her magenta blouse.

'You match, here, with the flowers,' he told her, just to be cheerful.

'What flowers?' she asked.

He followed her gaze, over the side of the mountain into the forest, and realized the flowers were above and therefore she had not seen them.

'Not much further to go, I think,' he said.

Alice stood up and began to walk slowly again, cradling her elbows in her hands. The rain had let up a bit and all the leaves glistened. Ronit turned and looked back. The town was covered in clouds, and it seemed now that they were high up in the sky. If he hadn't been so worried about Alice, he would have taken out his camera and tried to capture the breathtaking view. But he reasoned with himself, everyone takes the same photographs up here. It would only be a disappointment.

As they rounded the next bend, they saw a group of shops. There were two tea stalls, a dry goods store and a post office. Under awnings, groups of people drank tea and glowered at the damp weather. The road was now flat, and they swung to the left, as the young woman at the hotel had advised.

'Very close now,' murmured Ronit. Alice didn't respond. He wondered if she could even hear him.

The road curved along and presently, to the left, there was a small weather-beaten sign that read in raised lettering: COSMOS COTTAGE.

'This is it!' exclaimed Ronit, far more delighted at the sight than he'd imagined he would be.

Alice's face brightened. Holding onto his arm, she made her way with a livelier step down a steep drive that curved along the edge of the mountain. At the bottom was a long, thin bungalow that hugged the mountainside. It was painted white, with a red tin roof, and surrounded by cerulean hydrangeas. The bank above was thick with more cosmos.

'So beautiful!' cried Alice, her voice faint. She stumbled and grabbed his arm.

Once they'd followed the path down to the house, it wasn't immediately clear where the door might be. Alice seemed upset by this.

'It's so confusing,' she said, tears welling up in her eyes.

'Why don't I look over on this side, and you sit right here, and I'll come back and get you when I know where it is.'

Alice nodded, and Ronit strode quickly towards the side that faced the slope of the mountain. The bungalow was curiously shaped, probably due to its precarious perch on a terraced bit of mountainside. He walked around a jutting addition, which looked like a sunroom of some kind, and presently came upon an entryway. There he knocked, and even called out, but to no avail. He tried the door. It was unlocked. Gingerly, he pulled it open, called out again, and stepped inside. Just then he heard a woman scream, a long, piercing scream. It seemed to come from the front of the house. He turned and ran back around the sunroom, worried that it might have been Alice. But Alice was not where he had left her. Nervously, he walked around the side of the house to the front. There, on a small, well-tended rectangular bit of lawn, lay Alice, a heap of crumpled lavender, and bending over her, gazing with great curiosity, were three women.

# 27

Ronit stopped for a moment, startled at the sight. Then he returned to his senses, called out 'Alice!' and rushed forward. The three women, just as surprised as he, turned with alarm when they heard his voice and jumped back. A strange man was charging at them in their own yard, but they also felt an immediate proprietary responsibility towards the young woman lying in a swoon upon their lawn.

Ronit knelt by Alice's side and felt her pulse, which he found. She had fainted.

'Water?' he asked, looking up. 'Can you bring a glass of water?' He spoke in English, as the women were elegantly dressed and lived in this place high above the clouds, but they stared back at him, their eyes unblinking. He repeated his request in Hindi with the same results. Suddenly, the oldest of the three, a very old woman, he noted as he looked at her, snapped out of her attitude of shock.

'Yes, yes,' she quickly answered in English. 'Lulu, get a glass of water, there's one on the tray,' and she waved towards a small tea table across the lawn near some rattan easy chairs. The more slender of the two younger women, who was still rather large, hurried across the lawn at this command, picked up the glass and rushed back to Ronit. Ronit sprinkled some drops on Alice's face and spoke to her softly. Her eyes opened slightly. She had the look of a drunkard, no ability to focus, her limbs limp. Ronit tried to get her to sip some water, holding the glass up to her lips. A bit went in, but the rest trickled down her cheek. She closed her eyes again.

'I'm afraid she's rather ill. Might I put her in the house on a bed? And would you mind calling your doctor?'

The most elderly of the women agreed and motioned him to follow her into the house. Ronit picked Alice up; she was curiously light for a woman of her height. She flopped over in his arms like a doll, and he had no trouble bringing her inside to the daybed in the glassed-in porch. Lulu fussed around with some pillows, and the larger of the two younger women stood nearby, watching, expressionless. The elderly hostess rushed off to phone the doctor and returned shortly thereafter with a thick quilt.

'The damp creeps up at this time of the afternoon,' she explained pleasantly. Ronit nodded. He arranged the quilt around Alice, caressed her forehead gently and picked up her hand and kissed it. Alice murmured slightly and turned onto her side. He was glad for this sign of life.

'Dr Sharma will be here shortly,' the woman said. 'Please do take a cup of tea while you wait. So good for the nerves.' She smiled affably and waved her hand towards a stiff armchair covered in a nubby fabric the colour of pea soup. The seat held a quantity of small cushions, each with a neon-coloured crocheted cover. The prospect of trying to find a perch among these seemed daunting to Ronit in his current state and he demurred.

'Lulu, do move the cushions for our guest,' the hostess directed.

Lulu gathered up all the cushions and carried them from the room.

'No need, no need, too much trouble,' mumbled Ronit.

'Please sit,' she said firmly, and patted the seat as though he were a small child or a dog and might not know where she meant unless she showed him through clear gestures. He sat. It did feel better to sit, even if the chair was small and stiff. But he felt awkward sitting while his elderly hostess continued to stand. Lulu brought him tea on a tray and their hostess carried over a small table on which to place the tray, lugging it with some difficulty as though it were tremendously heavy. Ronit suspected that this was not the case. He started to stand, to help her, but she objected strongly, demanding that he regain his seat.

The tea was served in a small yellow teapot, sugar and milk separate. Ronit mixed himself a cup and helped himself to a biscuit, a small plate of these having been provided by Lulu. It was only then that it occurred to him that he had not bothered to introduce either himself or Alice, nor had he thought to explain their presence in the home of these women. He looked up and saw that the older woman had settled down nearby on a small wooden chair, and that the other two stood in the doorway. Lulu, who must have been around sixty, held onto the door frame and gazed at him with undisguised curiosity. The other, larger woman stood near her, but inside the adjoining room, which made her features indistinct in the dim lighting. It was discordant to see her gaze fixed somewhere along the frame of the door, bisecting Lulu's gaze at him.

'Do you usually take just one spoon of sugar?' asked his hostess, politely. 'I always have two, and the girls generally have three.'

'Minnie likes four,' corrected Lulu.

'That's true,' the hostess conceded, 'but we've asked her to consider three.'

Minnie betrayed no reaction to this conversation and continued to stare at Ronit impassively.

'I'm sorry,' Ronit began, 'I've been very rude. I should have introduced myself.'

'Poor Alice was so ill, we've all been distracted,' she smiled encouragingly.

'How did you know her name?' asked Ronit, confused.

'Well, you did call out to her, you know,' she said, then paused. 'But of course we have been expecting her. We just didn't know that you would be with her.'

# 28

Ronit's face assumed something of Minnie's blank, slack-jawed expression at this piece of information.

'You've been expecting Alice?'

'Well, of course. But,' she added hastily, 'do tell us about yourself, how do you know Alice?'

'I'm, well, I'm her fiancé,' said Ronit. 'My name is Ronit Roy.'

'Oh, how lovely! I'm so glad she brought you with her. I imagine she's eaten some outside food, isn't it? She's quite ill.'

'Yes, I did advise against it, but she can be stubborn,' said Ronit, temporarily distracted from more pressing questions by the topic of gastrointestinal parasites. 'I'd imagine it's giardia or dysentery. Something like that.'

'Oh yes, I'm sure you're right. Are you a doctor, then?'

'I am, although not that kind of doctor.'

She looked at him quizzically.

'I'm a psychiatrist.'

'Oh, I see! We don't have so many of those around here.' She smiled. 'Do take a biscuit.'

Ronit took a biscuit and chewed it slowly, trying to think of how to turn the conversation back to the woman's assertion that they had been expecting Alice.

'You say,' he said slowly, '… you say you were expecting Alice. But how do you know of her? She didn't know what she would find when she came here.'

'Ah, I'm afraid the message might have been a bit garbled then, but it's all worked out, hasn't it?'

'Well, yes, but which message are you referring to? Had Alice written to you?'

'Oh, dear, no. I mean the message from Him. He said He would ask Alice to come, to sort things out. But it is hard, you know, for Him to travel in this state.'

'For whom?'

'For Him. My late husband, you know. The girls' father.' She motioned towards 'the girls' standing in the doorway. Ronit realized she was adhering to the custom of not mentioning one's husband by name and he would have to try to get the information by some different tactic.

'Did your … your "late husband" know Alice in some way?'

'Oh, dear me, yes, of course. He was her grandfather, you see.'

Before Ronit could pursue this startling revelation further, the doctor arrived to examine Alice. He prescribed a round of antibiotics and pronounced her acutely dehydrated.

'Should we bring her to the hospital?' asked Ronit.

'I shouldn't think so,' said Dr Sharma. 'She'll be more comfortable here.'

'But shouldn't we be giving her fluids intravenously?'

'Is that really necessary?' responded the doctor evasively. 'You can just feed her plenty of water and tea, then try introducing solids. Curd. Then after a day or so some khichdi. The antibiotics will start to do their work and she'll be on her feet in no time!'

Ronit looked sceptical. 'She's not able to drink on her own very well right now ... an IV drip ...'

'Are you a doctor?' snapped Dr Sharma.

'A psychiatrist, so ...'

'Ah, a psychiatrist! We don't have many of your kind around here. I've some interesting cases up here I'd love to get your opinion on.' He sat on the edge of Alice's bed, comfortably crossed his legs and began to give Ronit a rundown of several of his mental health cases. Lulu was instructed to bring Dr Sharma some tea, and more tea for Ronit, who was now being called Dr Roy.

Ronit was exhausted, not to mention beside himself with worry. He could think of nothing more unappealing than hearing an exhaustive account of local mental illnesses, but Dr Sharma had warmed to his subject.

'Perhaps we could bring an IV drip up here?' he interrupted. 'Hook her up to that?'

'Bhai, where will we get such a thing from? You Americans have so many fancy machines that can be brought from here and there. Here in the hills we manage as best we can,' he replied jovially in Hindi.

'Doctor sahab, will you take a cocktail now that it's gone past five?' asked the hostess, whom Dr Sharma had addressed as Mrs Ramsey. It appeared he was no stranger to the hearth at Cosmos Cottage. He stretched out his feet on the carpet and sighed appreciatively.

'Don't mind, don't mind,' he said, turning back to Ronit. 'Shall I tell you about the man who went mad from fiddleheads?'

'Ah, if you don't mind,' inserted Ronit quickly, 'I would like to start Alice on her course of medications. Where is the nearest pharmacy, or do you have them in your dispensary?'

'Yes, yes, let us do that.' Dr Sharma looked disappointed. He drew himself up, picked up his bag with one hand and patted Alice on the knees with the other. 'She'll do just fine,' he said. 'Just fine. I'm off to the dispensary then.'

'Shall I come with you?' asked Ronit.

'No need, no need,' said Mrs Ramsey. 'We'll send Ramdas for that.' And with this, she walked down the steps into the garden, now cloaked in purple dusk, and called out to Ramdas in a surprisingly hearty voice.

# 29

Mrs Ramsey insisted that Ronit stay for dinner and asked Ramdas to prepare a bed for him for the night. Ramdas, nearly as old as his employer, was a small, wiry man with bowed legs. He shuffled about on flat surfaces, sometimes with a cane, but Ronit had seen him gambol nimbly up the hill to fetch the medicine, taking a shortcut of steep steps cut into the side of the mountain. At dinner, Ronit watched him shuffle back and forth between the kitchen and the table, his eyes filled with rheum, and wondered how well he could see the table or the food he had placed upon it. Periodically, Mrs Ramsey interrupted the conversation and leapt up to go into the kitchen where she would roundly abuse Ramdas for some small mistake in colourful language. Then she would return to sit serenely at the table, replacing her worn linen napkin in her lap.

'Now, where were we,' she asked, after one such interruption, this time to a discussion of the weather. Ronit saw an opportunity to get back to the topic of Alice's grandfather and seized it.

'Might we return to the topic of Alice's grandfather, if you wouldn't mind?' asked Ronit.

'Oh yes, quite right. We were interrupted before, I think,' she replied.

'The doctor.'

'Yes, the doctor.'

'Yes, you had mentioned that Alice's grandfather was ... that he was your late husband?'

'Yes, that's right,' she said, neatly slicing at a chicken leg with her knife.

'But,' began Ronit, hesitantly, 'Alice's grandfather was married ... was also married, to her grandmother, who recently passed away.'

'Yes, yes, He told us about her passing. We did observe mourning for the month following.'

'I see,' said Ronit, though he did not. He wondered how to get beyond this stage in the conversation.

'But we don't stay in mourning for longer than a month nowadays, of course,' she added, when she'd finished chewing a bit of potato.

'Minnie wouldn't wear black,' interjected Lulu in the tone of a tattletale.

'No, she couldn't be persuaded,' acknowledged Mrs Ramsey. 'But we decided her aubergine sari was close enough.'

'Hardly respectful,' mumbled Lulu, as though she felt Minnie's whims were indulged more than necessary.

'But darling, really,' Mrs Ramsey sighed, 'how was Minnie to understand?'

The subject of this minor dispute was seated right in their midst, staring off somewhere over Ronit's shoulder, chewing her meat methodically, and already well into her third helping.

Something developmental, Ronit conjectured to himself, turning once or twice to see if it was possible to guess what she was looking at.

'I don't believe,' he said, after a pause, 'I don't believe that anyone in America was aware that he had been married twice.'

'Well, his parents knew, of course, but they kept it quiet. It wouldn't have done, you see, because they had arranged his marriage without consulting him.'

'So, you were married to him first?'

'Yes, that is correct. His father sent him here when he was just eighteen, to look after the office here. In Muzaffarnagar. We met soon after, in church, at a tea. And I don't mind telling you,' she added, batting her eyelashes coquettishly, 'that it was love at first sight.

'I was a nurse in those days, fresh out of training. He came each day in the afternoon to the hospital where I worked with fresh-cut flowers. The days were crisp and lovely. It was fall ...'

Lying in the adjoining room, Alice could hear Mrs Ramsey's words as they floated into the semi-darkness where she lay. She felt utterly light, the roiling of her intestines like the sounds of some far-off storm that need be of no concern to her. She imagined the young Mrs Ramsey, in a crisp white uniform, smiling shyly up at Grandfather as he handed her a great bunch of flowers. What kind? Lilies, perhaps. Or maybe they didn't grow here. Alice would have to ask her later. And Grandfather, neatly turned out in a suit, perspiring slightly even in the fall – he never was a slender man – might doff his cap and gaze wonderingly into her large eyes. A sea of love where there'd been none in his severe New England upbringing.

'"Violet," he said,' continued Mrs Ramsey, revealing her first name, '"please marry me and make me a happy man for the rest of my life." I was an orphan; my parents had died of cholera in an epidemic. I was raised by nuns in Trivandrum and sent north to work as a nurse. So, I had no one, you see.'

Mrs Ramsey broke off to cry out to Ramdas to clear the dishes, and when he didn't immediately appear, she excused herself from the table and went into the kitchen where she unleashed a torrent of choice insults.

Ronit and the women sat silently around the table. They had all finished their meals and Ronit racked his brain to think of some topic or pleasantry with which to break the heavy silence. Thinking of none, he was saved by Alice, who just then called out to him from the other room. He excused himself and went to see her.

Alice held out a hand to him and he took it and sat by her side. She looked up at him. Her large eyes might have been tearful, or perhaps they were just watery. Her skin had taken on an almost waxen cast with her illness, and in the twilight of the sun porch, with her shining eyes, she looked exceptionally beautiful, if ill.

'What is it, Alice? How do you feel?' he asked, smoothing back her hair.

'Ronit, I saw him,' she said softly.

'You saw whom?' asked Ronit, though he felt sure he knew the answer. After all he had learned since entering the cottage, he was resigned to it.

'Grandfather. I saw Grandfather. Just as I rounded the corner into the garden, I saw him there. Sitting in one of the chairs. Not jumpy or unclear at all, just sitting there as real as when he was alive.'

Ronit shivered at this phrasing.

'What was he doing?' he asked.

'Reading the paper and having a drink, just as he always did.'

'Is that why you screamed?'

'I wasn't afraid. But I felt so ill, and it made me confused. I didn't know I screamed.' She stopped for a moment to reflect. 'Did I scream?'

'At the top of your lungs; and then you fainted.'

'That doesn't seem like something I would do.' Alice thought for a moment, her eyes seeming to explore the ceiling, but Ronit knew this meant she was thinking.

'It seems like a very Victorian thing to do, doesn't it? Like those women who were always fainting because their corsets were too tight.'

Ronit laughed. 'I'm sorry we didn't have smelling salts on hand, but you did come round all the same.'

'Am I very sick?' she asked.

'You'll be getting better soonish, with the medicine.'

'Yes,' she said. 'So, we'll stay here?'

'Until you're well enough to move, I'd imagine.'

'And until we know the whole story,' added Alice, happily.

'Yes,' said Ronit. 'And that shouldn't take too long,' he added.

# 30

Alice's recovery was slow but smooth enough. The next day she was moved into the guest room and Ronit was moved to the daybed on the porch. The guest room was neat and sun-filled. Though it was kept fresh and clean, it was curiously filled with the accoutrements of boyhood and adolescence. On her second day in the room, Alice, feeling rather more conversational than before, speculated to Ronit that there must also be a third sibling, a brother.

'All the adventure novels,' she gestured weakly towards the opposite shelf, 'and the cricket bat, and so on. Have they mentioned a brother?'

'Not a bit,' said Ronit, 'but I can try asking. What you can't see,' he added, 'from your vantage point, is all the romantic poetry. And there are French poets too, Baudelaire and so on,' he said, tipping a volume from the shelf and holding it up for her.

'A poetic son, then,' mused Alice.

When next Mrs Ramsey, whom Alice had come to think of as a sort of grandmother figure although she was still hazy as to all the particulars, entered bearing a tray with tomato soup and hot tea, Alice broached the subject.

'I've been wondering,' she began softly, 'whose room this is. Perhaps you have a son as well?'

'Oh yes,' Mrs Ramsey smiled pleasantly. 'This is Biju's room – Biju – Minnie and Lulu's older brother.'

'Does he live nearby?' asked Alice.

'No, no, he's not been by for some time,' said Mrs Ramsey with a little laugh. 'He's gone abroad, you know. He's a writer.'

She smoothed out Alice's quilt, adjusted the curtains and turned to leave.

'What does he write?' asked Alice.

'He's written a novel,' she replied, smiling brightly, and stepped from the room before further conversation was possible.

When Ronit returned to the house from a walk around the chukker, Alice told him of the existence of Biju and his novel.

'What sort of a novel must it be, I wonder?' asked Ronit with some curiosity. 'And why didn't she want to talk about it?'

'Why don't you try to find it?' suggested Alice. 'Maybe it's around somewhere.'

'Most definitely,' said Ronit. 'I'll do some sleuthing.'

Alice didn't feel well enough to read yet and mostly lay and stared at the cracked plaster ceiling where resided a handful of spiders of the most extraordinary size she had ever seen. She would have felt threatened, but they seemed to never move. Outside the window, she could see a patch of blue sky and the great conifers that covered the hillside.

On her second morning in the room, Alice asked Mrs Ramsey what they were called.

'They are Deodar cedars,' she told her. 'Lovely trees. Your grandfather adores them.'

'He adores them? Do you still see him? Does he – does he appear here?'

'Oh yes,' replied Mrs Ramsey matter-of-factly.

'Then when I saw him …'

'Ah, you've seen him then?'

'When I first arrived, he was sitting on the lawn, reading the paper. He didn't look funny at all.'

'Funny?'

'At home, at Nanette's house, he was hard to see. Blurry, jumpy, almost disappearing.'

'Poor thing,' sighed Mrs Ramsey. 'He tried so hard to reach you, but the journeys are difficult.'

'So he speaks with you too? He doesn't just appear?'

'Well, naturally, he's been anxious for us, you see. So he can't leave until we're seen to.' She smiled.

'I had thought,' began Alice, not sure which of Mrs Ramsey's utterances to pursue first, 'I had thought that spirits haunt, or stay, close by the place where they died.'

'Oh yes, that is correct.'

'But Grandfather died at home – at our home.'

'Oh no, indeed not. He died in his bed, here in Mussoorie.'

'How could I be mistaken? I'm quite sure he was at Nanette's house.'

'Doubtless that was what everyone was told. But the funeral there would have been a memorial. Your uncles had the body shipped back at great expense, but the soul, the spirit, *that* has stayed here, at Cosmos Cottage.'

'Can you tell me,' Alice was not sure how to phrase this, 'can you tell me what Nanette knew? Of you? Of the family here?'

'Well, at first she didn't know anything.' Mrs Ramsey spoke comfortably as though the whole thing couldn't be more ordinary. 'When your grandfather and I married, he did not immediately inform his family. He didn't think they'd understand, and he was quite right about that.

'He travelled back and forth once a year. We'd been married two years and Lulu had been born, when his father wrote and informed him that his marriage had been arranged with an heiress whose father planned to buy a large stake in the family business. It seemed that unbeknownst to him, the business was not faring well. This was the solution his father had come up with.

'He responded by return post, revealing to his father that he was already married and had a child. His father was furious. He said he would disinherit him if he didn't return at once. What could he do? He told me he would go home and sort things out. He stayed away a year and a half. He never stopped writing, and he always sent enough money, so we'd be comfortable. Finally, he returned. When he arrived, he admitted to me that he had been unable to dissuade his father from his plan and instead had lied and promised to get a divorce, which of course he never did.

'He had no choice really. The family business would have gone bankrupt without the investment of Nanette's father's money, and without the business he'd have no means of livelihood that could keep him in India.'

'Did he tell Nanette then? How did she know?'

'Oh, no, he told no one that he was still married to me. By then Lulu had been born. With the new investment he was able to rent this house for us in the hills and he came up here as often as he could. He just adored Cosmos Cottage.'

'But then she found out somehow?'

'Oh yes, eventually she did. They'd had three sons by then, but it was not a happy marriage, you know. His heart was always here. I don't know how she found out at last. Perhaps some business partner who'd been here, perhaps a letter, but she never forgave him, of course. I don't think I should either.'

'When was that, that she discovered the truth?' asked Alice.

'Well, Minnie had been born by then, and perhaps your oldest uncle was ten or so, just a year or two younger than our Biju.'

'So before my mother and aunt were born?'

'Yes, of course. You see,' and here she lowered her voice to a whisper, 'they never shared a bed again.'

Alice's eyes widened. She was shocked both by the intimation of her mother's unknown paternity, but also by the manner in which Mrs Ramsey made the revelation, as though she was sharing the salacious gossip of a neighbour or acquaintance and not speaking of the woman her own husband had committed bigamy to marry. Mrs Ramsey was sitting back now, a look of triumph playing around her lips. So that was it. She saw Nanette's affair as a moment of vindication.

'And so,' said Alice slowly, piecing the story together in her mind, 'and so, that man, a man that came to the funeral, I was told he had been her ... her lover – was he the father of ...?' She wasn't sure how to finish the sentence.

'He never knew for sure, you know,' whispered Mrs Ramsey, whose eyes had begun to glow with a sentiment that almost seemed like greed, a lifetime's greed to reveal the dirty secrets of her rival. 'But when he'd return, he'd hear rumours, of parties, of a certain man, and she didn't bother to hide them. But they barely spoke by then, you see. Till his death, they barely spoke.'

'Yes, even I knew that, as a child,' said Alice, thoughtfully. 'He had his "wing" of the house; the rest was hers. I rarely saw them in the same place.'

'And then she bore two daughters, your mother and your aunt.'

'Didn't he ask? I mean where they had come from?'

'She gave them his name, of course, and said they were his, though of course he knew that wasn't true.' Mrs Ramsey added with a sly smile, 'And didn't the daughters look rather different to the sons?'

Alice pondered this obvious truth. In her mind's eye, she saw the five children of Nanette, lined up in the pew, at her funeral. The three heavy, square backs of the sons, and the two whisper-thin daughters. In her imagination, she'd always foolishly attributed these differences to their genders. The boys had taken after their father, and the girls resembled their mother. More than ever now, she wished she'd gotten a closer look at the strange man who'd been shooed away. She wondered now at the vehemence of her uncles. Had they known? She was sure that if her mother ever had an inkling of her father's identity it would have come out. She felt weak now, her brain racing, and sank back into the pillows. A peripheral movement made her turn her head, and in the dusky light of the adjoining dining room, she saw the bulky figure of Minnie, standing quietly, staring at her. She must have looked startled, for Mrs Ramsey looked too and when she saw Minnie, she got up busily and started giving out orders and making preparations for tea.

# 31

'So what is your son up to these days?' asked Ronit at lunch the next day. He'd tried more subtle methods of learning more about the missing son but had got nowhere. His curiosity having got the better of him, he'd resolved to try the direct approach.

'He's a writer,' said Mrs Ramsey primly, pursing her lips.

'A writer! I'm not surprised,' said Ronit enthusiastically.

Mrs Ramsey raised her eyebrows in query.

'Such an interesting array of literary tastes,' said Ronit. 'In his room, I mean.'

'Oh yes,' she said, relaxing slightly. 'Biju was always an avid reader.'

'What sort of writing does he do?'

'He's written a novel,' she said firmly, as though such a revelation was certain to put an end to the conversation, which of course it didn't. Ronit's curiosity was now much greater, and Alice, lying on the daybed on the porch, turned her head so she could hear the conversation better.

'A novel! How wonderful. Is it published?'

'Yes,' she replied.

'Have you got a copy?'

'I have,' she said, clearly displeased at the information being dragged out of her. She paused, as if still hoping the topic had been terminated, but Ronit's expectant expression made it clear she would now have to reveal the location of the novel in question. 'It's in the drawing room,' she said. 'I'll just fetch it now.' She got up slowly from the table as if to make a show of the inconvenience of the thing and left the room. Ronit looked up at the two sisters of the novelist. Both stared at him placidly.

'Have you read it then?' Ronit asked Lulu, as he wasn't convinced that Minnie knew how to read.

'Oh no,' said Lulu firmly. 'Mother says it's not for us.'

'Oh, I see,' said Ronit, taken aback.

Mrs Ramsey re-entered the room bearing the novel in question. She handed it to him. 'I'll just go see Ramdas about the washing up,' she said, signalling the end of lunchtime. Ronit still had some rice and dal left on his plate, but he stood up all the same and took the novel into the other room, where he knew Alice would be anxiously awaiting its arrival.

The title of the book was *Himalayan Rhapsody*, and the author was G. Thomas Ramsey. It had been published in 1975 by an English-language press in New Delhi.

'What is it about?' asked Alice, propping herself up on her elbows eagerly.

'Shall I read you the blurb?'

'Yes, please.'

'*In this coming-of-age novel, Joseph Lanscome discovers a dark secret about his father's past and comes to terms with hidden areas of his own psyche.*'

'"Hidden areas of his own psyche?" I wonder what that means!' Alice was thrilled and held out her hand. 'I saw it first,' said Ronit, eagerly flipping through to the first chapter.

'But I'm sick!' pleaded Alice.

'I could read it aloud,' Ronit was about to say, but then glanced up to see Mrs Ramsey glowering at him from the doorway between the kitchen and the dining room. The dining room was poorly lit and the kitchen sunny, and thus her facial expression was difficult to discern.

'Or perhaps we should take turns,' he added, dropping his voice to a near-whisper.

'What?' asked Alice, craning her neck. But she couldn't see to the kitchen doorway, and at any rate, Mrs Ramsey had already disappeared. Ronit pulled his chair closer and leaned in towards Alice.

'I don't think,' he said softly, 'that our hostess approves.'

Alice, who had missed much of the subtext of Ronit's earlier conversation with Mrs Ramsey about the novel, looked at him mystified. Ronit wondered if she had missed all this because she hadn't been able to see Mrs Ramsey's body language or if there was some cultural misunderstanding.

'I'll explain later,' he said softly. Then, reluctantly, 'You can start reading it first. I need to take a walk anyway.'

'You just want to use the internet,' said Alice accusingly.

'That too.'

The novel got off to a rather slow start with lyrical descriptions of the mountains. Alice felt her eyelids growing heavy, which was typical these days with her illness. She rarely made it past two or three pages into a book before she started to nod off. But this time, somewhere between waking and sleeping, she suddenly found herself seated on the lawn, on a rattan chair, next to her grandfather.

# 32

'Ah, there you are!' said Grandfather, beaming. 'Would you like tea? Or drinks?'

Alice looked at him, her eyes shining with excitement.

'I can hear you! Is that because I'm asleep?'

'Yes and no,' he said, smiling jovially. 'What will you take? Tea? Gin fizz?'

'I've been ill, so perhaps tea?'

'Quite right. You really must avoid that outside food. You'll soon be well again, my dear.'

He patted her affectionately on the arm, or at least he appeared to, though she couldn't feel anything.

'Ramdas,' he called out, 'Chai le aao! That means "bring the tea". I'm sure you didn't know your grandfather knew a dab of Hindi, did you?'

'No,' said Alice, happily. 'I had no idea.' She paused and thought for a moment. 'But if you don't mind my asking, are you really my grandfather?'

'Ah, so you've been hearing all the stories from Violet. Never mind, dear, never mind. I was never, well, *technically*, your grandfather, or "biologically", as they say, but you've always been my favourite grandchild.'

Alice beamed happily at him. Ramdas appeared, walking with a more spritely step and sporting a tidier-looking suit than usual. He held a tray in one hand and a teapoy in the other, and setting the teapoy down with a flourish, he placed the tray upon it and began to pour out the tea.

'You know,' continued Grandfather, 'you're by far the best and brightest of the lot, children and grandchildren inclusive.'

He looked around furtively, as though suddenly worried someone in the excluded group might be passing by. 'How your mother managed to raise such a sensible girl, I've no idea. But she did marry well.' He winked and handed her a cup of tea.

She took a sip. It tasted real, more real than dream tea, and also much better. She wondered if they were in heaven. If ghosts could invite the living for tea in heaven.

'My father, you mean,' said Alice, suddenly attentive to his last remark. 'Did you like my father?'

'Lovely fellow. Bright, charming, from an excellent family. Poor chap, your mother was too much for him. No surprise there, I'm afraid.'

Alice sipped her ambrosia-like tea and pondered this notion. She had not seen her father since childhood. When they'd spent time together the occasions had been brief, fraught. Her father had forsaken the field of battle and left her mother victorious. Thus, all her perceptions of him were coloured by her mother's insinuating remarks.

'I wonder where he is now,' Alice mused. 'Do you know? Do you think he wonders about me? Do you see him?' she added, wondering if ghosts spent time together.

'To be sure, my dear, to be sure he does. But I'm afraid I can't help you there. And as it happens, our time here is limited, so if you don't mind,' he said, reaching down by his chair and pulling up a tan leather briefcase, 'we'll continue on to the business at hand.'

'The business at hand?' asked Alice.

'Yes, the reason I've called you here.'

He opened the briefcase and withdrew a thick file held together with a rubber band. He handed it to Alice. Alice put her cup and saucer down and looked at the file, which was marked 'Ramsey Trust'.

'In here,' he said, 'you'll find all the documents to a trust I set up in the name of Violet and the children. According to the terms of my marriage to your grandmother, all financial arrangements in the will would only carry over until her death. We had a complicated financial relationship, you see. She would have very much liked to have stopped the annuity payments to India, for she suspected whom they benefited, but this was not possible until her death. Now they have stopped, of course, and Violet and the girls will soon be destitute if you don't find it in your heart to do something. Your grandmother, of course, didn't anticipate that you would be able to restore the annuity without any knowledge of my family here, and that is why I've had to call you all this way to make you see how important it is that you continue the support of your cousins.'

Alice listened to him gravely, holding the folder in her hand.

'Are they really my cousins?' she asked, a little confused at the last bit.

'Well, in a manner of speaking,' he said confidently. 'And more importantly, they've no means of support, which is why I've turned to you.'

'What has happened to their brother?' asked Alice, suddenly remembering the novel she'd been reading before she'd nodded off and found herself on the lawn.

For the first time since their conversation had begun, her grandfather looked displeased.

'Well, he's of no use, is he? First, he got the idea of being a writer and next thing you know, he's gone.'

'You mean he disappeared?'

'After the book, he thought himself very fine and wanted to be considered a novelist. I told him he needed to learn a trade, finish school, earn an income to support his mother and sisters after I was gone, but he never listened for a moment.'

'That must have been a long time ago,' observed Alice.

'It might have been. One loses track up here.'

'I would imagine so,' said Alice, wondering what he meant by 'up here'.

'But let's return to the annuity,' said Grandfather, eagerly getting back to the subject, 'I don't have much time to explain.'

'All right,' said Alice, though she had to admit she was more interested in the flight of Biju than the dusty old legal files he held in his hands.

'I would like most humbly to request of you, my dear,' he said, holding out the files to her, 'that you take these files into your custody and keep them safe. On your return home, you must visit with the attorney, eh, Drawbridge, I think?'

'Yes, Lawrence Drawbridge.'

'Ah yes, the son. Take these files to him and ask him to reinstate the annuity at the appropriate rate to remain in place for the lifespan of my youngest survivor, that is, whichever of my children, the ones here, should live the longest.'

Alice thought for a moment.

'What would be the appropriate rate?'

'That I couldn't tell you, my dear. One cannot keep track of market rates and so on in one's current state. You must ask Violet and then set it up with Drawbridge.'

'Do you know,' she said slowly, not quite sure how to express what she wished to say, 'do you know that Nanette left almost nothing to the other children? Except for five thousand dollars apiece,' she paused again, 'everything else she left to me.'

'And she did quite right, my dear, quite right. They can all survive in their own way, somehow or another. You are the best custodian, and you will take care of everything properly, the house and so forth. I should have done the same. You were always our favourite. We may have agreed on very little, your grandmother and I, but certainly, Alice, dear Alice, was something on which anyone could agree.'

Alice blushed and he patted her shoulder. His touch felt comforting, though non-corporeal, like a blessing, or fairy dust. Alice's knowledge of theories of life after death and theology was dim and she wasn't at all sure if any of the world's religions had accounted for the kinds of things she was experiencing.

'I will do as you ask, Grandfather,' she said solemnly, holding the file to her chest.

'So delighted, my dear, so delighted.'

'Can I ask one other thing?'

'Please, please.'

'Can you tell me anything about my real – or biological – grandfather?'

'Ah,' he said, sighing philosophically. 'I wasn't around for much of that, I'm afraid. No, you'll have to go elsewhere for that information. Your grandmother fell out with him, I believe, though I don't know what for. He was, you know, banished from the kingdom.'

'He came to her funeral, you know.'

'Did he? So he is still living? Or was he making a visitation, like me? I do recall hearing he was considerably younger than her, so perhaps that makes sense. But, my apologies, my dear, I must be going.'

'Thank you for trusting in me, Grandfather.'

'The pleasure has been all mine; Violet and the girls will be much obliged.'

He stood, without much trouble, called out to Ramdas to clear the tea things and then leaned over and planted a kiss on her forehead. With this, her eyes fluttered open and she found herself again on the porch. By the light it seemed to be late afternoon. Ronit was sitting in a chair nearby, his brow furrowed, his head resting in his hands. On his knees lay open the novel by her maybe-cousin Biju. She felt she was clutching something in her hands which she had assumed, on waking, was the novel. Looking down, she saw it was in fact the sheaf of files that her grandfather had just given her.

'It wasn't a dream,' she whispered with delight.

'What's that, Alice?' asked Ronit, startled out of his deep reading concentration.

'These papers! I was just discussing them with Grandfather. He gave them to me and explained why he'd called me here and everything. When I woke up just now, I thought it had all been a dream, but it wasn't.'

Ronit looked stern but then softened his pose. He really didn't know what to think anymore, now that everyone else in the household was talking to the ghost.

'I thought maybe Mrs Ramsey had given them to you,' he said.

'No, they were from Grandfather. He wants me to continue the annuity that supported Mrs Ramsey – Violet, he calls her – and Lulu and Minnie.'

'Aha,' said Ronit, immediately worrying what the financial implications of this might be, not knowing for certain exactly how well-endowed Alice's trust was. 'Is there enough money for that?'

'Oh, I imagine so,' said Alice, vaguely. She stared out the window and happily thought about the kind words her grandfather had showered on her, about his magical touch and that delicious, delicious tea.

'Isn't it teatime yet?' she asked.

# PART THREE

## THE OTHER SIDE OF THE MOUNTAIN

# 33

'I wonder if he knows about me,' mused Alice. She was half-heartedly unpacking her suitcase, folding what now seemed like an endless supply of saris. In Kolkata's humid weather they had felt barely enough to keep her clothed.

'I don't think that's how you fold those,' observed Ronit as he watched Alice haphazardly bunch together the yards of hand-loomed silk and cotton. She didn't seem to hear him.

'And Bix's children too – I wonder if he knows about all of us.'

'Who do you mean?' he asked, pointlessly, as he had already been forced to discuss the mysterious biological grandfather countless times. He was perplexed by the rapidity with which one grandfather obsession had been replaced by another.

'My grandfather, of course,' said Alice. 'The real one. That we don't know. I keep wondering if he knows about us.'

'Well, you don't even know if he knows about his daughters.'

'I'm sure he does. Sure of it. How could he not? He must have loved her very much.'

'How do you know that?' Ronit paused, trying to think of the best way to put it. 'I don't mean to discourage you in your new quest; I just don't want you to be disappointed.'

'I know, he might have been a bounder and a cad. Maybe he left her, and not vice versa. But Grandfather – other Grandfather – said she had "banished" him, or so he thought. And anyway, please don't forget, *he came to her funeral.*' She placed particular emphasis on this last phrase because she considered it irrefutable evidence.

Ronit had, by now, accepted the possible existence of the ghost of her non-biological grandfather. He'd even accepted that a version of that ghost with poor reception due to being out of contact with his transmitting tower had dispatched Alice on some sort of mission, and that

that mission was now nearing completion. After all, they had found Cosmos Cottage and Alice had been given a folder of documents. But he wasn't yet ready to accept as evidence hearsay and gossip heard from the mouth of said ghost, who was in any case, biased against Nanette. As this image popped into his mind – of the ghost grandfather operating outside of his transmission area like a lost cell phone – he chuckled to himself.

'What?' asked Alice.

'Nothing,' he said, knowing any ghost-related jokes would displease Alice. 'Are you meeting with the attorney today?'

'Yes, at two.'

'You know, maybe he can help with tracking down Biju.'

'Why would he do that?'

'Well, because he would be an interested party in this annuity business.'

'But he left them high and dry. I don't think he deserves an annuity.'

'I didn't say he did, particularly. I mean, who knows how many people the trust can support, but one might want to look into how much of a claim he would have and whether he is living or dead, and so on. Maybe,' he added, 'your uncles would like to meet their half-brother. If he's in the US.'

'Well, that hardly seems likely. I can't help but think they all knew, at least a little bit, that Grandfather had another family, or something more than just his "business" that kept him going back to India.'

'Perhaps, but I just can't stop myself from feeling for the guy after reading his novel, and saying he left them "high and dry" seems to be slanted towards a particular version of events, doesn't it?'

'Perhaps you're right. Violet – Mrs Ramsey – was so vehement about it, as was Grandfather. And anyway, as you'll remember, I never finished the book, because you took it from me and then we had to leave. I don't know all his dark secrets and whatnot.'

'Well, that part was just that he was gay.'

Alice had finished stuffing the saris willy-nilly into a drawer. Fatigued by the effort, she lay down on the bed among the piles of debris from her suitcase. She was still short of breath at times, and even though it had been a month since she'd fainted on the lawn at Cosmos Cottage, she didn't feel herself.

'I know that part, you had told me, but there must be something more.'

'Well, there is. Do you want me to try finding you a copy on eBay or something? Or maybe in a library.'

'No, not really.' Alice closed her eyes. Finding something on eBay sounded simply exhausting and tracking down an obscure novel in a library unthinkable.

'Can't you just tell me what happens?' she asked tearfully.

Ronit was concerned about Alice's continued weakness. She didn't have health insurance at the moment, nor a primary care doctor, and she had so far been unpersuadable in the argument that she should find one. He also knew Alice was not very good at using the internet. Her whole family seemed to have a horror of modern technology, and he knew finding a doctor or a book, two activities that would take Ronit no more than ten minutes each, would take Alice the better part of a day and likely end in failure or even tears.

'I can tell you.' He cleared a space on the bed for himself, then lay down next to her and put his arm around her. 'Do you feel tired again?'

'Yes.' Alice's eyes were firmly shut, but tears were forming about her eyelashes.

'It takes a while,' he soothed. 'I love you. Everything will be all right.'

Alice started to sob at this. She turned onto her side and rolled herself into a little ball, still holding his hands tightly. As her sobbing crested and subsided, she began to hiccup.

'Don't worry,' said Ronit, wiping her tears. 'You'll be well soon.'

'I just – I just really want to find him,' she said, and began to cry again.

Ronit sighed and put his arms around her.

# 34

On the train to work, Ronit held a book open in his lap, a work of literary criticism his father had urged him to read. He couldn't focus. The text was too dense for a non-specialist, in his opinion, though his father had sworn up and down that it was lucid and accessible to the layman. Instead, his thoughts kept returning to *Himalayan Rhapsody*. It was beautifully written, he thought. The passages describing the protagonist's sexual awakening were haunting and written with a fresh and unpretentious eye.

As they were leaving Kolkata, Ronit had asked his father if he'd ever seen the novel. He remembered reading of it at the time, he thought.

'But in those days,' he added, 'one hadn't the same interest in queer theory one has today.'

Ronit hadn't known his father had an interest in queer theory and was only dimly aware of its existence. His father was always interested in the newest ideas, so he wasn't surprised. He had recommended a theoretical work on the topic and Ronit had ordered a copy on his return. He liked to read things that preoccupied his father as it gave him something to discuss with the otherwise taciturn man.

It was in fact this book that lay open on his lap now, and he wondered if his father had managed to track down a copy of *Himalayan Rhapsody.* Then he wondered if he should himself try to find a copy for Alice to read. He was surprised at her apparent indifference to her mysteriously missing not-quite-uncle-and-sort-of-cousin. Was it because he was not a blood relation? Or was it because she had already embarked on a different missing person search?

At the office, he spent a few minutes looking for copies of the novel on the internet. He found there were at least three in the Boston area. One at a community branch library within walking distance of his office. He'd go at lunch, he resolved, and see if he could take out that copy, not just for Alice, but because he wanted to re-read some particular passages that he'd found striking.

*

Outside the city, but not too far, Alice walked slowly from the train station, down the streets of a suburb for the comfortably well-to-do, to the familiar door of her Aunt Bix's house. Bix lived on a hill, in a newer townhouse made to look vaguely Victorian. The houses in the row were painted in pastel shades with white trim and matched in every respect, including the plantings. It was early December, and so the only flora in evidence were the small spruce trees that dotted the yards, each bedecked with strings of white Christmas lights which must look attractive after dusk.

It was chilly and a damp wind blew. Alice had grown thinner than usual and despite her pea coat, her heavy, knitted scarf and hat with earflaps, she was freezing. Ordinarily, she would have walked briskly to counteract the cold, but she was still too weak. She felt it was all she could do to shuffle along.

She had emailed Bix a few days before, not knowing if she'd hear back. Bix was ordinarily prompt in every communication she undertook, but Alice remembered, as she walked up the hill, the icy stare she'd fixed her with at the reading of the will. She shivered.

'Enough, enough,' she said softly, slightly out of breath, as though scolding the cold, or her own poorly insulated body. In subsequent group email exchanges, if they could be called that (some messages might be more accurately characterized as ad hominem tirades on the part of her uncles), Bix had never crossed any lines, but Alice felt the distance. She was being cut. Bix would never raise her voice or make a direct attack. She was always correct, perfectly poised and well behaved; Nanette's daughter in every way that Clare had never been.

Alice stopped for a moment and held onto the railing. This made her colder, but she was short of breath. She watched her breath leave her mouth in small puffs of steam. Somehow this was reassuring – a reminder that even if she was cold on the outside, she was still warm on the inside. She was definitely still alive.

As she rested, she wondered at the difference between Clare and Bix and shuddered. Did this mean Clare took after her father? Is this what Alice would find on her quest? Clare in the form of an elderly man? This thought was too much, and she resolved to erase it from her mind.

One more block and she had reached her destination. Bix had asked her to come at teatime, and from Nanette, she knew this meant four o'clock. She hoped she wasn't early. When she turned the corner and saw the house, she was surprised to see a for-sale sign in front. She hadn't known Bix was moving. She walked up the stairs and rang the doorbell. Bix appeared at the door almost immediately. Her bobbed hair was pulled back in a smooth, tight ponytail, and she wore a lemon cashmere sweater set with a sky-blue woollen skirt.

'Alice, Alice, you're here already! How lovely to see you,' she cried out, always the gracious hostess, and clasping Alice's hands, she planted a kiss in the air somewhere near her left ear. Alice briefly smelled her scent, which had always been Chanel, like Nanette's, but a different number.

She led Alice into the kitchen where she had been gathering things for tea. This was a pointed reminder that Alice had arrived five minutes early. As Bix walked briskly ahead, her voice wafted behind her, recounting trivial information about the house and her preparations for the holiday.

'Do be a dear and put these cookies out on the plate,' she said, handing Alice a package of shortbread cookies in a tartan box. 'I just love these cookies around Christmas, don't you?'

Alice nodded and carefully placed the shortbread wafers in concentric circles on the plate. She did like shortbread. Nanette had always served it in December as well. Bix's similarities to Nanette only seemed to grow as she aged. Her choice of colours, of foods, of turns of phrase – and yet, she lacked Nanette's charm; her poise and posture announced primness rather than regal mystique. Where Nanette was an oracle, a high priestess of decorum and taste, Bix was a petty acolyte who carried out her edicts in her every deed because they were doctrine, not because she had the transcendent sense of what was right and graceful that her mother had. Dusting the shortbread crumbs from her fingers, Alice worried briefly if this prosaic quality might have been inherited from the biological father but then reflected that at the very least it could never be that Clare's flamboyant teetering at the edge of sanity and Bix's perfect adherence to tradition could both be inherited from the same man. And such things, after all, might not be genetic. Nanette had been an overwhelming influence on both their lives, and an example that neither could live up to, a paragon with which it was impossible to compete.

Tea now prepared, Bix carried the tray into the living room and set it down on the coffee table.

'Darling, you look awfully chilly,' remarked Bix as though noticing Alice's state for the first time since she'd arrived. 'Are you ill?'

'I had been,' said Alice, who was, without noticing it, hugging herself for warmth. 'In India. I'm still recovering.'

'Oh dear, oh dear,' tutted Bix. 'Didn't that happen to you once before? Why ever did you go back?'

'Well, Ronit's family is there, you know,' replied Alice, affronted.

'Oh, of course they are, darling, I am so sorry. Couldn't they come here to visit? Or are they infirm?'

'I'm sure they'd love to come,' said Alice uncertainly. She was trying to steer the conversation towards the real reason she'd gone to India. All at once this seemed impossible. How might one discuss *a ghost* with Bix? Or question her paternity? She wondered why she had felt so sure of herself in coming here.

Bix poured out the tea and appeared scandalized to see Alice clutching the teacup for dear life, as if it was her only source of warmth.

'Darling, perhaps you need a blanket,' she said, standing up abruptly. She sped out of the room and returned with a woollen lap robe of a similar tartan to the shortbread packaging. This she tucked around Alice's knees and over her lap.

'There you go,' she said, satisfied with the results. 'Now, do tell me, when are you going to marry that nice young man? It seems as though you've been engaged ever so long. You mustn't let him get away, you know,' she added with a bright smile.

Alice shifted uncomfortably. This was not a topic she liked to discuss with anyone, even Ronit, or maybe especially not Ronit.

'There's no hurry,' she said vaguely. 'Maybe in the spring.'

'Well, if it's spring, you need to get moving, choosing dresses, invitations, the church – or will it be in a church? Now what faith does he – your fiancé, Rabeet, is it? What does he practise? Aren't they Buddhists over there?'

'His family is Hindu, but he's more of an atheist.'

'Ah well, then that's good. You can go have it in a church,' said Bix brightly.

'Well, we're not sure, I'm not sure what we will do,' said Alice, squirming slightly under the interrogation. An hour was quickly eaten up in this way. With tea done, the clock striking five, Bix sat up straight and said the perfect phrase for ending an afternoon engagement.

'Well, Alice dear, I must thank you so much for coming all this way. It's been an absolute delight.'

And perhaps it had been a delight for her, no doubt still resentful about the terms of her mother's will. And since it was impossible for Nanette to do any wrong and the blame must be laid at somebody's door, she laid it at the door of the heiress, Alice, who had by some hidden wiles forced the pen of a defenceless elderly woman. And thus, an hour of tea and cookies during which she grilled and caused the wily heiress to squirm and had the opportunity to witness from close quarters her feeble physical state was an hour happily spent indeed.

But the afternoon, it turned out, was not to be so purely enjoyable after all. As Alice stood in the hallway, fumbling on her light-blue, hand-knitted mittens, she looked up and saw her reflection in the mirror. Skinny, maybe even sallow, her hair hanging lank about her face, and her knitted cap, that matched the mittens, looking foolish on her head, with its earflaps and jaunty pompom. *I can't let this go just like that*, she thought. *It's now or never*. With Nanette gone, the family, never cohesive to begin with, was already splitting apart. The house was for sale, and she might never stand in this hall again, never sit drinking tea in a tartan lap robe, never spend an hour with this ersatz Nanette; they would all pull apart and the distance would grow too great to bring up intimate subjects and family secrets again.

'There's something I wanted to ask you,' said Alice, turning abruptly towards Bix, who was fussing with an arrangement of holly in the urn on the hall table.

Bix looked up at her sharply. She didn't like the change in tone from helplessness to defiance. 'What is it, my dear?' she asked, cocking her head to one side like a sparrow.

'At the funeral,' said Alice, clasping her mittened hands together to feel her own strength, 'a man came, an elderly man. I saw the uncles, your brothers, say something to him and then he went away. Do you know who that man was?'

A mask fell across Bix's features. She registered no reaction to Alice's query.

'No,' she said firmly. 'No, I'm afraid not. No doubt he was some kind of intruder, or … or a homeless person,' she added, less convincingly. 'Now, do wrap up and hurry home. I do wish you'd waited to come 'til you were better.' She fussed over Alice's scarf in a show of solicitude, while gently applying physical pressure to effectively push her out the door, or at least that's how it felt to Alice.

Alice knew this was now a dead end. But she had also learned something valuable: Bix was lying; she knew who the man was and thought him important, and Alice would get to the bottom of it, she was determined.

'All right, then,' said Alice, with false brightness. 'So lovely to see you. Thanks for tea.'

She gently placed her woolly hands on Bix's shoulders and kissed her on the left cheek. The touch and the feel of that kiss made Bix start and withdraw slightly, as though she might catch whatever ague it was that Alice suffered from.

'Goodbye, then,' said Alice. As she pulled open the street door and stepped back out into the damp chill, which had increased with the darkness of early evening, she noticed the for-sale sign again. 'Oh, I noticed you're selling the house,' she said, turning back. 'What made you decide to do that?'

Bix clenched her jaw, glared at Alice, and then pulled the door firmly shut.

As Alice walked down the steps and turned once more to look up at the attractive but unremarkable house, she felt a pang of guilt. Was it her fault? Were Bix's finances also affected negatively by the terms of the will? Then she noticed Bix's silhouette in the window gazing out – not at her, it didn't seem – but at something far off in the distance.

# 35

By the time she reached home, she was chilled to the bone. Her fingers felt so stiff it was an effort to get the key in the lock of the apartment. When she opened the door, she felt a rush of warmth and smells. Ronit was cooking something. When he heard the door shut, Ronit bounded into the hall. He was wearing his thick, brown wool sweater and brown corduroy pants; an outfit that always made him look like a soft, velvety teddy bear to Alice. His face was wreathed in smiles, as though he'd had some special triumph that day.

He helped her off with her coat, hung it up on the hook, then pulled off her mittens and hat for her.

'I'm so cold,' she said, almost shuddering. 'So, so cold.' She buried her face in his shoulder as he took her in his arms and felt the warmth of his body and his teddy-bear costume slowly melt through the outer layer of frost.

'Why did you go out today?' he asked. He put an arm around her and led her into the living room–dining room area. 'I thought you'd been feeling poorly this morning.'

'I was, but I'd arranged to have tea with my aunt Bix, to ask her about my grandfather,' said Alice.

Ronit settled her on the sofa and wrapped a red chenille blanket around her body all the way up to her neck. Then he went into the bedroom and brought back her slipper socks and gently put them on her feet, which she lifted to help him, as though she were a small child.

'Now I'll make a small "fire",' he said, indicating the scare quotes with his tone, as he went across the room to the gas-powered fireplace and flipped the switch.

Alice had been averse to installing the fireplace at first, because, she said, 'It isn't a real fire, it's just gas.' Ronit had pointed out that burning gas was in fact, technically fire, but she had asserted confidently that a real fire was built only with logs.

'Where would we get logs in the city?' he asked.

Alice had no answer, but after she'd seen how cozy a gas fireplace could be when they were having dinner at a friend's house, she'd agreed on the stipulation that they weren't to pretend it was a real fire. They would just enjoy it for what it was. Ronit had agreed and had henceforth referred to the gas fire as a 'fire'.

'I got a nice wine for tonight, but if you'd prefer, I can make you a toddy.'

Alice smiled. She was beginning to warm up. 'A toddy, please,' she said.

While he was heating up the toddy, Ronit switched on some madrigals that he knew Alice liked. He brought out the toddy and placed it on a coaster next to Alice and then got a glass of red wine for himself and sat down next to her and reached out to clasp her hand.

'I've made a pot of chilli,' he said, 'and there's fresh bread and salad.'

'And for dessert?' asked Alice, only partly joking.

'For dessert, chocolate amaretto bars from the bakery.'

'Why are you so good to me?' asked Alice, tears suddenly starting in her eyes. She leaned against his shoulder and closed her eyes to keep herself from crying.

Ronit turned his head and kissed her on the forehead. He put his arms around her and held her close.

'Because you are my most precious treasure,' he said. 'Also, because I love you.'

Alice murmured that she loved him too, her voice muffled by his sweater. After nearly two years together, it was still difficult for her to accept such open expressions of affection. In her family, it simply wasn't done.

'I have a surprise for you,' said Ronit.

Alice looked up, excited.

'What is it?'

Ronit got up and went across the room to his backpack, unzipped it and drew out a book. He held it up triumphantly.

'*Himalayan Rhapsody*,' he said. 'I found it at a community library, of all places, right near my office.'

Alice was disappointed, but she successfully hid her feelings. She had hoped, despite the fact that such an outcome was unlikely, that Ronit had somehow succeeded where she had failed and brought her some information about her real grandfather.

'Oh,' she said. 'That's fun.'

'You're not excited,' he said, crestfallen. 'I was sure you'd be excited. I don't know why you're not more intrigued by Biju. Your missing pseudo-uncle! Why are you only interested in missing grandfathers?'

Alice smiled.

'Missing grandfathers and pseudo-uncles,' she said.

'I'm sorry,' said Ronit. 'I know you really want to know about that man who may be your grandfather, but is it just not possible for you to be interested in more than one mystery at a time?'

Ronit came back to the sofa and sat down, but farther away from her. He held the book petulantly in his lap.

'You really must read this,' he said.

'I will,' said Alice, sorry she had not been able to show more excitement. She reached out and took the book from him and held it to her chest. 'I promise I'll read it, and then I'm sure my interest will grow, and I'll see things your way.'

Ronit sighed. He didn't know if he felt like sharing the rest of the information he'd found that day.

'What is it?' asked Alice.

'Well,' said Ronit, still feeling peeved, 'you might not really want to hear the rest.'

'What? Tell me. I'm sure it's very interesting,' said Alice, trying to look attentive.

'Well,' said Ronit, 'a few different name combinations and I might have found him, or traces of him, anyway.'

'Oh! Where is he?'

'He might be nearby. I found a few people that could be him, a Tom M. Ramsey, a Matthew T. Ramsey, but I also found an M. Thomas Ramsey in the Boston area, and I thought maybe that would make sense, that he'd go to Boston, near to where his father was from, even if he never looked him up. Or maybe he did look him up, and your grandfather didn't tell you that.'

'Where does he live? Could you tell?'

'Well, there were many past addresses. Probably he's moved around a bit. Also, in one spot, I saw his employer listed as Macy's.'

'Macy's …' Alice tried to piece together in her mind the disparate puzzle pieces. A childhood in Cosmos Cottage, a well-received novel, a mysterious disappearance, a job at Macy's.

'What do you think he did at Macy's?' she asked.

'I don't know. I might be able to find out, if I can track him down there, or if they'll give me information about an employee.'

Alice's interest in her missing pseudo-uncle was sufficiently piqued.

'Tomorrow is my meeting with Lawrence Drawbridge,' she said. 'I'll ask him if he knows anything too. And you know,' she added, 'I got nothing out of Aunt Bix. Except that she was upset by my mentioning that man. And she's selling her house.'

'Well, that's something, I suppose,' said Ronit. 'She must not have been as well off as you thought,' he added.

'Yes. She didn't seem entirely happy with me.'

'If she was counting on getting some money from the will, I'd imagine not.'

Ronit got up and put supper on the table, and Alice, her attention not all there, opened the novel by her not-quite-relation and began to read.

# 36

Alice walked down the steps from the train carefully. It was not a popular stop, and they were partially covered with slush and ice after last night's snowfall. She headed along the same route to Lawrence Drawbridge's law office she'd traversed before in summer in a sundress and sandals. Now it would be just her, and although some of the topics would be awkward, she'd worked out a way to discuss everything so as not to mention things the attorney might find questionable, such as ghosts.

'You'll not want him to doubt your mental wellness,' Ronit had suggested, tactfully.

'Do you think he'd be less helpful if he thought I was crazy?' asked Alice, genuinely curious.

'I don't know him, but I think it's best not to test him too much if you want his sympathy.'

They had walked through the story until it was all set in her head. She wondered if she should have done this before visiting Bix as well, but she also felt fairly sure she'd have got nothing from her no matter what.

Alice trudged through the slush to the door of the office building and went in, wiping her boots on the mat by the door. She rode the elevator to the ninth floor, then down the hall to the law offices.

The secretary seemed to recognize her and told her Mr Drawbridge would see her in a moment. She was ushered into an empty conference room. The secretary closed the door on her way out. It was a different room from the one in which they'd heard the contents of the will, a bit smaller, but just as bland, and smelling rather strongly of new vinyl seats and carpeting. Alice removed her coat and hat and mittens and sat down in an empty chair in the corner. Then she took out *Himalayan Rhapsody* and began to read.

After some time, Alice thought she heard raised voices. A woman speaking loudly to a man. Alice tried to drown it out and keep reading, but the woman's voice grew louder. After a while, she was forced to admit that the woman whose voice she was hearing was her mother. The room was moderately soundproofed and so the exact wording of Clare's tirade was unclear to her, but it was easy enough to guess. She must be back from her stay in upstate New York, thought Alice. Ronit had not mentioned this, but perhaps he didn't know how long the programme would last. From the sound of things, it had not been a resounding success.

Alice sighed and stared at the words on the page, but they blurred and formed patterns. There was a blood-curdling scream, and many more voices were added to the growing cacophony outside the room. Alice imagined this to be the police and her mother's scream a response to their arrival. She would probably call them 'the men in white coats' at some point and tell them that if they wanted to put her in a padded cell, they'd have to take her in a straitjacket first. Alice wondered if she should go and help, but as was usually the case during one of Clare's rants, she felt perfectly frozen in place. She was grateful for her hiding place.

Alice mused over these turns of phrase that Clare liked to use, 'men in white coats', 'padded cell', 'straitjacket' – they all came from movies and novels from the early days of psychiatry, and though the concepts described by the terms were not completely fictitious, they did not accurately describe Clare's usual treatment plan. The men who usually took her away wore blue, for one thing, because they were policemen. And they didn't need a straitjacket to take Clare away, both because she was small and thin and not totally out of control. It was all a performance that made her seem so, involving endless streams of insults at the policemen, and whichever people had called the police. These insults were delivered in a high-pitched scream and laced together with streams of profanities. For the policemen, it was never so much a physical challenge to take her off to the squad car and get her to an emergency room as it was a psychological one. Clare's insults, while launched as rants to people personally unknown to her, were razor-sharp and amazingly accurate.

Somehow, she could guess at the secret anxieties of two burly Boston cops wrestling her into the car and cry out all manner of revelatory insults about their deepest fears, hopes and anxieties. Ashen and unmanned, they would finally deliver her to the intake people at the emergency room, where she would not, in point of fact, end up in a padded cell (and this much Alice only imagined, for her role in all this, when she had the ill fortune to play a role, was to remain in the hard plastic turquoise seats of the ER waiting room and stare around the room at the people who had been brought in for all manner of ills, most of them involving bodily harm of a more life-threatening nature than Clare's). Then the police officers would return to their squad car, silent, unable to look one another in the eye, especially if Clare had raked up some unspoken tension between them. They would quickly drive away, searching for an excuse to separate so they could re-inter the horrors she had dug up and thrown in their faces. As the noise outside the room died down, Alice wondered what these policemen would do. Would they go to a doughnut shop? Buy a pack of smokes and sit by the river's edge, pretending to conduct surveillance on the few students who were rushing along in the biting cold? How long would it take before they could look one another in the eye and converse as they had before?

A tap came on the door.

'Come in,' said Alice.

The receptionist put her head in.

'Mr Drawbridge has just finished with a client, and he'll be with you shortly,' she said evenly. She patted her carefully coiffed, short grey hair as though she wondered if anything was out of place. Alice took the gesture as her way of indicating that she was not altogether telling the truth, but she didn't blame her. What could one say in such a situation? She was only glad she'd been allowed to remain protected in the vacant and characterless room. She felt a dark burning in her gut, a familiar sensation. Her hands were red, and her knees felt as though they were trembling, although when she looked down, she saw that they were still.

'Thank you,' said Alice. The secretary looked at her face searchingly for a moment. Perhaps she had intended to offer some sort of comfort, but Alice's thin, pale features offered her a blank wall. Her hands were resolutely clasped about her book. Her posture was erect, her knees together. The receptionist softly closed the door.

Alice looked down at the book again. She looked at her hands holding the book and wondered if they were still attached to her body. She started reading again, automatically, not really understanding, just doing it, as she had always done in these situations. She read some things about the protagonist's feelings of loneliness. She found her eye scanning. There would be a new tutor, it seemed. A young man. Maybe this was where the 'gay part' would come in.

There was another knock on the door. Alice looked up. It was Lawrence Drawbridge.

'So sorry to have kept you waiting,' he said, uneasily. Was it Alice's imagination, or did he look a bit dishevelled? Probably. Clare was like a cyclone. During these phases, it felt like she was flinging and ripping and spinning, but Alice had to remind herself that this was not so.

'My mother was here,' said Alice.

'She was,' replied Mr Drawbridge, brushing his pink striped tie as though it had crumbs. 'Unexpected.'

'Naturally. I didn't know she was out.'

'Nor did I, but I imagine that won't last long.'

'I wonder if she'll go back to the same place.'

'I don't know. That's beyond our purview. But if you like,' he added, 'I can make a call and inquire …'

'No,' said Alice. 'My fiancé will take care of that for me.'

'Ah, yes, the psychiatrist. Very useful,' he added, undiplomatically. 'Well,' he said, changing the subject, 'Are we ready for our meeting?'

Alice was grateful he did not tell her why her mother had come, although she realized this information might have been confidential.

'Yes, I'm ready,' she said.

'Very good.' He sat down casually in a chair near her.

'How can I help you?'

'Well,' said Alice, 'in India, I went on … on a kind of quest,' she began. Then she stopped, worried he might think she meant a spiritual quest. 'A quest to find family information,' she clarified.

Lawrence Drawbridge squinted sensitively but did not respond.

'I had found,' continued Alice, 'some addresses in India related to my grandfather's business dealings there.' Alice felt pleased with the phrase 'business dealings', which she had rehearsed with Ronit. 'And so, my fiancé and I went first to one of the addresses, in a town called Muzaffarnagar, which led us to a building that was no longer there, that used to be where his business was.' And then we went to Mussoorie, which is a town in the Himalayas, and at that address …' she paused to see if Mr Drawbridge registered any recognition of these facts. He was squinting and patted down his tie again. '… and there, we learned some very interesting things.'

'I see,' he said.

'We met a woman who goes by the name of Violet Ramsey, who said she had been married to Grandfather for forty-five years. Living with her were two women whom she referred to as their daughters. I believe that she was telling the truth,' added Alice.

'I see,' said Drawbridge again, now noticeably uncomfortable. His father had been Nanette and Grandfather's attorney until his retirement some twenty-five years before. Mr Drawbridge, the younger, had assumed the mantle at that time. He'd known the family his entire life.

'Were you aware of the existence of my grandfather's second family?' asked Alice suddenly, staring directly at him with unblinking, clear eyes. The directness of the question made him flustered.

'Well,' he said, 'with the death of your grandparents, I suppose – I imagine – there's no reason to shield you from this sort of information,' he said.

'Who else had knowledge of this?' she asked. 'Do any of my uncles know? My mother? My aunt?'

'I believe,' he said, 'I believe that your uncles might have some inkling but only vaguely so. They were involved in – in bringing the body – back to the United States as your grandmother did not wish – wish to be involved.'

Lawrence Drawbridge was clearly uncomfortable with the subject. Alice wondered how he would handle the next parts of her query.

'Violet Ramsey and her daughters received an annuity which has ended with Nanette's death,' continued Alice, feeling calmer. The situation was under control, she felt. The shock she had felt from hearing her mother's screaming in the other room was wearing off. She pulled the dusty files from Mussoorie out of her shoulder bag and handed them to Mr Drawbridge.

'These files contain details of the annuity. I'd like to have that reinstated.'

'I see,' he said, placing his reading glasses on his nose. He pulled the papers from the file and began glancing over them. 'Of course, this will be something you would also need to discuss with the bank.'

'Of course,' said Alice, though it hadn't really occurred to her to think of the lawyers and the bankers as separate entities. 'But,' she continued, 'there's one other thing I want to discuss, something else I learned in India.'

Lawrence Drawbridge, who had been slowly taking the previous topic in his stride, eyed her uneasily.

'Yes, please, ask away,' he said. He crossed his legs theatrically and clasped his knee in his hands. The pose was meant to convey a casual attitude but the bulky envelope of files was still in his lap and Alice wondered if it might fall.

'I learned as well that in all likelihood, my grandfather is not really my grandfather at all, and that my mother and aunt might have a different father than their siblings.'

Lawrence Drawbridge blanched. Nothing immediately suggested itself to him as a suitable response. The words Alice had just spoken existed in the collective Drawbridge psyche only as a darkly whispered rumour that was never spoken aloud, alluded to through gestures and veiled innuendo.

'At Nanette's funeral,' Alice continued when it became clear he had as yet no words to add to the topic she'd introduced so delicately, 'a man arrived who was older, perhaps in his seventies, tall, thin, well dressed. I never had a chance to see him up close. My uncles, I observed, persuaded him to leave, and a woman I was talking to at the time, a friend of Nanette's, told me when I asked who the man was that he had been Nanette's lover. She told me his name, too, Smith, I think.'

The files slid from Mr Drawbridge's lap, his legs uncrossed; his hands weren't sure what to do with themselves and became occupied with imaginary adjustments to the pink striped tie. Alice was surprised at the unease of this usually professional man. She had expected something more along the lines of a confirmation or denial, but so far, she'd gotten nothing at all, only a glimmer of some aspect of his soul, which, despite its sudden nakedness, she didn't feel prepared to interpret at that moment. She focused on storing as much of this information as possible in her mind for a later conversation with Ronit, who was sure to come up with something sharper than her woolly impressions.

'What I would like to know,' she said slowly and carefully, as though speaking to a small child or someone hard of hearing, 'what I would like to know, is whether you know who that man was.'

This clear-cut question provided Mr Drawbridge with a point of focus. It made him regain his former posture, let go of his tie, straighten his legs properly. Colour returned to his face and his evenly trimmed and unobtrusive moustache suddenly looked crisper.

'Who he was,' he said authoritatively.

'Yes, do you know?'

'His name is James Smith, III,' he said briskly. 'He was at St Paul's with my elder brother. I am the youngest, much younger, of four. My elder brother Bannister was with him in school. My brother went on to Williams College, then Dartmouth Law, after which he took the bar here in Boston. He's retired now.'

'And where did Mr Smith go to college?' asked Alice.

'Ah, somewhere in Maine, I think. Bowdoin, I'd imagine.'

'And do you know anything further? Do you know of his relationship with Nanette?'

Lawrence Drawbridge was not about to be drawn back into the abyss of sordid secrets and libellous rumours.

'I am aware that they moved in the same social circles,' he said definitively, as though that were clearly the end of it.

'Do you know,' continued Alice, not to be put off so quickly, 'do you know the woman with whom I spoke at the funeral? She was Nanette's age, or maybe slightly younger, white hair, lavender-tinged, pulled back, in a bun. She had a black straw hat pinned to her hair, with a small veil which came down to just above her eyes. She wore a black silk dress to the knees with a black wool jacket, bolero cut.'

'Gracious! What an eye for detail you have,' cried Mr Drawbridge with what seemed to be genuine admiration. 'I wouldn't have thought I'd be able to tell you which woman was which, but from your description that could be none other than Hyacinth Butterworth. A very old family, hers. She was a very close friend of your grandmother's, and I did specifically talk to her right after the service, so I know that she was dressed more or less in the manner you describe.'

Alice took out a small notepad from her shoulder bag. In it, she wrote: *James Smith, III* and *Hyacinth Butterworth*.

'Thank you very much,' she said, with a finality that seemed soothing to Lawrence Drawbridge.

'You're very welcome, my dear,' he said, rising quickly from his chair. 'You must excuse me now. I have another appointment coming right up.'

'But do you have addresses for either of them?' she asked suddenly, realizing the names were not very useful without any addresses.

'I'm afraid not. It's been ages,' he responded briskly.

Alice stood too and followed him from the room. Out by the secretary's desk, she held out her hand and thanked him for his help.

'Not at all, not at all, we're always at your service. Cheerio,' he returned, shaking her hand briskly.

'Don't forget the files,' Alice added, pointing towards the conference room where the files from Mussoorie still lay on the floor.

'Of course not, of course not,' murmured Mr Drawbridge, and he lurched back into the room, returning with the files under his arm. Before heading down the hall, he winked at her in an avuncular fashion, then turned on his heel briskly and made a hasty retreat.

Alice stood silently, donning her coat, hat and mittens in the presence of the secretary, who watched her only obliquely as she shuffled through a stack of papers.

'Goodbye,' said Alice, and turned towards the door.

'Have a nice day,' returned the secretary doubtfully.

# 37

Ronit generally only scheduled half an hour or forty-five minutes for himself to eat lunch, so he'd had to wait for a couple of cancellations in a row to be assured enough time to take a bus to Macy's to make some inquiries and return to the office in time. His schedule was particularly backed up due to his long absence. Colleagues had covered for him to be sure, but many long-time patients were eager for an appointment after his lengthy absence, so he squeezed them in as best he could.

A week or more after he'd made the initial discovery about Biju's possible connection to Macy's, he finally found such a block of time. Quickly bundling himself up in his parka, hat and gloves, he set out for the bus. He'd forgotten it was close to Christmas, and the bus was crammed with shoppers bearing large parcels. He wondered what he should get Alice for Christmas. Anything sold by Macy's was not likely to do the trick. Alice liked odd things, old things, like the curios found in *The Old Curiosity Shop*. Ronit had yet to find a proper curiosity shop for buying presents for Alice. One had to hunt year-round in all sorts of out-of-the-way places and then save things up for Christmases and birthdays and so on. And then, she had a child's uncanny knack for discovering his stashes of presents in their small condo. He wondered sometimes if, like a child, she found the things on purpose, or if it was always an accident caused by her wandering about looking for something else as she said it was. Probably a little of each, he thought.

Last year, he'd given her a small wooden box of old chandelier pendants, a nicely preserved edition of *A Girl's Guide to Camping* from 1947, and a taxidermized hummingbird in a glass box on a gold stand with a dusty label that read *Eric*. The label was stuck with two golden straight pins into the discoloured velvet cushion on which the unfortunate bird was perched. All these items he'd hidden throughout the year in various spots in his office, the one place into which Alice was least likely to wander accidentally.

Would any of these do? As Ronit exited the bus, he wondered if Alice would find them Christmassy enough. *Christmassy* for Alice was not the spectacle he beheld right at this moment as he rounded the corner and crossed the street to an entrance of Macy's. Salvation Army Santas, armies of consumers laden with bags and parcels, every conceivable surface bedecked with red and green ornamentation, the incessant loop of carols, pop songs and re-recorded standards. His ears were assailed with a particularly egregious example of the latter genre as he selected one of the many entry doors to this temple to consumerism. He shuddered as he listened to, or passively was caused to hear, a fresh reinvention of 'Rudolph, the Red-nosed Reindeer'.

As usual, Ronit found himself immediately bewildered – he now realized this happened by design – among the bottles of scent. Cologne girls, sharply dressed, wafted in clouds of artificial odours that were meant to attract, beguile and bewitch hapless shoppers.

*Breathe*, thought Ronit, stopping to gather his wits about him and find some orientation that might lead him to an information kiosk. *Breathe* – and no sooner had he uttered this mantra to himself, although he would prefer not to call it a mantra, because, technically, it wasn't one, he realized its futility. For here he stood, a bewildered-looking man, possibly married, probably attached, totally still among the scent vendors, nostrils flared as though inhaling some celestial aromas. The cologne fairies were upon him, atomizing, spraying, compressing and squeezing shiny dispensers of all kinds. 'Passion', 'Obsession', 'Profusion', 'Deception', they called out lists of abstract nouns. *No, they couldn't have just said some of those,* thought Ronit, happy to find he still retained a sliver of humour. This thought, giving him hope, made him raise his head high, and looking directly into the eyes of one fragrance temptress with light-red hair and plump, powdered cheeks, he asked, 'Which way to the information desk?'

Her eyes glassed over as he evaporated from potential target to nothing, nothing at all, and he wondered if some part of him didn't secretly wish this soft-faced woman would appreciate him. What would it be like to reach out and softly squeeze the powdered cheeks and have those pale eyes ringed elaborately in green turn to him with a look of unbridled desire? She held out a pale, plump finger to indicate some indistinct point, an invisible vista somewhere at the end of the scent gauntlet.

'After perfumes?'

'And make-up,' she responded brusquely, walking away before the sentence had fully cleared her lips.

Ronit sighed. Still in the midst of the odoriferous cloud, he already felt a little hungover. A sort of chemical haze. He walked straight, with purpose, through the lines of women, who showed less interest in him by the time he reached mascaras and eyeliners and even less in foundations and blush. He wondered, as he regained some measure of confidence after being temporarily unmanned by the scent apsaras, if that sensation he had just undergone would appear anywhere in the DSM-V.

Reaching the end of make-up, Ronit stopped and looked around. He'd expected the information booth to pop up like a shimmering mirage, but it did not. Finally, he noticed a thin, blonde woman dressed in black and wearing a Santa hat. She was seated in a small booth made to look like a chimney. She must be the keeper of information. In fact, the word 'Information' was written across the front of the kiosk but was partially concealed by a festoon of artificial holly. Ronit approached the woman, who was talking on a headset, and cleared his throat. She leisurely excused herself from her conversation and turned her heavily lined eyes towards him.

'Yes,' she asked flatly.

'I'm trying to find someone – a relative – who I believe works in this store. His name is Thomas or Tom Ramsey – he's Indian, like myself.'

The woman glanced to the left and to the right and then said, 'Sir, we wouldn't give out that type of information. That's confidential.'

'Even just a confirmation that he works here?'

'That's right, sir,' she said, sullenly fixing her gaze on a rack of sharply reduced handbags to Ronit's right. Another employee came up with a stack of men's socks and asked the woman a question in Spanish that Ronit couldn't understand. Only then did he realize that despite the woman's hair colour, she was not really white at all. In fact, her blonde hair resembled the synthetic tresses of a Barbie doll and might even be a wig. Ronit thought he'd try just one more time, despite the stonewalling. Raising his voice slightly, he asked, 'So you can't tell me if a Tom Ramsey – T O M R A M S E Y –' (he said, spelling it out) 'works here at this Macy's?'

The woman looked up at him suspiciously from the pile of socks she was examining. She blinked. Her eyelashes were enormous and were probably also not real. Ronit looked at the other employee, who he was surprised to see staring at him with frank interest. The young man cocked his head, looked him square in the eye and then motioned several times to the right with his eyes only, after which he looked down again and busied himself in the socks.

'I see,' said Ronit to the woman again. 'Well, thank you for your time.'

What had the young man meant to tell him? That Biju was nearby? No, that couldn't be. There were only women clerks as far as the eye could see. Perhaps he wanted to meet him in the direction he'd indicated with his eyes. Ronit decided that was the case, so he sauntered over to the right, a jungle of women's accessories. Bags of all sizes, hair ornaments, caps. Everything a jumble from the excessive handling of holiday shoppers. He settled on a rack of travel-sized cosmetic bags, and pretended to pick them up and examine them, all the while furtively glancing over towards the information kiosk so he wouldn't miss any movements on the part of the young man with the socks.

What would Alice think if he brought her home one of these small, brightly coloured bags with slick plastic lining to prevent damage to one's luggage from leaking beauty products? It was hard to say. He'd never seen Alice use beauty products at all, and she only travelled with essential items such as toothpaste and shampoo, and even these she used erratically. It was he who had persuaded her to visit a dentist, something she'd not done since shc was a teenager. Nanette had periodically made her appointments with her own dentist, and paid for them, as Alice and Clare had no insurance to speak of. For all he knew, Alice would be pleased by a cosmetics bag. He carefully examined a turquoise-blue model with pink stripes, on sale for $10.99, then glanced up again and saw that the young clerk was walking away from the kiosk. He looked back at Ronit, shrugged a shoulder and squinted, then proceeded towards the down escalator.

Ronit took all this to mean he should follow him. He set off quickly but circuitously through the display racks, feeling every bit as though he were engaged in some kind of drug deal or assignation. As he stepped onto the escalator, he glanced back one more time towards the woman charged with dispensing information. She was engaged with another customer by now, and he wondered, after all, what need there had been to escape her notice in this manner. She wasn't a security guard after all.

At the bottom of the escalator, Ronit looked around for his informant and saw him straight ahead arranging rows of men's dress socks on hangers, occasionally applying a small, gun-like device to their labels. Ronit approached him, suddenly concerned that he had mistaken the man's gestures and expressions for acts of communication with him, when he might just suffer from spasmodic tics or even Tourette's syndrome.

Drawing close to the young man, Ronit cleared his throat and said, 'Excuse me.'

'Oh, hey,' responded the clerk, whose name tag read, Ronit noticed, 'JESUS – PUERTO RICO.'

'Did you happen to hear my question upstairs?' asked Ronit.

'Yeah, man, that guy, Tom, he works down here in men's,' he said, squeezing his small gun at a pair of argyle socks. Did men still wear argyle socks, wondered Ronit. It seemed old-fashioned.

'Is he here now?'

'No, no, he comes evenings – four to nine – last shift,' he said. 'You a relative of his? Cousin?'

'Something like that,' said Ronit.

'I knew it!' cried Jesus, suddenly enthusiastic. He warmly grasped Ronit's hand in an inventive sort of handshake that was more contemporary than anything Ronit was accustomed to.

'But your name tag?' asked Ronit, bewildered. 'You're Puerto Rican?'

'No, man, they just write that shit so folks have an easier time – shoppers. Most folks see brown-skinned dudes like me and think *Latin*, so they say, let 'em.'

'But you were speaking Spanish upstairs.'

'Yeah,' he said non-committally.

'But you're Indian?'

'What, Indian folks can't learn Spanish?'

'Oh, I didn't mean that …' Ronit felt fully sidetracked.

'What part of India is your family from?' he asked.

'Kerala!' he replied, triumphantly, raising his fists in the air, as though he were associated with a winning team.

'Aha, I believe Tom Ramsey's mother was also from Kerala.'

'No doubt, no doubt. Dude is old but he's cool,' replied Jesus/not-his-real-name.

'Well, I'm looking for him, long-lost kind of thing, can you tell me what he looks like?'

'Big dude. Big. Dude.'

'You mean tall? Or heavy?'

'Both, man,' said Jesus, approvingly. 'No one messes with that dude. Big.'

'And do you know what days he works?'

'This week probably Thursday, Friday, Saturday – all weekend. Monday off, I think. It changes.'

'Thanks so much,' said Ronit, and then, as an afterthought, he asked, 'What's your real name then?'

'Venkat. But everyone calls me Jesus now. It's a cool name; I'm down with it. Even my mom calls me Jesus sometimes.'

Ronit chuckled. He held out his hand and said, 'Ronit. I'm from Kolkata.'

'Oh, that's cool,' said Jesus-Venkat. 'I knew a dude from there once. Smoked major weed.'

'That is true of many Bengalis I know,' responded Ronit, feeling jovial at his successful sleuthing mission. Bidding his new young friend adieu, he walked back through the socks, half wondering if he didn't need a few new pairs himself. But he would be back, so he decided against it. He made his way up the escalator, past the woman at the kiosk, who was glowering sullenly at a middle-aged woman brandishing a receipt. Was the information woman then not Latina either? The idea that all the staff in the store might be mislabelled as to their country of origin was decentring.

With greater confidence and poise, he walked back through the make-up and scent gauntlet, regarding the clouds of perfume now as a kind of breadcrumb trail marking his path out of the forest of Macy's. Outside, jostled by shoppers, he rounded the corner, crossed the street and walked to the bus stop. He would make it back to the office just in time for his next appointment.

# 38

Alice's next move, she decided, should be to go to Chichester to see what she could learn from Nanette's friend Hyacinth Butterworth.

'But it's so close to Christmas,' objected Ronit.

'Let's do Christmas there. I'll open up the house; you come when you can.'

'How will you get a tree?'

'I'll chop one down from the woods and drag it into the house.'

Ronit looked sceptical. 'Can you do that?'

'I know where the saw is.'

The location of the saw was not so much an issue for Ronit as the idea of taking a tree from a forest, though he couldn't actually think of an argument against it.

'Okay,' he said. 'If you think that would be Christmassy.'

'Oh, yes, I do,' she said firmly.

Alice took the bus to Chichester. She would use Nanette's car if need be, as it was still parked in the garage and now belonged to her, along with everything else on the property. When she reached the village, she called for a taxi at the drugstore and waited outside in the dusk for the local taxi driver to appear. A thin layer of snow had fallen, and the main street was festooned with white Christmas lights that made it look like the whole town had become a haven for fairies. Alice wouldn't have been surprised if she'd seen a group of snow fairies arrive in a cloud and alight in front of the bank. *Very Christmassy*, she thought.

The house, when she reached it, was totally dark. The snow was fresh in the circular driveway, unmarred by tracks. There was a caretaker who came regularly, but she hadn't thought to inform him she was coming and therefore no arrangements had been made for her arrival.

'Will you be all right?' asked the driver, dubiously.

'Oh, yes,' said Alice.

The house looked haunted, but Alice already knew it was, and she had missed it so. She paid the driver, stepped lightly across the snow and walked to the side door, the one they'd always used, and fitted her key in the lock. The driver was still there. She waved to him and smiled broadly, to show him that she was fine. With her pale skin and long, brown hair, she looked a bit of a ghost herself, thought the driver. *The ghost returns to the haunted house*, he thought, and shook his head as he drove around the driveway, leaving two black tracks behind him.

Alice breathed in the cold air. It was crisp and did not carry with it the damp of Boston's winter air. Somehow this felt healthy to her and didn't fill her weakened body with chills. She glanced back at the prints her feet had made walking up to the door. *I'm home*. Then she slipped the key into the lock, turned it and entered the kitchen through the mudroom.

Inside, she reached for the switch and flicked it on. The kitchen looked neat. She went into the hallway where the thermostat was and turned up the heat. It was set at forty-two degrees, just enough to keep the pipes from freezing. She set it at seventy-two as they always did in their condo and then remembered that this thermostat might heat the whole house. She was pretty sure it did. *Must do something about that*, she thought, with a slight thrill, like a child who has been left alone in the house for the first time without an adult, even though she had frequently been left alone in this and other houses without an adult from a young age.

She kept her coat on and went back to the kitchen. She hadn't thought of getting groceries – that was silly – and by now the village store would be closed. She looked in the fridge, her expectations low. There were things like mayonnaise and peanut butter, and even an unopened stick of butter. The fridge looked emptier than usual. No dodgy cheese remainders now. The caretaker or perhaps the cleaning staff may have removed all the unsightly bits of food.

Alice went to the pantry next to investigate. There were canned soups and some boxes of crackers, one of which had been feasted on by a mouse or something. A few other things had been tampered with: a box of cookies, some teabags, there was a bit of a mess around the sugar too. Odd mouse, thought Alice, and selected for her dinner a can of tomato soup and an unopened box of crackers.

These she ate at the small, white enamel kitchen table, which looked downright barren. She didn't know the last time the surface had been visible. Usually, she'd balance her plate or bowl on a stack of magazines, old newspapers and the like and try her best not to spill her coffee all over the seed catalogues, and, depending on the season, seed packets as well.

When she was done, she washed up, stacked her dishes in the dish drainer and took the rinsed-out tin can to the back sun porch where the recycling bins were kept. Without turning on the light, she tossed the can into the bin for cans and bottles and turned to go back into the house, when it occurred to her that the can had not made the sound she'd expected it to: a rattle of tin against the side of an empty plastic trash bin. She switched on the fluorescent grow light, the only one on the porch, which doubled as a greenhouse, and peered into the recycling bin. At the bottom were three empty bottles of pinot noir.

She picked one up and looked at it carefully to get a sense of how old it was. There was no dust on it. It must be recent. *Clare*, she thought, unsurprised. Clare probably still had a key. Alice hadn't thought to change the locks. With the trip to India, this was really the first time she'd had a chance to visit the house as its owner. She felt more surprised that Clare had left the kitchen so clean and even rinsed and recycled her wine bottles. She couldn't be here now; it was much too cold, and the house felt empty.

Alice wondered if Clare had merely come to assert what she perceived to be her rights, or if she had come with some specific mission in mind. Alice took a flashlight from the porch, switched off the light, and set out to investigate the house. The sitting room was as it had been, and the bed had been removed from the dining room now that Nanette was no more. The dining table and chairs were back in place and the sombre ancestors stared down at little Alice playing house with marked disapproval.

She moved on down the hall, inspecting rooms and confirming the hall locks were secure. The library seemed untouched, as did the music room. Then she made her way up the staircase. Here she decided to check Grandfather's wing first, not because she thought Clare had any interest in it, but because she was curious if he would still be there. She switched on the wall sconces one by one and walked slowly down the corridor to Grandfather's study. Here she flicked on the overhead light and looked around. She had taken a number of files from here after the funeral, but Alice could tell someone else had been rummaging around as well. She knew how she'd left things. She didn't think this was Clare. Clare had no interest in dusty files, nor in her father, for that matter. *Because he wasn't her real father*, thought Alice with a small thrill. She ran her finger over the red leather seat of Grandfather's chair, leaving a clean trail in the layer of dust that had settled there.

Grandfather was no longer there; she felt sure of it. The room had an emptiness she had not felt before. She wondered what the intruder had taken or wanted to take. *I must remember to change the locks in the morning*, she thought.

Alice switched off the lights, went back down the corridor and entered Nanette's wing. She turned on the sconces here and went first into Nanette's room and turned on the bedside lamp. Nanette's bed looked slightly dishevelled, the imprint of a head on a pillow, a glass tumbler, empty, with an orange lipstick mark on the rim. Peeking out from under the bed was a novel by Anthony Trollope – from the *Barchester Towers* series. *So Clare has finished the Palliser novels*, thought Alice.

Alice crossed the room and slid open the door that separated Nanette's bedroom from her dressing room. As a child, Alice had considered it the greatest possible privilege to be allowed into this sanctum sanctorum. In spring and summer, Nanette always placed a vase of fresh-cut flowers atop the high chest of drawers along the left wall, the scent hovering harmoniously in the air with a rich concentration of Nanette smells: lavender water, Chanel no. 5, talcum powder, the rose sachets in the top drawers where she kept her brassières, underwear and girdles. Nanette was thin as a post, like Alice, Clare and Bix, and as a little girl, Alice used to watch with fascination as her grandmother pulled and prodded her scant flesh into the mould of those body-shaping devices that no one else she knew seemed to wear. Nanette's underwear and brassières (she always used the full word, with the French pronunciation) were of the very best quality, decorated with subtle, lacy edging and tiny rosettes. Alice liked to sit in the large, faded mauve velvet wingback chair in the corner, holding her knees to her chest – she must have been five, six, seven, eight – and watch Nanette pour her small, thin breasts shot through with blue veins into her brassière, then carefully fasten it in the back. The girdle, then the slip, then an atomizer puff of lavender water to her armpits, then the ritual inspection of her gowns in the large wardrobe opposite the door to the room, pushed against what used to be a communicating door to her husband's bedroom, now closed off from Nanette's quarters, a rock across the entry to the tomb of their marriage. Grandfather had not, in Alice's lifetime, ever slept in that room on the other side, nor even entered Nanette's part of the house. Though the room had lain vacant for decades, it had always been referred to as Grandfather's room. As a child, Alice had been told that the communicating door had been blocked off because Nanette had needed a second wardrobe to keep her dresses. So many dresses! And that Grandfather did not sleep in there because the bed was lumpy and the windows south-facing. He preferred east, to watch the sun as it rose.

Who had told her this, Alice wondered, as she fumbled for the switch in the darkened room. It was hard to imagine anyone but Nanette saying those words. The switch seemed not to work, so she walked across the room to turn on the lamp on the vanity and tripped on something in the middle of the floor. She switched on the small table light with a tangerine shade and turned to see what had made her stumble. She gasped. The wardrobe doors hung open and the room was strewn with Nanette's clothing and personal effects. It was as though a small band of monkeys had been through and callously ripped apart the room, looking at pretty things and flinging them every which way. All over the floor. The upper drawers of the bureau were pulled open, Nanette's delicate undergarments cascading out. To the usual Nanette smells, rendered now musty without their owner, was added the smell of stale red wine, of old cigarette smoke, of sweat, of Clare. It was all Clare, Clare, Clare. Tears started from Alice's eyes. Tears of shock. She felt she might vomit and rushed from the room, down the hall, to the bathroom at the end, with the yellow walls and the claw-foot tub. Here she regurgitated the contents of her stomach, the crackers, the soup, a granola bar from the bus ride; really, she thought, she hadn't eaten much, not much at all, to warrant such insistent retching.

When nothing was left, she turned on the tap in the low sink and splashed water on her face, repeatedly rinsing the putrid taste of stomach acids from her mouth. She wiped her face carefully with the hand towel near the sink, now suspiciously inspecting it for signs of the desecrations of Clare. But there were none: no orange lipstick, no mascara. She was still crying, lightly. She went back down the hall, forgetting to switch off the lights, and down the stairs, back to the kitchen phone, and carefully dialled the number of the condo in Boston.

When Ronit answered, he heard nothing but soft breathing at first. Irritated, he took a confrontational tone, and thundered, 'Who is this!'

'She's been here,' Alice whispered softly. 'She's been here.'

Recognizing Alice's voice and troubled by its faintness, he asked gently, 'Who? Who? I'm sorry I yelled. I didn't know it was *you*.'

'Clare. She's been here.'

'What did she do? Is she there now?'

'No. A mess. She made a mess.'

'All over?'

'No. In Nanette's room.'

'You must change the locks, right away, in the morning.'

'Yes,' said Alice, and then her breathing became laboured; it felt like her throat was closing up. 'Can't … talk …' she said haltingly, and hung up, sinking to the floor below the phone, rocking slightly on her heels. The phone kept ringing and ringing, but she didn't really hear it. She rolled herself into a little ball, like a mouse or a guinea pig, on the floor beneath the phone and fell asleep.

She dreamed vivid dreams again, of dances, boating parties, picnics, but now there was something that felt sinister, some spirit that was not right, that floated through all the gaiety and laughter. In a room full of people laughing, she felt a chill. She saw a streak of green, a green dress perhaps, and followed it. Someone beckoned her, drew her away, but no matter where she ran, from room to room in the giant house, she could not find the person or thing, and then suddenly there would be a new party, a musical, Nanette playing the pianoforte, and it would begin again.

Before the sun had fully risen, Ronit pulled into the driveway. He'd spent an hour packing, calling in favours for the next day's clinic at the hospital and cancelling appointments at the office. He tried the door in the dim light of dawn. Finding it open, he slipped inside. There she was, curled up in a ball beneath the phone, twitching slightly in her sleep. The hall was freezing.

'Alice,' he said, 'Alice, I'm here.'

# 39

Ronit had not realized how dire the food situation would be. He seated Alice in a kitchen chair, wrapped her shivering legs in a blanket, and fed her some stale crackers. Her words were incoherent. He feared her losing her speech again, knowing fully well that despite the fact that he was credited in Alice's family with curing her, he'd accomplished nothing at all as her psychiatrist besides harbouring inappropriate thoughts about his patient.

'Let's go out,' he said, suddenly, and Alice looked up at him, surprised out of her incoherent state. 'Let's have a fancy brunch,' he said. 'Change of scene.' He felt, though he would not like to admit it, that the air in the house was thick with ghosts and that Alice had the look of someone suffering a spirit possession. He thought this not because he knew anything about spirit possession himself, or even believed in it, but because he'd once seen a documentary on Haitian spirit possession with his ex-wife. For months after, they'd argued about whether the phenomena chronicled in the film were real or if they could be explained as medical or psychological phenomena. He'd argued for the latter, of course. As he looked at Alice now, pale, dishevelled, eyes frightened, mumbling disjointedly, he could hear his own pompous voice calmly lecturing Malini about hallucinations and hysteria. *No wonder she left me*, he thought to himself, and a wry smile passed momentarily across his lips. Alice seemed to notice this and looked at him searchingly.

Ronit held his hands out to her. 'Come,' he said. He led her out of the kitchen door to his car. It was only eight o'clock in the morning, he realized, after he'd got her into her seat, belt fastened. It was a Tuesday. Who would be serving brunch? Perhaps he'd spoken too soon. He didn't know the area well at all. There was a large inn at the centre of town, which they could try. He drove the two and a half miles into town, Alice silently staring straight ahead, him chattering lightly about the weather. He pulled up in front of the inn, came round, unbuckled Alice and helped her out of the car.

'I bet they have a nice breakfast here,' he said cheerfully. He led her up the front steps, across the porch, and through the large doors. Inside, the inn was done up within an inch of its life for Christmas. Not Macy's style, he observed, but New England picture-postcard style. A huge fir tree, covered with antique-coloured glass pendants and blinking white lights, stood in one corner. A fire blazed in the fireplace. Garlands of evergreen boughs decked the mouldings around the room. Christmas choral music blared. All this at a quarter past eight in the morning.

Ronit asked the hostess for a table, and they were led to a comfortable spot near the fire. The tablecloth was spotless white linen, and two teacups sat ready at each setting.

'You sit near the fire, sweetheart,' said Ronit, and placed Alice in the warmer seat. Alice looked around. Ronit ordered her a cup of Darjeeling tea, a two-egg omelette and scones, as he wasn't sure if she'd speak to the waitress. For himself, he ordered a tomato–broccoli frittata, bacon and a cup of coffee. When the waitress was gone, he reached across the table and gently took Alice's left hand in his. It was the hand that would bear the engagement ring if she would only wear it.

'Now try to tell me,' he said softly. 'Try to tell me what happened to make you feel this way.'

Alice stared him directly in the eyes, her gaze glassy.

'Please try,' he coaxed. 'Tell me how you knew Clare had come.'

'The recycling,' Alice whispered.

'She'd left something in the recycling bin?'

'Wine bottles.'

'Are you sure those were new?'

'Yes.'

'Anything else?'

'Yes.'

'Tell me, what else.'

In a whispered monotone, Alice enumerated the disturbances she'd found, including those to her grandfather's study. She even managed to indicate that that intrusion did not seem like Clare. But when she got to Nanette's bedroom, she stopped, shuddered and covered her face in her hands.

'Did it remind you of last time? Right before you first came to my office?' he asked.

She nodded and then began to sob.

The dining room had been slowly filling with well-heeled vacationers. The sobbing was soundless, but Alice's shaking shoulders, her hands held over her eyes and Ronit's stricken expression all created a legible tableau of grief for their fellow diners. Such public scenes are riveting, like roadside catastrophes: an ambulance, a police car, orange reflectors, bits of broken tail lights and fender. The seemingly healthy and well-to-do couple breakfasting at a country inn only to suddenly erupt in expressions of sorrow was, if not worthy of Greek tragedy, at least as exciting as a televised serial.

Ronit didn't know what to do. His solution, to remove her from the house, had seemed to be working, but he hadn't considered the possibility of a public scene. A couple of retirees in red turtlenecks and dark-green corduroy pants murmured and glanced their way. What did they speculate? That he had broken off an engagement? Chosen breakfast on vacation to reveal an affair or terminal illness? Was she mad? Ronit stood, picked up his chair and placed it gently at the side of the table next to Alice. He put his arm around her and steadied her shoulders. The feel of his arm against her back, his hand gripping her shoulder, was comforting to her, and gradually the sobbing slowed, and she leaned her head on his shoulder. In the midst of this, the food had arrived. The waitress set it down on the table awkwardly, not knowing if the standard, 'Can I get you anything else?' was really the right question to ask. She settled for raised eyebrows and a bright smile in Ronit's direction to give him the opportunity to make further requests.

Ronit smiled blandly and shook his head slightly to indicate that nothing more was needed at this time, although he could have used some coffee. Better not to disturb Alice with extra conversation. When she had left, he picked up a white cloth napkin and wiped Alice's face carefully.

'Want to eat?' he asked softly. Alice turned her gaze upon her omelette and looked at it carefully as if it were a foreign object.

'Why don't you have something to eat?' he asked again. Alice nodded, picked up her knife and fork, and started slowly to cut the food and lift it to her mouth. Seeing that she was beginning to eat and be more present, Ronit decided it was time to move his chair back. Once he was seated back in his place, he glared up at the festively clad onlookers. One woman gave him a tentatively censorious glance, as though she had settled on a narrative in which the fault in the situation was entirely his.

Alice was now eating heartily, and he began to feel reassured. Changing the topic seemed like the best bet now.

'Shall I tell you about my trip to Macy's yesterday?' he asked.

Alice looked up. Her eyes brightened.

'You went back,' she said, her voiced hushed and a bit hoarse.

'Yes! I went back in the early evening. Right after my last appointment.'

'Was he there?' she asked. He was glad to see her taking an interest in the Biju story now.

'Hold on,' he said. 'Let me tell you what happened.'

'Yes, tell me,' she said, slathering whipped butter over her blackcurrant scone.

'So, I went back down to men's shirtings – or haberdashery – or whatever it's called.'

'I don't know if they call it haberdashery anymore,' she said musingly. 'But I like that word.' A line of crumbs trickled down her chin and he reached over and wiped them away with his napkin.

'I saw Jesus, folding blue shirts, and he was with a large man in his sixties, grey hair, slightly balding. Could have been Indian or Mexican.'

'It was him!' said Alice excitedly.

'So I went up and greeted Jesus/Venkat, and he said he'd like to introduce me to someone. "Tom," he said, "here's the Bengali dude I told you about." And Tom looked up, maybe a little suspicious, and asked, "Can I help you, sir?" And I said, "Hello, my name is Ronit Roy, I'd like to talk to you about something, if you don't mind."

"What is it?" he asked. He was guarded.

"Maybe you'd like to talk privately?" I suggested.

"No need," he said, like he didn't want to go anywhere with me.

"Okay," I said. "I'll give you the gist. I was just in India. In Mussoorie. I believe I met your mother and sisters there."'

'What did he say?' asked Alice, now speaking at normal volume.

'He looked even more suspicious. He said, "How did you know where to find me?" As though he'd been intentionally hiding all along. What, thirty, forty years? Still in hiding?'

'How strange!'

'Yes. So I said, "Well, my fiancée is related to you in a way. She's American, and we went to Mussoorie to learn more about her family and ended up at Cosmos Cottage." So all this time, Jesus had been busily folding shirts but listening closely with great interest. Then Tom-Biju turns to him and says, suddenly, "I'm going on break, Venkat, you mind the shop." Did I mention that he has a really sharp upper-class British accent?'

'Do you mean like Indian English?'

'No, like completely British, like BBC.'

'Why would he have a British accent?'

'No idea. I couldn't very well ask though, could I?'

'No, I suppose not.'

'So then he says, "Let's go somewhere we can chat." So I followed him and we went this way and that, up and down

– I had no idea where I was, and it was extremely crowded. We ended up in some Starbucks in the bowels of Macy's. There were no free tables, but there was a counter to stand at. I said, "My treat, what would you like?" and he looked annoyed, like he didn't want a treat from the likes of me. He said, "Venti Americano." I guess he goes there a lot. So I got us two coffees.' Here Ronit paused and motioned to the waitress, who'd been a bit skittish about visiting their table, that he'd like his coffee cup refilled.

'What did you say then?' asked Alice, who had thoroughly polished her plate and was still feeling a bit peckish.

'I brought over the coffees and he went and put milk and sugar in his, and then came back, and said, very bluntly, "What do you want from me?"'

'Oh!'

'And I said, "Oh, nothing! My fiancée, Alice, is a granddaughter of your father's. She was curious about her grandfather's life in India, so …"'

'Did you tell him about the ghosts?'

'No, I didn't tell him about the ghosts,' said Ronit irritably, but then he thought how nice it was that Alice now seemed so well he had inadvertently snapped at her.

'Why not?' she asked, disappointed.

'Because I didn't want to scare him away.'

Alice scowled and picked up her teacup to drink but found it empty. 'Do you want more?' asked Ronit.

'Yes, and another scone.'

Ronit hailed the waitress again and continued.

'So then he said, "Oh, she wanted to see her grandfather's third-world family?"'

'What did you say to that?'

'I said, "On the contrary, she knew nothing about it. She'd discovered his connection to India among his files and she wanted to know more now that she was planning to marry into an Indian family."'

'But that's not true!'

'I know, but it sounds plausible.'

Alice grimaced and stirred milk and sugar into her tea.

'He seemed to calm down slightly, so I added, "… and then she became interested in meeting you after reading your wonderful novel."

'And then he looked quite surprised and maybe a little bit pleased, and he said, "Oh, you've read it?"

'And I said, "Yes, it's wonderful and we felt inspired to find you."

'After that, the conversation got much more fluid. We discussed the novel, mostly, but I didn't get much other information. He had to get back to work, so he gave me his phone and email, and I promised we'd have him over for dinner after Christmas.'

'How lovely! You've been so successful. I've accomplished nothing except having a tantrum,' said Alice ruefully, picking at her second scone.

'I think it was a bit different from a tantrum,' said Ronit carefully.

'I don't know what happened to me,' said Alice, suddenly frightened. When she cast her mind back to the previous evening, to last night, to this morning, she felt like she was gazing at the experiences of some other person. 'I saw what she had done in Nanette's dressing room. It was a horrible nest, like a rat had been there, or a monkey or a poltergeist.'

'But you know it was Clare.'

'Of course it was.'

'How did it remind you of before?'

'That time she stayed in my apartment, when she got angry because I interviewed for that job at the children's library, she did similar things. To my clothes, to my photograph albums. She ripped all the family photos in half and threw them around the room. They were all I had, of my childhood, of my father …'

'The same kind of invasiveness.'

'Yes, but this time I felt – the way that Nanette's death has unmoored us all in a way – she was expressing her grief by sort of forcing her way into … into a kind of shrine.'

'A desecration?'

'Yes, like that. Maybe she wanted to punish Nanette for dying, or for writing them all – but her specifically – out of the will. And to punish me for inheriting it all. It's another abandonment – on top of death.'

'Yes, I see that.'

'It was too much, too much to bear to see that destruction. I don't even know if she took anything, probably she did, but it looked mostly like she was trying things on and then throwing them around. We're all the same size, you know, although I'm taller.'

'Didn't you say she was wearing something of Nanette's when the will was read out?'

'Yes, yes, she was.'

'Could this all have happened as far back as then? After all, you haven't been back.'

'That's true. It could have. But we know she's been out recently and not well.'

'But did it seem like she'd just been here?'

'Well, not from the recycling. But I just don't know. It made me feel as though the house were haunted.'

'But you thought that before.'

'Before, there was a ghost. This is different.'

'How so?'

Alice had throughout this exchange been carefully creating a growing crater in the middle of her scone with her index finger. The waitress had come by several times, hoping to bring the cheque, but felt put off by the intense conversation. She hovered in the vicinity, bee-like, with a pot of hot coffee in the offing. Ronit wanted to give her a break, but the conversation was productive, and he didn't want Alice to lose her train of thought.

'Before, there was a ghost,' said Alice in a tentative tone. 'He was not alive, but he was just another person in the house. But now – now I feel unseen presences – spirits. I dreamed of something like spirits last night. It was the same very real sort of dream of parties and so forth as before, but there was a malign presence moving through the dreams.'

'Was it a person? Or a feeling?'

'Somewhere in between. Dressed in green. I mean I saw flashes of green in the peripheries but could never see what or who it was.'

'Do you think it was Clare?'

'Sort of. I'm not sure. But Grandfather is definitely gone. I feel sure of that.'

'So the ghost is gone and now the house is haunted by the living?'

'Something like that.' Alice suddenly felt foolish and very tired. 'Maybe we can go home now?'

'Yes, yes, let's get the cheque and some groceries and then see if we can exorcise some of these spirits.'

Alice smiled.

# 40

Over the next few days, Alice and Ronit worked on their exorcism. They stocked the kitchen, changed the locks and kept the house locked, contra the norm in those parts. They aired out rooms, exposing dust and spirits to the chill December air. A cleaning lady was hired for just after Christmas. They chopped down a skinny pine in the wooded area behind the house and dragged it inside, where they decked it from the treasure trove of ornaments collected by the family over generations. Some were damaged and moth-eaten, but Alice felt nostalgia for these and wasn't prepared to part with any of them just yet.

Nanette's suite of rooms remained shut. To stay clear of the whole corridor, they slept on the third floor, in the old maid's quarters Alice had always inhabited as a child. For this, they rearranged some beds so that a not-quite-double bed with a white metal frame was switched for the two narrow single beds in Alice's old room. It felt awkward to Alice to change anything, even the locks. She was moody during these days, not the most cheerful holiday companion, but she strove always to be kind to Ronit even if a dark cloud hung over her head.

Ronit, leery of leaving Alice alone again, had cancelled some appointments in his schedule and taken others over the phone. The library, a room he'd always liked, became his office. Better this than Grandfather's study, which still felt a bit creepy to him even if Alice said its former occupant was now gone.

On the afternoon of Christmas Eve, Alice suddenly got it into her head to go to church that evening.

'It would be Christmassy,' she said.

Alice had never before expressed any desire to step inside a church or any other place of worship, but, Ronit thought, in the spirit of exorcism, it might just be a good idea. In the late afternoon, they wrapped their presents for one another and placed them under the tree. Then they dressed up a little – Alice wore a wool skirt and a sweater with her boots, and a long, black wool coat she'd found in the hall closet, and Ronit wore his brown tweed suit with a red and green striped tie which Alice said would be suitable. It was a country church, after all.

They arrived just in time for the service to begin and sat towards the back. The atmosphere was magical: candlelit, and just how Alice had remembered it. Nanette had not been a particularly religious person, but she had been a regular churchgoer and always took Alice with her to the Christmas Eve service. Ronit was pleased by Alice's glow of happiness, and he found the service a pleasant one. Towards the end, four parishioners approached the altar to take the golden collection plates around to the congregation. As the four wove their way about the pews, Alice clutched Ronit's sleeve and whispered, 'That's her!'

'Who?' he asked softly.

'The woman I was looking for, Hyacinth something. Butterworth.'

'Ah, yes.' Ronit, feeling already obtrusive enough as the only brown-skinned person in the church (and perhaps the town?), was uncomfortable with the volume of her whispers and didn't want to attract further attention. A little girl had turned to stare, although perhaps she was just restless from sitting still in a pew for so long.

'I'll try to get her attention,' whispered Alice, still too loud.

Ronit put his fingers to his lips and whispered, 'After.'

Alice looked slightly perturbed at this delay but nodded. In truth, she'd meant to call Hyacinth Butterworth immediately upon her arrival in the village, but her episode of shock and the 'exorcism' they'd been undertaking had derailed her plan. Despite the fact that before arriving, she had been obsessed with her new quest with every particle of her being, the shock had truly distracted her. Now she was back on target, and

Ronit could see that the gleam had returned to her eyes. He was happy her excitement was rekindled, as it might inoculate her against the forces that had disabled her earlier in the week, but the prospect of her pursuing her quest with renewed energy seemed exhausting.

The moment the service ended, Alice scurried from the pew to stand in the aisle, scanning the crowd. She was not sure where her target sat. Small groups had formed, and people were annoyingly sticky, in Alice's view, wasting time exchanging Christmas greetings instead of proceeding to the exit. The minister spied Alice, whom he hadn't seen since the funeral, and breaking away from the receiving line, came to greet her warmly. He shook her hand and touched her gently on the shoulder. Alice felt as though he was performing some sort of laying on of hands, and, uncomfortable with overt displays of affection and the touch of strangers, she jerked away instinctively. The minister smiled benevolently at her twitch and inquired after her well-being and her mother's. Alice wondered how much he knew about her mother. It was hard to imagine Nanette confiding her troubles or the shortcomings of her family members to a clergyman.

'And have you opened up the house for Christmas?' he asked. Alice was craning her neck, as subtly as she could, searching the sea of faces for Hyacinth Butterworth. She thought she saw her on the other side of the room.

'Have you met my fiancé?' she asked hurriedly. 'Ronit Roy?' And with this, she slipped away into the crowd. Ronit, who had been hanging awkwardly at her elbow, was now in the even more awkward position of being thrust into the arms, so to speak, of the minister, whom he had in fact met at the funeral some months back. At that time, he'd been told about Reverend Myrtle's colleague and school friend, who'd taken up a missionary post in Pondicherry, a place Ronit had never been to and knew nothing about. To be fair, Reverend Myrtle knew even less about Pondicherry than he, except that his friend had eventually been medevacked out of nearby Madras for treatment of dengue fever.

Now, on this re-encounter, the good reverend thankfully seemed to remember the previous conversation and did not repeat any of it. Instead, he told Ronit of a new Indian restaurant in the area that served very nice curries, for which Ronit thanked him politely. After this, the reverend was interrupted by other members of the congregation offering him the heartiest of Christmas greetings, and Ronit was able to shimmy away to stand in a shadow by the side of the sign listing the numbers of the hymns that would be sung later that night.

In the meantime, Alice had wriggled her way through the crowd, thankfully encountering no one who immediately recognized her. She was rewarded for her effort, for about halfway up the aisle she came upon Hyacinth Butterworth deep in conversation with an elderly couple, her bright blue eyes sparkling with gossip, her ears bedecked with large, clip-on Christmas wreath earrings that glinted and bobbed as she narrated.

Alice approached and tapped her on the shoulder.

Hyacinth Butterworth turned and looked at her questioningly.

'Alice Bloodshaw, Nanette's granddaughter,' said Alice.

'Ah! Alice! Of course. You look every inch your grandmother. I feel as though I'm looking back in time.'

Alice smiled at the compliment, though she knew it was not true. She lacked Nanette's elegance, and her wardrobe (although it was technically hers now), and she was easily six inches taller than Nanette had been, even in her younger days.

Hyacinth Butterworth introduced her to the couple she'd been talking to, who greeted her warmly and echoed the claim that Alice was an exact replica of her grandmother.

'Such a lovely woman,' everyone murmured with appropriate sadness, as six months had not yet passed since her death.

After a few more such pleasantries had passed between them, Alice turned to Mrs Butterworth and said she'd been meaning to get in touch with some questions about her grandmother. The other couple decorously excused themselves and continued down the emptying aisle, glancing briefly at the dark-skinned man lurking in the shadows near the hymn sign with a slight frisson of fear.

'But,' observed the wife on the way to the car outside the church, 'he was very well dressed.'

'He was, he was,' murmured her husband, who had already forgotten about Ronit.

Inside, after exchanging more pleasantries about the holiday season and her family, about whom she could only make the vaguest of reports, Alice got to the point as quickly as she could.

'Mrs Butterworth, I –'

'Cece, please. Everyone calls me Cece.'

'Ah, Cece, I wondered if we might get together sometime – soon – I'd love to talk to you about your memories of my grandmother.'

Cece Butterworth was a shrewd woman. She narrowed her eyes and looked appraisingly at Alice.

'You want to know more about your grandmother,' she said. She immediately knew that what Alice wanted were the secrets, the things Nanette would have told no one in her family, the things a very old friend would know, whether Nanette would have wished it or not.

'Yes,' said Alice firmly. 'I have some questions.'

Cece Butterworth did not actually recollect telling Alice that the stranger who'd shown up at the funeral had been Nanette's lover, but she did remember that he'd come, for nothing could rip that memory from her consciousness. And she suspected that Alice's questions had something to do with him. If this was the case, she was fully prepared to answer them all. *It would do no harm*, she thought. After many decades, secrets outlive their usefulness.

'Perhaps you can join me for tea on Boxing Day,' she said. 'I've a do at seven that evening, a small party at an old friend's house, but you may come for a visit at four.'

'Oh, thank you so much!' cried Alice with glee.

'I'll see you then, darling,' said Mrs Butterworth, patting her on the shoulder with a gloved hand. 'And do bring your young man. So handsome. Italian?'

Before Alice had a chance to answer this perplexing query, Mrs Butterworth was waving to a friend across the room and was over there in a flash, despite her dependence on a polished wooden cane adorned with the painted head of a parrot.

# 41

On Christmas day, Ronit and Alice exchanged their gifts in the parlour next to the Christmas tree before a fire which had taken them a while to build, but after about forty-five minutes of labour, it burst into a cheerful, roaring blaze, 'Just like in a picture book,' said Alice.

Alice had given Ronit a biography of Copernicus she'd found at an antique bookshop. It had looked very serious, which she thought he'd like, and he did enjoy the history of science so far as she could tell. She also gave him a periwinkle-blue scarf which she had knitted herself from skeins of angora she'd found at a yarn shop in Cambridge. Alice was not an especially accomplished knitter, despite Nanette's best efforts to instruct her in the fibre arts.

Ronit was not sure what had prompted the gift of the biography, a thick, musty book, but he appreciated the sentiment. The scarf he received happily. It was lumpy, and the fluffiness of the wool seemed sure to shed upon one's clothing, but he was touched by the notion that she had spent quite a bit of time making something just for him, in his absence, and even managed to keep it a secret. In his imagination, Alice spent much of her time wandering about the apartment, a novel held loosely in her hand, dreaming about her next obsession. The idea that she'd spent so much time thinking about him moved him, and he hugged her and thanked her profusely for the gift.

To Alice, Ronit had given a set of green Bakelite decorative combs with pink roses on them, and an antique music box that played a waltz when wound up. It was the size of a cigar box, but a dancing couple was somehow ingeniously folded up inside it and when the box was closed and opened, the couple danced back and forth in a figure eight across a red felt floor. Alice was suitably delighted by both, and Ronit heaved a sigh of relief, for both gifts had taken a considerable amount of effort to find (not, of course, that he had been looking for these particular items all along, but that it took much effort for him to hunt through curio and antique shops looking for something appropriately unusual and beautiful for Alice).

When they were done marvelling over their gifts, they moved on to the kitchen. Ronit was going to make an eggplant pumpkin dish he'd been working on, dal and rice, and Alice, after looking through Nanette's recipe cards, would make English trifle, which she had never really liked but which reminded her of Nanette, and of Christmas. They switched on the radio, which was playing seasonal choir music, of course, and set to work.

It was around the time that most of the meal was cooking on the stove and Alice had just refrigerated the trifle that they heard a thump, and the sound of someone knocking snow from their shoes. Alice looked at Ronit in panic. Ronit moved close to the door. Of course, they'd already stopped locking the doors, just four days after the locks had been changed. The door at this time was unlocked and nothing could be done about that now.

The door rattled, then burst open, and in walked Clare, carrying a poinsettia wrapped in a wide red velveteen ribbon with gold trim. Her hair was pulled back tightly in a chignon, and under a large men's black overcoat she wore a dark-green velvet sheath – Nanette's Christmas best. Alice recognized it instantly. The chunky rhinestone clip-on earrings were Nanette's too, as was the rhinestone necklace. On her feet were an old pair of running shoes. Her black stockings had ladders up the sides.

'Am I late?' she asked, with a pleasant smile.

That remark, and the subsequent blandly appropriate behaviour, disarmed Alice and Ronit, preventing them from taking any aggressive actions. How could they call the police? The door had been open, her behaviour inoffensive. How could they tell her to beat it, scram, when she'd done nothing wrong? Both realized they were being manipulated, but they saw no escape. Before they knew it, they were setting a place for Clare at the table and almost feeling the setting for two had been some embarrassing oversight.

Throughout dinner, Clare spoke evenly about this and that, current events, family news, her plans to enrol in an arts conservation course at the museum in Boston – 'Might be a good career choice for me,' she'd said pleasantly.

Alice was composed, but in her mind, she could still hear Clare screaming in the lobby of the lawyer's office. The memory was present and audible, and yet her brain was being forced to tell her that this woman was perfectly reasonable. *She's all better now*, was what she was supposed to think, even though she understood, more than anything else she knew, more than she knew her own psyche, that this was classic Clare, that she would soon feel pain, that something would be asked of her, that a dramatic betrayal would take place and that the betrayer would be Alice. Alice's role was always Judas in these stories. And Ronit was growing into the role of Roman Soldier Number One.

They continued to break their bread, to behave as normal; a small family celebrating a holiday together. But no wine was drunk, and none was mentioned. The bottle they'd chosen remained unopened in the cupboard.

Clare spoke of herself as a recovered alcoholic, making little jokes to put them at their ease, 'Why do you need to call a paramedic when an alcoholic tries to screw in a light bulb? Because they try to use the corkscrew!'

After dinner, they refreshed the fire and sat by the tree. Clare complimented the tree, the decorations. Alice waited, waited for it to happen.

It was late afternoon now. Dusk was falling. Ronit needed to go out back to get more logs but was uneasy about leaving the two of them alone. He glanced at Alice, but she was perfectly composed. Unreadable. Perhaps it would be all right.

'I'll just be a minute,' he said. 'We need more wood for the fire.'

'I think I'll get my bag,' said Clare. 'I could use a nap.' She stood up, stretched and left the room.

Alice sat frozen on the sofa. Where would she go? What room would she choose? She heard the kitchen door slam, once for going out, a second time for coming back. She felt suddenly cold. She heard Clare's steps go by the parlour door, slightly ajar, but she couldn't see Clare. Footsteps, up the stairs. Back door slam. That was Ronit. A moment later, he entered, three logs balanced on his arm. He saw that Clare was not there and that Alice was sitting perfectly still, a look of terror on her face. He dropped the logs quickly on the hearth, and roughly dusted bark, snow, splinters from his arms.

'Alice,' he said, alarm in his voice, 'what's wrong? What is it?' he shook her slightly, put his arm around her.

'She's upstairs,' she whispered, her face drained of colour.

'What's she done? What's she doing?'

'Going to take a nap,' said Alice flatly.

There were footsteps overhead. 'Shhh,' whispered Alice, putting a finger to her lips.

'Do you think she'll go to Nanette's room?' asked Ronit softly.

'Shhhh.' Alice knew the pattern of footsteps in the rooms of the house intimately. She sat, listening to the pattern. A moment later, she relaxed her posture.

'She's taken the green room,' she whispered.

'Which is that?'

'Down the hall from Nanette. It's where she used to stay.'

'So that's good then?' asked Ronit nervously.

Alice inclined her head slightly, still staring straight ahead.

*

After nap time, an hour or so later, Clare came down to the living room with a book. Alice recognized it as the Trollope she'd seen peeking out from under Nanette's bed. Alice was sitting with a copy of *Martin Chuzzlewit* open in her lap. She'd pulled it out at random from a shelf in that room. They sat and read for a time, and soon after, Ronit made tea. There was more reading – they could have been any family on Christmas except that one of them had received no presents or invitation.

Evening came and Ronit warmed the leftovers from earlier. They ate them in the parlour, their plates in their laps. No trifle was left and at any rate, it was full of alcohol so best not to have around. Alice brought out some cookies and put them on a tray. Clare disappeared for a time, mentioning the bathroom. Alice could hear her in the kitchen. *She's looking for the alcohol*, she thought. She waited to hear the pop of the bottle uncorking, but there was no sound. Had she been wrong? Was Clare actually cured?

After a time, Clare returned. She seemed more restless now. She sat with her book in her hand, but her eyes darted about the room. She got up and began to walk around, picking up objects, turning them over, weighing them appraisingly in her hands. For what? To steal? Alice couldn't figure out where this was going, but she knew the transition had begun. Such behaviour as had been exhibited heretofore could not last more than a few hours – certainly not an entire day.

Clare began to talk about the restoration class again, how it was just the thing for her. Her speech became more animated, her movements more jolting. Alice's anxiety had spread to Ronit. He was not scared of Clare, but her pressured speech and increasingly manic behaviour did not bode well. Christmas night would be busy at the emergency room if it came to that, and the police would be none too happy to be called out here for this sort of thing.

It suddenly occurred to Alice that Clare must have been at the brandy she'd bought for the trifle. That's why there'd been no cork sound. Brandy would be worse than wine. She tried to remember how much had been left in the bottle. She looked up at Clare. Clare was holding a figurine of a shepherdess in her hands, rolling it from one hand to the other while she talked about the process of cleaning oil paintings, as though she were already an expert, even though the course had yet to begin. She must have looked these things up on the internet, thought Alice, and wondered if Clare had a computer or used someone else's. Maybe they had them set up in the rehab. Or at a public library.

Clare spoke faster and faster. The shepherdess rolled back and forth rapidly. Alice felt mesmerized by the movement of the figurine, back forth back forth, between Clare's long, bony fingers so like her own. Ronit kept his eyes fixed on his book. The letters were blurry, and his mind was focused on contingency plans. How to protect Alice? When to intervene? Suddenly, there was a crash. He looked up. Clare was standing still, a wild look in her eyes, darting from Alice to Ronit. *Recording our reactions*, he thought.

The figurine lay in pieces on the floor about her feet. Only then did he notice she had put on mismatched Christmas socks, striped red and green, but definitely not a pair.

Alice was staring at Clare, perfectly still. *Like she's in a hypnotic state*, thought Ronit.

Clare laughed, high-pitched. 'It dropped,' she cried, almost gaily. 'I'm so sorry!' but this too in a tone of good cheer. 'I'll go get the dustpan.' She rushed from the room, and they could hear the banging of brooms and mops in the hall closet. Ronit went and sat by Alice on the sofa. He put his arm around her. He didn't know how much of this either of them could take.

Clare returned with a dustpan and small brush. She knelt and swept the particles of the figurine into the dustpan along with a moderate quantity of dust.

'Maybe I could fix it,' she said, turning her head to look at them, her eyes popping out a bit. 'My first restoration project!' She chuckled. 'Who would have thought, my first job as a restorationist and I'm working for my own daughter, breaking her beloved objects d'art. Of course,' she added in a tone that was warm and confiding, 'of course this figurine couldn't have been worth much. It's just a crappy collectible. Everyone always said Nanette liked nothing but the best, but that's not true of *everything* she owned. She collected these junky little figurines, picked them up at knick-knack stores, gewgaws – gimcracks. This little shepherdess is just a piece of shit. Look how easily it broke!'

She picked up a few pieces roughly from the dustpan and brandished them as she said this through clenched teeth. 'These shitty little sheep-herders break so damn easily,' she said. Blood began to trickle down her hand, down her wrist, and with the blood came tears. Ronit felt this was enough. Alice hadn't moved a muscle.

'That's enough, Clare,' he said, standing up. 'I'll finish cleaning. You let go. Go clean yourself up.'

'Oh, Mr Shrink has had enough,' gloated Clare through her tears. 'This is just too much for Mr Shrink!' she repeated, and now Ronit didn't know if he'd imagined it, but he felt fairly certain she'd said this last in a fake Indian accent. He walked towards her, his hand out, either to ward off a blow, or to pick up the dustpan and the fragments of the broken figurine.

Clare stared him square in the eye, judging, judging what he was made of. She slowly put the fragments in his hand, and even more slowly wiped the smaller blood-flecked splinters of china from her hand over his outstretched one.

'Do you think it's genetic, Doctor?' she whispered, her gaze jumping over to Alice sitting on the sofa. 'Do you? That would be scary, eh?' She smiled. Ronit felt chilled. He had indeed been turning this over in his mind. Just the notion of hereditary mental illness. And of course she had guessed this.

Clare stood to one side while Ronit cleared up the rest of the bits of china from the floor. Then he carried them down the hall and threw them in the trash. Currently, his mind was racing between two options: Call the police? But for what? She wasn't totally out of control, and they had even broken bread with her. It was Christmas. People don't have their close relations forcibly removed on Christmas. Should he call the inn and see if there was room? Maybe he could move Alice out of the house. But that would be abandoning the field of battle, Alice's own legal territory, to the enemy.

He dumped the shards into the trash and jumped with fright when he turned around and found Clare standing directly behind him in the kitchen.

'Help me clean the wound, Doc?' she asked, in an almost seductive tone.

'Clare, you'll have to leave in the morning,' he said decisively.

'What, is that the punishment around here for breaking your shitty collectibles? I guess I should be thankful you're not going to cut my hands off like they do wherever you're from, Mr Fiancé.'

Ronit knew that this strange hodgepodge of insults signified that Clare realized she was on thin ice.

'You know what you've done. You weren't invited, and if you stay beyond 9 a.m. tomorrow, we'll have you removed.'

'Is this what Empress Alice has decreed?' snarled Clare. 'Since when do you get the rights? I don't see a ring on your finger; not yet.' And she grinned. She could see her insult had squarely met its target.

In the early days of his practice, Ronit had accepted a few patients with such disorders because he needed the money, and as they weren't wanted anywhere else, they or their families were willing to pay him quite handsomely. But taunts and manipulation like this had soon cured him of the habit. They didn't need psychiatrists anyway. Drugs wouldn't cure them. Probably nothing would, certainly nothing he had on offer.

And now here he was again, and having experience with this sort of behaviour was only helpful insofar as that he knew he had to remain mindful of who he was, where he was, and not let his opponent set reality spinning so hard he wound up thinking the ceiling was the floor and the floor the ceiling. *I'm a mental health professional*, he repeated to himself over and over. *A seasoned mental health professional.*

Out loud, he said, 'Tomorrow. Nine a.m. Time for bed now.'

Clare almost seemed to growl at him, like a beaten beast. She grabbed the brandy bottle, then turned to saunter out of the room and down the hall. He would have to follow her, to make sure she did no more harm to Alice than she already had. But he would wait a moment longer.

# 42

After returning from the second floor, where he locked Nanette's suite (they'd had the locksmith install a lock there, but it had remained unlocked until now), and made sure Clare was in the green room, Ronit returned downstairs. Alice was not in the living room. Ronit hurried down the hall, where he found her in the kitchen, looking around for the brandy bottle. He went to her and put his arms around her.

'She took it with her,' he said. 'Don't worry about it now. I'll deal with everything. Why don't you go get some rest.'

Alice slowly and mechanically started to rinse some dishes as though she didn't hear him or feel his touch. She placed the dishes in the drying rack. Then she went over and reached up to the shelf where they'd put the bottle of pinot noir and pulled it down. Holding the bottle in one hand, she began to open drawers and fumble around.

'What are you doing?' asked Ronit. 'What are you looking for?'

Alice held the bottle upside down over the sink and shook it.

'You want to empty it out?'

Alice nodded and continued to look through the drawers.

'No, no, Alice, don't do that, it's not necessary. I'll hide it.' Ronit picked up the bottle. Alice looked at him sceptically but appeared to acquiesce. She glided from the room and disappeared down the hall.

Alice felt like she was in a dense fog. It was not a painless fog: everything seemed out of focus and woolly. Like a sinus headache, when one is aware of intense pain, but also not aware of much at all. She walked up the stairs to the third floor, slowly and deliberately. In the bedroom she changed into a nightgown, folded up her clothes and placed them in a neat pile on a chair. Then she went and brushed her teeth and washed her face. She lay down under the covers, her palms resting on the counterpane.

When Ronit came upstairs ten minutes later, he was surprised to see that she was sound asleep, her lips parted, snoring softly. The light was still on. Alice was usually in the habit of reading before bed, often until quite late. How could she sleep under such stressful circumstances? She must, he realized, have some sort of shutdown response when Clare behaved this way. He was worried by the fact that she hadn't spoken since the breaking of the figurine, and wondered if there'd been some such incident, perhaps a particularly bad one, at the time she'd stopped speaking before. *How odd*, he thought, *that I, a seasoned mental health professional, albeit perhaps not a very good one, am so filled with anxiety. I'm not likely to get a wink of sleep, and here is Alice sleeping peacefully.*

Ronit decided to read for a while to calm his nerves and then try to get some sleep. As a precaution, though it made him feel foolish, like a character in a thriller, he barricaded the door by placing a chair under the handle, even though this would make it inconvenient and noisy to go to the bathroom if anyone woke in the night.

After reading for about forty-five minutes, he did begin to feel sleepy and decided to turn off the lights and try to rest. He felt reassured that the house had been quiet all this time. Perhaps Clare would simply go to sleep, wake up in the morning and then leave. Maybe he'd overreacted with her. Maybe she was just tipsy. *She's just ill*, he told himself. With this mildly reassuring thought, he drifted off to sleep.

*

They were awakened in the night by a persistent rattling sound. Alice sat up first, suddenly, her back straight. She gasped and put her hand over her mouth, afraid she might scream. She'd been dreaming she was drowning, and the rattling had pulled her up from the floor of a turquoise sea that was filling her lungs.

When she knew she was awake, at night, in bed, she put out her hand to see if Ronit was there. This was when Ronit woke up as well.

'What, what?' he asked, flustered. As a resident, he'd trained himself to sleep during an ongoing case, or crisis. He could keep it filed away in his consciousness so that he was prepared to access it the moment his beeper went off. He had done that this night without realizing it and mentally grasped now for the relevant file. Clare. Lilac Hill.

'Is it Clare?' he asked, reaching for her hand, which felt chilly and damp.

'It's Nanette's door,' she said softly. 'She's trying to get in.'

'I locked it,' said Ronit. 'So, she can't.'

The rattling was constant, rhythmic, almost like the sound of the wind rattling the trees at night, the kind of repetitive, insistent sound that humans generally don't make, since they usually give up and try another tactic. But now, all of a sudden, there were bangs; they moved, up and down the corridor on the floor below them, systematic, repetitive.

'She's banging on all the doors,' whispered Alice, barely audible.

'Why?'

'She's mad she can't get in.'

The bangs echoed down to the landing and continued on Grandfather's corridor, then returned. There was a light tread on the stairs. Creaking floorboards. Alice grabbed Ronit's arm and clung to it.

'She's coming up here,' she said.

'I've barricaded the door,' he whispered.

Alice didn't respond. He couldn't even hear her breathing, as though she were holding her breath.

Now the bangs were loud and near, four or five per door. Clare's footsteps were soft; she padded towards their door. *Bang, bang, bang, bang, bang*. Surely she knew they were in there, thought Ronit, his body shot through with fear, despite himself. He felt as though his subconscious was unable to deliver to his brain the message that this was not a poltergeist but his mentally ill mother-in-law-to-be. *Bang, bang, bang.* She was not trying the door, but the force of her blows made the door handle jiggle against the top of the chair that was serving as a lock.

Now the steps shifted away again, onto the next room, down the other side, down the hall, down the stairs again, receding. She'd probably not spent more than three minutes on their floor, but it had seemed much longer than that. Ronit could hear Alice breathing again. She filled her lungs, gulped in air, blew it out, artificially, as though she was practising breathing exercises.

'Now what will she do?' asked Alice.

'What do you think she'll do?'

'Ruin something. Make me pay.'

'Pay for what?'

'For inheriting the house. For being the owner.'

'But you didn't do anything. It was a surprise.'

'She doesn't see it that way. She can't. I did it. I did it to her. I did it to hurt her. I betrayed her.'

'What madness,' said Ronit, though what Alice said made perfect sense, given what he had seen and heard so far.

Alice had said it all so quickly and simply, as though this were a thing that was always known and discussed, but in fact it was something that was only ever known and said inside Alice's head to Alice, when she was alone. Now she'd said it out loud, she felt a strange sensation, like air rushing through her. She imagined a medieval painting of an exorcism, with demons pouring from a sinner's mouth, their eyes bulging, blue tongues hanging out, faces distorted in ghoulish, maniacal laughter.

That is me, she thought, I am the person they've possessed. She held onto Ronit, crying, gasping. She imagined the ghouls rushing around through the same corridors just traversed by Clare, rushing around corners, sliding up and down walls. One, she thought, was the presence in green, a green dress, a green velvet dress, who had haunted her dreams of a few nights ago, flitting through those wondrous parties and leaving a stench of poisonous vapour in her wake. *I will call that demon Clare*, thought Alice, *and I will make her leave my house.*

To Ronit's surprise and considerable anxiety, Alice now rose from the bed. Holding herself tall in her long, white flannel nightgown, she marched over to the door, where she proceeded to dislodge the chair from the doorknob.

'What are you doing?' asked Ronit.

'She must be stopped,' said Alice, firmly. 'She must leave now.'

'But I told her she could stay until morning …' his voice trailed off as Alice managed to wrench away the chair, turn the knob and disappear into the darkened hallway.

Ronit was stunned for a moment, then, realizing he could hardly let her go alone, he scrambled from bed and rushed out after her, fumbling with the electric wall sconces on the way. He didn't relish having this confrontation with Clare in the pitch-dark.

Somewhere down below, Ronit could hear Alice's light step padding down the worn Persian carpet covering the main staircase. He felt compelled to run after his beloved, to help her or save her, or whatever might need doing, but at the same time, he was repelled – from the thought of what they would find, of what they would have to confront. An ugliness, he feared, that might be easier to cope with by light of day.

At the second-storey landing, he heard a door slam – open or shut – and a shout; he wasn't sure whose. The sounds came from below. With trepidation, he walked as fast as he could will himself to do, down the stairs, into the hall. There was light coming from the parlour, and a low, angry voice. He still didn't know whose. As much as he'd hate to admit it, it was hard for him to distinguish between Clare and Alice from a distance. Their voices, their builds, were so similar.

He crept towards the door and pushed it open. Clare was seated on the floor near the Christmas tree. A fair number of glass baubles from the tree lay smashed around her. There was also a profusion of books, photo albums, perhaps, scattered about the floor, and snipped bits of paper. Clare herself sat in the midst of this, her hair pulled up on her head in a ponytail. Her face was heavily made up – but sloppily so – giving her a ghoulish look. Bright orange lipstick rimmed her lips but slid off and on in places as though applied by a small child. Her eyes were ringed with black eyeliner, and she wore a revealing red satin negligée trimmed with black lace. In her hands, she held the broken figurine, and by her feet lay a pot of glue.

Alice stood over her, talking in a low voice. On seeing Ronit enter, Clare turned her head and said with a bright orange smile, 'I was just repairing the figurine. I love restoration!'

Alice leaned down and picked up the pot of glue.

'This is rubber cement, Clare. Rubber cement is for paper. You know this. Get up.'

'Oh, is it? I thought it was something else!' Clare giggled. Her speech sounded babyish. Nothing else about the tableau was particularly logical to Ronit.

'Stand up, Clare. Stand up,' said Alice.

'But, sweetie … I …'

'Stand up. Stand up. Stand up.'

Alice reached out her hand and pulled the figurine from Clare's grasp. She placed it on a side table. Then she reached down and took hold of both her hands and pulled.

'Stand up. Stand up.'

Clare looked dazed now, and slowly, awkwardly, stood, small bits of paper and shards of ornaments sliding from her lap and landing on the carpet.

'Where am I to go?' asked Clare, vacantly.

'To the hospital,' said Alice. 'We can take you there or we can call the police. Which do you prefer?'

Clare looked around, glancing at Ronit with little recognition.

'I'll go,' she said without emotion.

'You stay here with Ronit,' said Alice. 'I'll pack your overnight bag.'

There was something in the way Alice said this, as though it had been said before, and would be said again. The hardened resignation of a child who had been her mother's keeper, and a middle-aged woman who was in some ways still a child.

Ronit came over to Clare, took hold of her hand and led her into the kitchen, where he seated her on a chair. She sat obediently, said nothing, looked nowhere. For lack of anything else to do, he poured her a glass of milk and handed it to her. She drank it quickly in a few gulps, as though it were medicine, and handed it back to him.

Alice returned with Clare's bag.

'Let's go,' she said.

# 43

It was noon by the time they awoke the next day. The visit to the emergency room had been predictably long and drawn out, and on their return, when a grey light bathed the roads and the house was outlined in the light haze of predawn, sleep had not come easily.

Ronit was the first to wake. He went downstairs and fixed Alice tea and toast and brought it upstairs to her. She lay in bed, staring at her fingers and turning her hands in the sun.

'What do you see?' he asked.

'I still have hands,' she said.

'So you do.'

'That means I still exist.'

'Indeed. Did you expect otherwise?'

'Yes. I didn't know if I could live through it. Or even if it happened in real life. So much happens in dreams here.'

Ronit set the tray down by her side.

'Bed tea,' she said, and smiled at him with such sincerity he felt overcome with love for her.

'I love you, Alice,' he said.

'I love you, also,' she said carefully, as though it were a tricky sentence she might mess up. And then she gazed seriously at the tea, checking in the pot to see that it had steeped enough, and looking around to see if he'd put sugar and milk on the tray.

At this time, and for many days after, they were very careful not to mention what had happened with Clare that night, as though any discussion was akin to reliving the experience. In the afternoon, Ronit would clean up the parlour while Alice was out, and a day or two later, when Alice was quite ready, she would open the door to the green room and survey whatever the wreckage might be. Only much later, a matter of months, would the lock to Nanette's room be opened, the knob turned, and a reckoning made of the damage there. That they would do together, when the season had changed to something brighter, and the memory of this night had begun to fade.

But now, by far the best thing was to turn to the future, and Ronit therefore sat down next to Alice as she took her tea and asked her about the plan for her visit with Mrs Butterworth that afternoon.

'I'm expected at four,' said Alice.

'Do you think she'll have leads?'

'I think she'll have something, though what, I don't know.'

'Do you want me to come, or do you think she'll be put off by the presence of a man, or an Indian?'

Alice looked at him, her head cocked to one side, as though she were assessing him for signs of off-puttingness.

'She won't know what to make of you,' she said after consideration.

'So best not to come?'

'Yes, although it would be nice if you could hear everything in case I forget some important details.'

'That seems unlikely,' he said with a smile.

'Yes,' said Alice firmly. 'That does seem unlikely.'

*

Later that afternoon, Alice dressed in a manner she thought Nanette, and therefore Cece Butterworth, would approve of. She wore a fawn-coloured cashmere turtleneck, a maroon boiled wool skirt, dark-brown wool tights and calf-length leather boots. She fastened her hair back in a ponytail with a wide barrette – it wasn't long enough for a bun – and she searched through her luggage until she managed to find a pair of pearl earrings Nanette had given her on her twenty-first birthday that she always wore when the need for jewellery arose.

Thus prepared, she presented herself to Ronit, who had rarely seen her dress so neatly. He voiced appropriate approval, though secretly he thought she looked like a stranger, perhaps a cousin of Alice, but definitely not Alice herself.

Alice then noted down the Butterworth address from Nanette's Rolodex which still sat on the phone table in the hallway and made her way out to the car.

Cece Butterworth lived closer into town, but on the other side. At one time, her family had probably commanded one of the handsome manses that lined the main street of Chichester, but now she lived in a small cottage with a neat garden from which one could easily walk into town to fetch the mail, if one were so inclined.

Alice parked her car and approached the side door. The walk was shovelled here and not at the front. She knocked, waited, then knocked again, and when no response came, opened the door and called in. Now she heard a small shriek and a shrill bark, and presently, Cece Butterworth, accompanied by a tiny white Shih Tzu, came trotting to the kitchen in Christmas-red pumps.

# 44

'Darling!' she cried, and kissed Alice firmly in the air beneath one ear as she clutched her arms in a surprisingly tight grip. Cece Butterworth smelled like Nanette, and her kitchen smelled of buttery cooking and roasts. Alice felt herself at home although she thought of Mrs Butterworth as a stranger – Nanette had never been inclined to mix her Alice visits with friends, although Alice was not sure why.

'Tea's out and ready,' said Cece. 'Come along, dear,' and then, to the dog, 'Now now, Fwitzi, she's a fwiend, no naughties!' as Fritzi yapped enthusiastically about Alice's ankles.

In the living room, tea was laid out in front of a gas grate fire. A small plastic Christmas tree stood on a side table, and the room was heavily ornamented with seasonal decorations, some of them quite ordinary, but others that attracted Alice's attention. She stopped to gaze carefully at a small Scotsman in a kilt standing by a nativity scene. All the figures were made of moulded plastic, but their clothing was made of fabric. They were all fixed to a round stand with a wind-up key on the side.

'May I?' asked Alice eagerly, pointing to the key.

'What's that, dear? Oh, the Scotsman? No one's tried that in simply ages, but I think he'll still do a jig for you if you ask nicely.'

Alice wound him up and watched enchanted as the tiny figure did a jig, rotating slowly as he circled the holy family on a small track.

'How wonderful!' cried Alice, in sincere appreciation. She clasped her hands together.

'Wee thing. It came with a bottle of whiskey, long ago, when the children were small. We used to wind it up again and again, didn't we, Fwitzi?'

She seated herself in a chair by the tea tray and started addressing the dog again, encouraging him to stand on his hind legs in exchange for a biscuit.

Alice turned away from the dancing Scotsman and went to sit on the edge of the sofa, near to Mrs Butterworth, who began to pour the tea.

'Do take a shortbread cookie, my dear,' she said.

When all was poured out, she balanced her cup of tea on one knee and looked Alice up and down as though for the first time.

'My dear,' she said. Suddenly her pale-blue eyes welled up with tears.

'You look so like her, you know. There's not a day that goes by I don't miss your lovely, lovely grandmother.' Her teacup rattled in her hands, and some of its contents sloshed into the saucer. Alice reached out to help but Cece deftly returned the cup and saucer to the tray and patted a mascaraed eye softly with a lace-edged napkin.

'They're all gone, you know,' she said in a quavering voice. 'Everyone's died.'

Alice felt awkward. Though she was able to muster a modicum of pity for this woman who claimed to have been close to Nanette, she felt, now in her presence at last, an overwhelming desire to extract the information she sought as quickly as possible. Not because she was in a hurry or wished to leave. On the contrary, she felt quite comfortable in her presence. She was simply impatient to hear the story and wondered how long they would have to linger over these mournful thoughts.

'I am so sorry,' she murmured.

Cece Butterworth wiped away another tear.

'Not at all, dear, not at all. And besides,' she added, suddenly brisk, 'you are young and beautiful! Let's not linger over the dead.' She took a shortbread cookie from the plate and Fritzi yapped.

'Naughty puppy! It wantses an ikkle bicky!' And she held the cookie over the small dog's head so that it jumped to its hind legs and began to prance. She dropped the cookie into his jaws and patted him on the nose.

'So, darling,' she said, turning to Alice. 'You had questions for me about your dear grandmother.' Her eyes suddenly sparkled at the thought of telling such stories, and Alice wondered at the range of emotions Mrs Butterworth could display in just a short span of time.

'Yes,' said Alice, happy to be on topic at last. Her words came out in a rush: 'I'd like to know specifically about James Smith and Nanette's relationship with him, and well, everything you know, if you don't mind.'

'Dear Nanette would be *furious* with me,' mused Cece, taking a sip of tea. 'After a certain point in time, Jim Smith was *absolutely* out of bounds in conversation. One had to tread very lightly. But then he did seem to evaporate from everyone's lives all of a sudden, after being such a fixture for so long. Gracious, I don't think I'd laid eyes on him for nearly, I don't know, it must have been over fifty years!'

'Until you saw him at the funeral?'

'Yes, until then. Of course, he was just as handsome as ever, wasn't he.'

'I didn't get to speak to him or even see him up close.'

'No, the boys sent him packing, didn't they! Not a terribly imaginative bunch, your uncles, but then look who their father was.' At this, Cece Butterworth winked at Alice just in case the innuendo was lost on her. Alice was happy for the opening.

'So, do you think it possible, then? That he was, you know, the father of the others?'

'Was it possible?' Cece gave a little snort. 'It had been many years since Nanette had been seen anywhere near Charles when she came up pregnant with the first of the girls.'

'Did everyone know that? That my grandparents were not …'

'I wouldn't say they *knew*. Good gracious, I can't imagine Nanette saying anything to anyone …'

'Not to you?'

'She *implied*, yes, but Nanette was never one to *say*.'

'Do you know why? Why had their marriage gone bad?'

'First, I don't know that it was ever good. It seemed most of all something that they'd been popped into. A business deal between the fathers, you know. They weren't the cheerfullest couple, but they were dutiful, and Nanette carried those three large boys – can you imagine how big they were as babies? The size of them, and your dear grandmother so petite. I don't know how she kept her figure but kept it she did. In those days, we didn't have all those things you see now in magazines – for the movie stars – the tummy tucks, the lifts and the like …'

'And then, something went sour?' interrupted Alice.

'Well, yes, and one really never knew what it was, but to make Nanette openly part ways with Charles – and of course there was never talk of divorce – one didn't do that then unless there was some sort of catastrophe – so it wasn't divorce, and they stayed on in the same house, but they never went out together unless it was a funeral or something that required them both to be present. Even then, it would not be unusual to see them arrive in separate cars. And Charles, of course, had the business concerns in India. He was away a great deal, and this provided cover, so to say, for the state of the marriage.'

'Were there rumours? Of why?'

'Darling, there are always rumours.'

Cece paused for a long wink and refilled Alice's teacup with tea, now grown quite dark and chilly.

'The rumour was, Charles had been discovered to have a mistress, or some such thing, in India. Other rumours were that he didn't really go to India at all, that that was just a cover, and he kept a girl, or something worse, in Boston.'

'Something worse?'

Cece lowered her voice to a whisper and leaned in, though there was no one there save the dog, to overhear the confidence she was about to share.

'Some said he kept a boy there.'

Alice laughed, both at the thought of her grandfather and a kept boy in some seedy flat in Boston, and at how far from the truth the rumour had strayed.

'… and that, of course, would be one way to explain why Nanette reacted so strongly!'

It was clear from Cece's tone that though she might not subscribe to this theory with fullest confidence, she certainly hadn't ruled it out. And so, thought Alice, it had never occurred to anyone that Charles Ramsey was a bigamist, and that Nanette was actually the second of his wives, not the first. But she must have known, Alice decided, or she would never have scorned Grandfather so openly.

'So then when did James Smith come along? How long after this separation became apparent?'

'Well, that I can tell you for sure, because I was there when they first met. My family always kept a house by the seashore in Maine. Just a small village, really, there, and such beautiful islands. There were a number of lovely old houses built up there by Boston families. My grandfather had built one – on a sizeable property – the house was on a cliff – called Winserly Bluff – Winserly is my maiden name. Of course, the house has long since been sold, the property cut up into horrid little *vacation homes* – such a shame, but the house – houses like that cost a fortune to maintain. My siblings and I had to sell it after my mother's death …'

Alice quickly pushed the conversation back on track: 'So this was where Nanette first met James Smith?'

'Ah, yes, yes. There was a wonderful house party. In those days, Nanette would always come up for a week in the summer with the boys. August she would come, to escape the heat in Massachusetts.'

'How old were they then? My uncles?'

'Ah, I'd imagine they were boys. The oldest perhaps eleven, the youngest five. And James Smith, well, he was recently out of college – a Bowdoin man – he's from an old Maine family … you can never tell, with a name like Smith … but it was a good family … and they had a house in the same town too. A charming house, mostly for summers. Not so large. And they wintered in Portland, if you can imagine that! Very hearty stock. So, James, Jim, he was called, was working for his father a bit. His father had a firm in Portland, but he was really very recently out of college, and they wanted him to go into law or some other profession, as he wasn't keen to stay in business as his father wished. But you know, for all that, he was a poet at heart.' Cece put down her teacup on the tray and sighed. '*Such* a handsome man, and *so* sincere. All the girls were mad for him in those days, but he was a funny one, didn't seem to really notice all the attention.

'And I can tell you, quite frankly, had I been just a little bit younger,' and with this she closed her eyes, set her hand across her breast and smiled, then continuing in a wistful tone, she said, 'but I was already married with two children by then.'

'So, when he came into town at the beginning of Nan's week, Nan and the boys, we decided to throw some parties, find people for tennis and swimming and sailing and the like.

'There were some very attractive girls up there at the time, the de Vois sisters, Miriam and Louise, they must have been in their late teens, long, auburn hair, lovely figures, very good at tennis but so charming to talk to, and another girl, just shy of twenty, Mary Ellen Gainsevoort – so charming, a petite blonde who'd had her heart absolutely broken in two by some cad from Yale and we thought her very likely for Jim – so poetic and soft-spoken.

'But Jim had eyes for none of these. Certainly, he was polite and charming as the day is long, but it was very obvious, from the beginning, you know, that he had eyes for Nan alone.'

'What was their age difference, do you think?' asked Alice excitedly.

'Oh, I'd think ten or eleven years. She had her eldest young – at twenty, maybe, so she would have been over thirty, and Jim not more than twenty-two or twenty-three.'

'Was Nanette very beautiful then?' asked Alice, caught up in the romance of the story. To this question, she already knew the answer, but she wanted to hear it anyway – feeling somehow wronged by the attention paid to the beauty and charms of the other eligible young ladies in Cece's tale.

Cece rolled her eyes at this and waved her bejewelled, veiny fingers in the air.

'Is there any question of that? Such elegance, such charm! You know, you might have compared her to other gals her age – and younger too – and said, "Oh, this one's got a better nose, that one has lovelier cheeks, or the other has a very neat figure," but truly, when you saw Nan, all put together, not taken apart like that, there was no question. You know,' here Cece dropped her voice to a stage whisper again, 'you know, she was often mistaken for royalty, or assumed to be from a very prominent family – not that her family wasn't known – but you know, people thought she must be a Vanderbilt or something along those lines …

'Now, mind you, I've known my share of Vanderbilts and Rockefellers,' and here her voice became rather loud, and she laughed the crackly, raspy laugh of a life heavily seeded by cigarettes and whiskey sours. 'They're a decidedly mixed bunch.' Cece grabbed hold of Alice's arm with her vice-like grip, and Alice wondered at how those at both extremes of the life cycle, newborn babies and elderly socialites, could hold on to strangers with such tenacity.

'In fact,' Cece continued, now dropping her voice again to a whisper and drawing her face close to Alice's, while still clutching her arm, 'you wouldn't know this, but when I was a debutante, Billy Vanderbilt had a thing for me, and he was always running after me at the parties in Boston: "Cece, can I get you a drink?", "Cece, are you cold, do you need a shawl?" And gracious me, you know he was always trying so hard to get me alone so he could steal a kiss, but I'd have nothing of it.'

'You didn't like him?' asked Alice, who felt that their faces were much too close right now, so close she could see the film of powder clinging to the wrinkles etched in her hostess's face, and the tiny specks of mascara that dotted the skin below her lower lashes.

'Darling! He was *hideous*! At least not my cup of tea. A great hulking fellow, so maladroit, always knocking absolutely everything over. He was fast friends with your grandfather, of course. They were two peas in a pod, were Charles Ramsey and Billy Vanderbilt.'

'So, then you were telling me about Jim Smith meeting Nanette. What happened then?'

'Oh, they were smitten – on both sides – and she as much as he, so graceful, ordinarily you'd never have known she had those sorts of thoughts about anyone, even though one was quite sure she didn't have them for Charles.'

'Did their affair begin then?'

'Possibly. They went on long walks, talked about poetry. Always a bad sign,' said Cece with a wink. 'She'd brought a girl along to look after the boys – a Belgian or something au pair – so she'd just disappear with him. And one day, I saw them – I'd been looking for my girls and I walked out to the garden, then started along the cliff walk – always so enchanting at sunset – and I looked up and I saw two people silhouetted at the Point, and I couldn't see their faces, but I knew it was them – two slender figures, and they were holding one another's hands and she was looking up at him, and it really did look like some sort of movie poster, for a romantic movie, not something in real life. And I thought, and I remember this well, I thought, *Well, this won't end well*, because I just knew Nan would never consider divorce, and Jim Smith, he was the sort, one could tell, the sort of man who could only fall for one woman. They say Prince Charles is like that with what-is-her-name? Carmelia? Something like that, and he could never let go of her even after he married that poor, sweet Lady Diana. You know, I've got a commemorative plaque from their wedding. Let me just find it for you.'

Cece hoisted herself up with the arms of her chair and was off to a series of glass-fronted cabinets filled with china and various knick-knacks.

Alice was anxious that this quest for the commemorative plaque not take up too much of their time, as Cece had only allotted her two hours. She got up and followed her over, so the plaque could be pointed to but not removed from the case. Clearly a time-consuming procedure. This move proved efficacious, for now the plaque was found and duly marvelled over, as were other bits of memorabilia concerning the royal family, and then Alice managed to steer the conversation back to the story of Nanette and Jim Smith.

'And so, there were more meetings after that?'

'Oh yes, many more, many, many more. I'm sure more than one ever knew about. Nan could certainly keep a secret. At first, there were parties at her house. When Charles was away, there'd be the most wonderful parties. Nanette invited many people, many mutual friends, so that it would be difficult to suspect, though many did, of course. But such delightful soirées she gave – it was like being teenagers again – we played games, like charades, blindman's buff, hide-and-seek. Of course, there were children there as well, and they were used as an excuse, but really it was as though Nan was making up for being married off so young. And there was plenty of drinking too, you know. In those days, people weren't so concerned over such things, and you'd find perfectly respectable bankers and so forth passed out on the lawn furniture in the mornings. Missing their shoes and socks, poor things, like little lost lambs when they woke up.

'And over time, Nan grew more brazen. She'd have parties when Charles was there – and he wouldn't come! People would ask, "Where is Charles? Will he be coming down for dinner?" And Nan didn't care a jot, "Oh, I don't think so," she'd say and just shrug.'

'How long did that go on?' asked Alice. 'I mean, until the girls were born?'

'Ah, two years, perhaps. Not more than three. How long can that sort of thing go on, after all? Eventually, the parties stopped, and I imagine they found some other way to see one another, less cumbersome, fewer people. It wasn't just an ordinary affair, after all. There was something between them, and I don't think others were any use to them in the end. It was just about the two of them.

'Charles would be away, Nan would send the boys off to her mother or to camp, and then who can really say where she went and whom she saw. She was free then.'

'But then she had a baby.'

'Yes, when it was clear she was pregnant, everyone wondered, but Charles said nothing, acted as though nothing odd had happened, and so the wondering remained just that. Whispers, rumours, but there was Charles at Bix's christening, and Jim notably absent, and there was Charles for the second, for Clare.

'And such lovely babies, so fine-featured and so unlike the other Ramsey babies. Certainly, they were girls, but they were such delicate, delicious little girls, and Nan so delighted to have girls, and perhaps to have loved the father too, who can tell?'

'And did it end there? Did they still see each other?' asked Alice, feeling slightly mournful now that they were reaching the end of the great love story.

'More or less. Jim was seen around a bit, but slowly he disappeared, and Nanette never mentioned him, and something about her changed. I don't know what it was. Something hardened. She was still and always would be the most charming and graceful creature, but she was more concerned about what was proper, about things being done the right way. And life went on and those girls grew up to be the very images of Nanette but also of Jim Smith, but after a time, people forget to notice these things, don't they? They say, those ones took after their father and these ones are the image of the mother, and the days are forgotten when Nan stopped doing the proper thing and took a risk.

'I sometimes think ...' she paused and looked thoughtfully at Alice. 'I sometimes think that when Nan hardened her heart and pushed him out of her life, it did something to her as a mother. The way Trixie turned out – Clare, I suppose – your mother, as much as Nan was irreproachable in every way, one always felt she saw him in Trixie and never gave the child much of a chance. She'd turned quite cold, you see.'

Cece Butterworth looked almost tearful again and lifted the tea napkin to daub the corner of her eye. Alice felt tears in her eyes as well. Poor Nanette. Poor Clare. And how must Clare have felt that her mother had no warmth for her, but plenty for Alice?

And now the massive grandfather clock, crammed into the corner, another relic of those days in large houses that crowded the small rooms of Cece Butterworth's cottage, struck six. Alice's hostess started from her reverie of past days and gathered herself together smartly. 'That's six o'clock now,' she said. 'I'm expected for dinner at the Forsters'. So lovely to see you, my dear.'

Alice rose and helped her from her chair, then gathered the tea things onto the tray and carried it into the kitchen with Fritzi yapping at her heels.

'Poor widdle Fwitzi,' cooed Cece, 'it wantses its sup sup.' And she busied herself with opening a small can of dog food and emptying its contents into a little white dish on the floor in the shape of a dog bone.

'I'm so grateful to you,' said Alice, after Cece had stood and placed the can in the sink. Cece came over to her, and taking hold of her elbows, her lacquered nails sticking uncomfortably into Alice's arm, she gave her an actual kiss on the cheek.

'Darling girl,' said Cece fondly. 'Such lovely memories today. And you are so like her. *Do* come again.' She trotted with Fritzi to the door and opened it up, though Alice had barely got on her coat. The next social engagement called, and one could never sacrifice one for the other.

Alice scurried out the door, breathing in one last time the scent of old lady and lavender, for each of the women had reminded the other of the one now gone.

# 45

Ronit could only take off so many days without seriously endangering his practice and his patients, and that fall and Christmas, he'd taken off far more than was wise. A few days after Christmas, Alice seemingly stabilized, he urged her to return to Boston with him and lock up the house. Alice was anxious about leaving the house again, even if she felt reasonably convinced that Clare would not be back now. But he argued that it was best for her not to stay there alone for the time being. And so, they returned to the city, after supplying the caretaker with new keys and instructions for dealing with family invaders. The draw in this for Alice was also the presence of working internet in their apartment – a modern convenience she'd always avoided as much as she could, but which she now wished to unleash, as was suggested by the ads put out by their internet service provider, in the hopes of turning up some clues about the whereabouts of James Smith.

'That's not a great name for turning up clear results on a search engine,' observed Ronit, worried at the disappointment Alice might face.

'But I know he's from Maine,' said Alice brightly.

'That's not going to help,' said Ronit. 'Even if you knew the exact town, there would probably be five Jim Smiths there, and …'

'… then I'd just call all of them and find the right one,' stated Alice.

'And ask what? 'Are you the one who had an affair with my grandmother fifty years ago?''

'I'll think of something.'

'And how do you even know he still lives in Maine, or if he lives there, that he lives in the same village or town he grew up in?'

'Oh, I just know. I'm sure he's in the place of his birth.'

'Why?' asked Ronit, exasperated. 'How are you so sure?'

'Because he would be faithful; faithful forever.'

Ronit worried at Alice's absolute confidence in everything to do with Jim Smith, a man she'd seen once, from a distance, and about whom she'd heard the romantic reminiscences of a dotty old society lady.

'I just don't want you to be disappointed,' he said carefully.

'I won't be. And look how we've found everyone we looked for so far. You even found Biju!'

'Speaking of whom,' said Ronit, eager by now to change the subject, 'I was thinking we might invite him to dinner.'

'Do you think that's a good idea?'

'Why not?'

'Well, you just met him once, I mean who knows what he's like. He could be an axe-murderer or something …'

'And now you're suddenly so cautious,' said Ronit, with irritation, 'after you wandered up a mountainside with acute gastroenteritis and fell over on the lawn of perfect strangers you were positive you'd like to meet.'

Alice scowled and her cheeks reddened. She stared out the window at the landscape whizzing by along the highway.

Ronit regretted his words. Alice was strangely innocent when it came to her obsessions, and it genuinely hurt her to have them criticized. He was silent for a moment, then suggested, in a conciliatory tone, 'Maybe we could meet him somewhere else for dinner. Or lunch.'

Alice didn't answer. Ronit thought she might have wiped away a tear, but he couldn't be sure, as he was busy dodging trucks.

'I thought you said he had a night shift,' she responded, subdued.

'True – maybe his day off, or lunch?'

'Doesn't he have anyone? In his life, I mean?'

'He didn't mention anyone.'

'Maybe he thought you'd judge. Because he's gay, I mean.'

'But I said I loved his book.'

'That's true. But all the same, you could tell him he could bring someone if he wanted.'

'Yes, that's fine. I'll tell him that,' agreed Ronit, relieved that the price for his earlier remark had not been heavy.

But when they returned, Ronit kept forgetting to call Biju in the mornings, and he didn't have an email for him. Alice, for her part, continued to feel doubtful about the whole thing and spent her days googling 'Jim Smith' + 'Maine' or 'James Smith Maine' on the computer with no clear results. It was during one such listless day that she received a call from the lawyer's office. She didn't pick up, even though she could see the law office's name on the caller ID, and she waited half an hour before listening to the voicemail, mostly because she didn't feel like talking to anyone, especially not about wills or trusts or whatever it was. She went and made a cup of coffee for herself and finally sat down with the voicemail password and called up to hear what the message was.

To her surprise, it was the secretary asking her to call back as soon as possible regarding the annuity to be sent to Violet Ramsey in India. Worrying that the lawyers or someone else might fail to send the payments she'd requested, she sat up and called the law offices back.

The secretary informed her that after the first set of cheques had been sent to Cosmos Cottage, they'd received word back via an attorney there that Mrs Ramsey had passed away just days after the annuity had arrived for her. Should the cheque be returned, they wanted to know, or could it be used to defray the costs of the funeral and burial?

Despite the clear fact of Violet Ramsey's very advanced years, Alice felt shocked – bereaved even. She toyed with the idea of going to India for the funeral, then realized it had probably already taken place. She felt she should do something to help 'the girls', and she called Ronit at the office to ask him what he thought she should do, and should she return to India immediately to help in some way.

'Well,' said Ronit, thoughtfully, since he could not gauge Alice's current mood over the phone, 'the funeral must be over. You've given them money. But maybe,' and here he paused to avoid sounding bossy, 'maybe what would be helpful would be to tell Violet's son of her passing and offer to buy his ticket home if he wishes to go and see his sisters.'

'Oh,' said Alice. 'Oh, yes. He'll want to know. And to go. Will you call him?'

And so it was that Ronit arranged for them to have lunch with Biju 'and a friend', if he wished, at a diner near his home in Somerville.

# 46

'I've been found,' said Biju.

He was squeezed uncomfortably close to his friend Ned in the booth where they usually faced one another with ample elbow room for each heavyset man.

'Ah,' returned Ned, conversationally, 'so you were lost then?'

Biju sat with his friend of many years at the diner where they had eaten lunch nearly every Sunday since they'd known each other, save on days of extreme weather, or sickness, or one or the other or both of them falling off the wagon they tried to stay on as best they could. Ned and Biju had met in Alcoholics Anonymous, a group neither of them cared for – too evangelical for their tastes – and they'd agreed over coffees following their first meeting together, and ever after, that they'd steer clear of the place except for when Ned's family or Biju's workplace firmly warned of consequences.

Today Biju had asked Ned to come fifteen minutes earlier than usual to explain what he knew of the situation, of the other guests, so he would feel fully fortified for the meeting about which he still felt unsure, despite the kind words that Ronit had showered upon his novel when they'd met at Macy's and spoken at the basement coffee shop.

'Lost – in a manner of speaking. I'd left home, you know, so long ago, but never wrote and so forth,' explained Biju, even now at a loss to formulate his sudden decision to leave his family and his country at the age of twenty and flee to Boston, the city his father used to mention most. And yet, despite coming to Boston, he'd broached no contact with his father or his father's family, knowing the former had been displeased by the revelations of his orientation that had inevitably come with the publication of his novel, and the latter of course most likely unaware of his very existence.

For though the notion that he, his mother and sisters were a 'second family' for his father flitted about their lives like a lean spectre, it was nonetheless never said, never broached. They were just two parallel universes that could never collide. And perhaps he'd hoped to collide with the other parallel when he came here – not literally, but simply to co-inhabit it, though the story he lamely told himself was that he'd come to a place where there'd be a more openly gay culture.

But then why Boston, why not New York? Why not London? There was no other reason but to live near his roots, even though he made no attempt to find them. Had he taken much advantage of the 'openly gay culture' once he'd arrived? Not particularly. Instead, he'd ended up at a men's haberdashery shop, his self-created British accent a plus in the field, and stayed there ever since, migrating thankfully to men's shirts in Macy's when the haberdasher's had finally closed.

He'd had troubles with drink, another legacy from his father, he knew, although his father had never been seen to have a problem per se, just a fondness. And he'd made a friend, Ned, a man of erudition with whom he could discuss art, literature and ancient Greece and Rome, Ned's speciality, and yet they'd barely ever discussed any personal matters, even their drinking problems – a topic best left at the doorway of the hated AA meetings.

Ned had only the faintest notion that Biju was from India; he didn't even know him as a once-successful novelist. And of course, Biju had scarcely written a word since those days. A journal he'd kept for a time, then notes to himself; nowadays, he belonged to some online gaming sites and occasionally went on dates with other lonely men who took a liking to him in men's shirts, although these encounters never amounted to much.

Ned took a sip from his coffee into which he'd dropped his usual three creams and two packets of sugar. He stirred and considered.

'What, or who has found you?' he asked pensively, trying, as a man who'd never been lost to anyone, who in fact had a tendency to turn up again and again on the doorsteps of his relations, to imagine what the state of being lost might look like. It was remarkable to learn that his closest friend, or at least the most reliable one, was now emerging from such a state and that, according to his testimony of moments ago, he'd inhabited a state of 'being lost' for decades.

'A man found me at work,' said Biju. And then, seeing that more information might be required, 'He's engaged to a relation. A cousin, or niece, of sorts.' And here the explanation was already getting murky, and he knew that this was why saying nothing had always seemed the better option.

'But how did he find you, er, or why?' Ned felt aware that these questions were somehow missing the mark, that they weren't helping.

'Well,' said Biju. 'Well. This cousin or niece went to India with him – he is also from India, though a different part, and she was in search of information about her grandfather – that's my father. She met with my mother and sisters, and they learned there was a brother.'

'– you?'

'– yes – me, and that the brother was long since absent. The fiancé –'

'The Indian fellow?'

'Yes – the Indian fellow – read a bit of something I'd written in those days, liked it, and decided to try and track me down.'

'Something you'd written? Well, that's something, isn't it? What sort of something? Essay? Journal entry?'

'A – a novel, actually,' said Biju, feeling bashful now, as he'd always known he would if he'd have to bring it up. A specialist in men's haberdashery as a novelist – he knew this would be too much to explain. But Ned was surprisingly sanguine on the subject.

'A novel,' he said, musingly. 'Isn't that something. Tom, you are a man of surprises! Of course, I want to know everything about this novel – want to read it too – but first things first. The people, then, who've found you, who are joining us momentarily, are these they then? The Indian fellow and the … the …'

'The cousin or niece?'

'Well, let's see, here, you've said she was looking for information on her grandfather, and he was your father, so wouldn't that make her – unambiguously – your niece?'

'Yes, I suppose,' said Biju doubtfully. Too much had been said already, and he wasn't prepared in any way to fashion into words the history, mostly unknown to him, of his father's twin families across the world from one another. Nor was he inclined to cobble together some explanation or description of what it was like to grow up in a parallel universe where the other side was only sensed but never seen or discussed.

It was at this moment, when the two men in their late sixties of indifferent health and formidable if largely unkempt intellects were sitting and mulling over the notion that one of them had been found, that Alice and Ronit walked in, looked around, and on Ronit's recognizing Biju, approached the table and introduced themselves. And here an odd coincidence occurred: for the introductions had only just begun when Alice and Ned suddenly recognized one another, as New Englanders of patrician mien and crumbling pedigrees often do. Ned stood and jovially kissed her on the cheek, shook her hand heartily and congratulated her on her engagement, for he presumed this was the lucky fellow.

'So how do you two know each other?' asked Ronit, bewildered at the way the meeting he'd set up had already turned into something else.

'Ned is a relative – my cousin Daniel's uncle from the other side, I think,' said Alice, faltering slightly, for she wasn't precisely sure.

'Yes, that's right,' said Ned, sitting down and rolling back his cuffs in a gesture of enthusiasm. 'My sister is married to one of Alice's uncles – one of her mother's brothers, you see. So that makes me sort of an uncle, perhaps.'

Ronit and Biju were both silent, not because they could think of nothing to say but because they'd arrived at the same conclusion at the same time, that this made Ned and Biju relatives of a sort. Ronit was not convinced that this was a fact known to either man before this moment, and not being sure of the nature of their relationship, thought it best to keep his mouth shut.

Biju was not sure what he felt – horror that he had run so far without running at all, happiness of some kind to find family after many years of solitude? He sat silently, a look of melancholy on his broad face, and turned away from the scene, to glance out the window – a place where this story was not unfolding. He felt the old urge to flee again, despite the cheer of the moment, but it was then that Alice turned to him – he sat diagonally across from her at the table – and reached across to his hand resting by his coffee cup. She took his hand in hers and clasped it warmly.

'I'm so glad to meet you, Uncle Biju,' she said. 'At long last.'

Her smile was wide and radiant, and her eyes shone as though she were close to tears. Biju felt unnerved to be touched in this way, offered familial love in a manner that for him had become the stuff of nostalgia, the kind of weepy sentimentality that overcame him when he occasionally watched videos online of old Hindi film songs. The scattered, forgotten memories of haunting melodies he was not even sure he'd heard when he was a boy in India.

'I have something to tell you,' said Alice, looking at him gravely. This is a woman who doesn't fear much, he thought; and then she said, 'Your mother, dear Violet, whom we came to know and love at Cosmos Cottage, has passed away. We've just learned this through the lawyers.'

She held his hand extra hard as though she wished to absorb the surfeit of sorrow she imagined he must be feeling, and this gesture alone, perhaps more than the news she'd delivered, which reached him as a distant echo from a far-off mountain peak, filled him with a rush of rarely accessed emotions, and he felt tears well up in his eyes. A sometimes drunkard, this emotion was reserved for those moments of excess, for transposed emotional events that couldn't immediately be identified as feelings of loss for what he'd left behind – a pious, tenacious mother, shadow wife; an American father, never quite here or there enough to amount to much of a parent in either place; two sisters, one odd, the other unpleasant; and a house perched on the edge of paradise. And this, he thought as he allowed the young woman whom he'd never seen before hold his hand; grip it, rather – this was what his heart ached for and missed, that perch on the edge of paradise.

'Bad luck, old man,' said Ned gruffly after a pause, and briefly laid a large pink hand on Biju's shoulder.

'She was a lovely woman,' added Ronit, unhappy with the Ned angle, which had made this lunch into a less manageable emotional experience than he'd intended when he'd suggested Biju bring a friend.

Biju looked out the window again, hoping to attenuate his tears. He blinked, carefully withdrew his hand from Alice's and fished out a paper napkin from the dispenser next to the window. With this, he daubed his eyes, sniffed, blew his nose, and then suddenly felt himself a great oaf for the gesture.

'I'm sorry,' he murmured. 'I didn't expect – and then one's memories surround.'

'How beautifully put,' said Ronit. 'I do hope you still write.'

'Not so much.' Biju wiped his nose again. 'There's work. One tires.'

'I'd no idea,' said Ned, eager to move from the topic of sorrow and death, 'No idea from Adam, this man's been touched by the muse! And to think! But now that I cast my mind back there have always been lovely turns of phrase. Don't suppose, old fellow, you'd be willing to allow friend Ned to see this oeuvre of yours, eh?'

Biju looked unexcited by the idea and Ronit felt unnerved when Alice drew a copy of *Himalayan Rhapsody* from her bag and handed it to Ned.

'It's really good,' she said, casting an encouraging glance towards Biju. 'This is a library copy, but there are others in the city.'

Ned picked the volume up and began to look it over eagerly. In the midst of this, the waitress came, and to Ronit's surprise, the two older men appeared not to be too overcome by emotion to order hearty meals, the usual for each, it seemed. Ronit then ordered tuna salad, which he doubted he'd like, and Alice asked for pancakes and tea.

The four ate their heavy meals slowly, the two regulars tucking into plates laden with sausages and potato preparations with accustomed gusto, and the newcomers, of a different mindset regarding fat and cholesterol content, carved away at the margins of their platters. Ronit was particularly appalled at the grotesque proportions of the tuna salad, an item he'd chosen with some misgivings, hoping it would live up to the menu subheading: 'On the Lighter Side'. An enormous scoop of canned tuna mixed with generous quantities of mayonnaise sat perched atop a sea of iceberg lettuce blanketed in shredded mozzarella cheese, extra-large croutons, with a slick of gelatinous orange dressing covering the entire dish. Alice, he now realized, had made a far wiser choice, a fully carbohydrate-based meal that caused no insult to vegetables or proteins.

As Alice daintily ate a bit here and a bit there from the stack before her, she narrated in some detail the trip they'd made to Mussoorie. In her usual manner, she showed no hesitation in sharing parts of the story many might have held back, of ghosts seen and stomach ailments experienced, so the two older men in her audience, despite their enthusiasm for their meals, gave her a rapt hearing. Most of the story she managed to tell with no interruption, and the content of the thing was revelatory to Biju for what it told of his father in America, of his life here and his reputation, and to Ned for the vista of astonishing surprises that were unveiled about a not-too-distant relative whom he'd thought he knew reasonably well.

It was late in the story that one item actually so caught Ned by surprise that he dropped his fork mid-bite. Alice was explaining what Violet had told her about Nanette's infidelity, when Ned cried out, 'Why! That's just it!'

'What is?' asked Alice.

'Jim Smith! Why, not the Smiths of Swinchendon, Maine, is it?'

'Is it?' asked Alice eagerly, seizing on this town name with a sudden zeal that surprised Biju, who had been marvelling at her even temper in narrating such complex family dramas.

'Swinchendon? Do you know him? Did you?' Alice's eyes sparkled with excitement, and she began to knead the napkin on the table just to the left of her plate, her knuckles clenched and white.

'Why of course! A lovely family, all! Swinchendon is really nothing more than a small fishing town, but it's a major draw for fly fishermen, and more than a few well-known writers have summered there as well. I knew all the Smiths! Of course, his younger sisters were dear friends of Daniel's mother. All lovely girls, don't know what became of them, but Jim Smith, a sportsman, but something of a bright light, everyone was surprised when he decided against Harvard, went back up to Maine, a man for his roots I guess. Always took him for a writer – perhaps the nature-writing type, thought I. Don't know what became of him in the end either. One loses touch, you know, but he must be quite old now, is he –?'

Alice listened with fierce attention to this. '– alive?' she asked. 'I think so. He was at Nanette's funeral, but they sent him away. That wasn't long ago.'

'Still carrying the torch, eh? Not surprising, not surprising, deep one, he was. A Homeric look to him, eh, I always thought.'

Biju listened to these fresh storylines and felt a new kind of sadness, as when a long-lost niece turns out not to be one's own relation after all. And yet, he thought, as he scooped up the remainder of his mashed potatoes, this she had already known when she came, so maybe kin such as this can also be lost and found and held close as easily as blood relations.

Ronit, next to Alice, sat anxiously anticipating what upheavals the new information in her quest might bring. He also dearly hoped the waitress would reappear sooner rather than later to remove the inedible and uneaten colossus that lay before him.

Alice had casually pushed aside her pancakes by now. She had chipped away at the sides of the stack, leaving a sort of butte formation in a syrupy desert. Ronit always marvelled at the way in which Alice seemed unaffected by unappealing food choices. If she didn't like it, she just didn't eat it, whilst he was left feeling somehow abused, degraded even, by his poorly chosen salad. He reached out for a roll, which looked safe, and buttered it lightly.

Alice had pushed aside the plate of pancakes to make room for her notebook, in which she now wrote, carefully: *Swinchendon, Maine*.

'Are there other family members still there, do you think? That I could search for?'

'Ah, don't know, don't know,' replied Ned pondering. 'One of the sisters, maybe? But then you'd run into the married names and so forth. Cecily married a fellow up there, what was his name? I'd have to think.' Ned, who'd once been quite good with names, now began to grimace as he attempted to recollect.

Biju had been silent for some time now, and as he'd finished his meal, he had nothing to occupy him. Ronit could sense his discomfort and felt anxious that Alice had dropped the news of his mother's death like a little bomb at the beginning of the lunch. Though he knew Biju had not seen or spoken with his mother for decades, he felt appalled at the shock such news could hold. At the same time, he didn't want to come off as behaving too much like a psychiatrist in this social setting.

'Do you think you will travel to India?' he asked, and then immediately regretted it.

Biju felt gutted by the question. He'd been turning it over in his mind throughout the intervening conversation.

'I don't know. Think not. Expensive,' he telegraphed, not sure if his heart could take a return, to see the changes and the absences.

Alice, now conscious of her error in allowing the conversation to stray so far from Biju, closed her notebook and laid the pen down beside it.

'You can go if you want,' she said, looking at him earnestly. 'I must tell you, everything's been set up, to care for your sisters – this is what Grandfather asked. The money is yours too if you wish. You are a part of the family. I can arrange with the lawyers. Even –' and she hesitated, not knowing the value of work so very well herself, 'even if you wish to retire, there can be an annuity for you too.'

Ronit was pleased by Alice's generosity, though he did wonder what the size of the estate must be. He hoped that the lawyers and financial planners would put a stop to things at some point if she began handing out too many annuities.

Biju felt flustered. 'Thank you, that's kind, but I don't know as yet.'

'Well, I wanted you to know, specifically, that that was an option. And you are welcome any time to the family house in Chichester. I'm sure you'd enjoy seeing Grandfather's study and so on.'

'That's very kind, thank you.' By this point, Biju felt he could tolerate no new information, no changes. 'I think now I've got to get to work,' he said, the prospect of leaving, of changing into his work clothes, somehow easing his mind. His accent became more clipped; words came more easily to him.

'Oh dear, have we been keeping you too long?' asked Ronit, happy as well to gain release from the emotional tension of the diner booth.

'Bit early, isn't it?' asked Ned, confused.

'Extra training today,' said Biju quickly, holding up his hand for the waitress, who obliged quickly, bringing them the bill.

'Let me,' said Alice, taking it. 'I don't want you to be late.'

Ronit, seeing the awkward look on Biju's face, added, 'You can treat next time.'

'Quite right,' said Ned, perfectly cheerful to receive a free lunch. 'Much obliged.'

Room was made for Biju to slide himself out of the booth, and after bidding everyone a hasty adieu, he scurried off down the street to his apartment, where he'd have time to think alone, then ready himself for work.

When Alice had paid the bill, she exchanged numbers with Ned, in case he should think of any more information that might be helpful to her. Then they parted, Ned for the public library where he spent his afternoons, Ronit for the office, and Alice for home and more searching. But on this afternoon, she dallied, flush with the notion that she held in her pocket a word, a name, that might hold the key for her quest. Somehow it wouldn't do to type it in too soon and lose the deliciousness of this moment.

# 47

Not more than four or five days after the luncheon at the diner found Alice driving happily along the highway towards the coast of Maine. She had cleared the noxious suburban roadways that belt the city of Boston without incident (on highways she was a nervous driver, having nearly always driven only around Nanette's home, and usually only in Nanette's car). The only problem had been the toll plazas. The 'UNITED WE STAND' banners were gone by now, but had been replaced with 'SUPPORT OUR TROOPS' and festoons of yellow ribbons everywhere. But since she was the driver this time, she couldn't squeeze her eyes shut to avoid looking at the signs.

She drove Ronit's silver Toyota, and since it had not occurred to her to choose any music for the drive (her tastes in music were vague anyway – she liked to hear what was on, if it was nice, and occasionally bought music on a whim, but did not possess in her much fannishness, nor the carefully curated aesthetics of the connoisseur), she listened to the CD set already in the car the entire way, Wagner's Ring Cycle, which had some nice dramatic bits that matched her mood.

She had searched, and found, two or possibly three matches for James Smith, Swinchendon, Maine, not long after she'd reached home after the lunch and had felt that the best solution was to simply get in the car and drive there, then figure out which one was which.

'But aren't there phone numbers? Attached to these names?' asked Ronit, perplexed. 'Don't you think you should call and figure out which one is which?'

'And say what?' asked Alice lightly.

Ronit considered this and offered some suggestions which were flatly rejected.

'I must surprise him,' she said with conviction.

'Why?' asked Ronit, growing exasperated. 'So, he won't run away?'

'No,' said Alice, taking no offence. Her vision was clear, and any other suggestions or ideas were simply white noise to her.

'Then why?'

'He must see me, then know.'

'You think he will somehow recognize you, even though he's never seen you?'

'Yes, I know he will. If he doesn't, then none of it is true. Then we're not related.'

'But he must be quite old!'

'In his seventies, I think.'

'What if he's got dementia? What if his eyes are failing him?'

'Then how did he come to the funeral, all alone? He must have driven, on his own. He must have read the news. How did he know to come?'

'I see you've got this all figured out,' sighed Ronit.

'Yes, I'll go in the morning.'

'Right away?'

'Yes.'

'At least wait a day or two. Prepare for the journey. We need to get the oil changed ...' Ronit was above all else horrified at the precipitousness of the plan. It was sudden even for Alice.

'Okay,' she said, irritable at the prospect of the wait. 'I do have a doctor's appointment the day after tomorrow. I'll go the day after that.'

'And what about your mother?' he asked suddenly. 'What about Clare?'

'What about Clare?'

'Are you going to tell her all this? Are you going to warn her? Are you going to find out what she knows? Maybe you should visit her at the Oasis before you go.'

'I can go after. I can bring him with me.'

'What if it destabilizes her further? Don't you think she'll react better if she has some kind of warning?'

Alice glared at him and continued to pack. In this moment of joy, the last thing she wanted was to take a detour to New Hampshire and visit Clare at the Oasis, where she was in another residential treatment programme, chosen by Ronit, paid for by Alice. In fact, she was still so shaken by what had happened over Christmas that she would prefer not to tell Clare at all. She would prefer if Clare didn't exist, and that therefore nothing needed to be explained to her. But she knew Ronit was right. It would be better not to surprise her.

'All right,' she said. 'How about this. I'll go visit her afterwards and prepare her before I introduce him to her.'

Ronit agreed to this, although he knew he really hadn't any choice in the matter. And so, she waited, arranging her affairs, as though, Ronit noticed with some trepidation, she were leaving town for an indefinite period of time, and would have no access to mail or phones or internet in the interim. She spoke with the lawyer and instructed him to release funds to Biju should he wish to take a trip to India. She spoke to Biju and notified him of the same.

She went by the bank and signed papers. She paid bills, even those that had not come due. She cleared out the refrigerator and washed and folded all her laundry, an activity she only engaged in when her lack of clean clothing made it impossible to leave the house. It wasn't that Alice didn't intend to return. It was just that she was of the firm opinion that this meeting would change her life forever. When she finally managed to articulate this to Ronit, it unnerved him.

What if she was horribly disappointed, he worried. Or worse yet, what if it was true? What would that mean for him? If her clothes were all clean and neatly packed, they could easily be removed permanently. Her knick-knacks would take longer to pack, but he was haunted now by the spectre of the dissolution of his first marriage, which began its slow decline with a transformative trip to Nicaragua that Malini had taken without him.

By the time everything was in order for her departure four days later, Ronit heartily regretted his earlier advice.

'Are you sure you don't want me to come?' he asked anxiously, the night before she left.

'Why?' she asked this lightly, as though his presence or absence were irrelevant to the trip.

'For moral support? To drive? For safety? What if this Jim Smith is some sort of shady character, what then?'

'It will be fine,' she responded absently, as she dusted off the top of her dresser. 'And anyway, you have work. You said you couldn't miss any more days.'

'But if it's a question of safety …'

'It's not.' She seemed disinterested in the conversation, her mind elsewhere.

Ronit got up from where he was sitting at the edge of the bed and put his arms around her. She was dusting off the tops of her jewellery boxes with her new feather duster.

'What is it?' she asked, almost irritable now that her range of motion had become limited by his embrace.

'I don't want to lose you,' he said despondently, almost in a whisper, somewhere along the collar of her sweater.

'Why would you lose me?' Alice was annoyed. She was busy, in her mind, checking off all the things that needed to get done, and she couldn't understand why Ronit was asking to come along when he'd said he couldn't.

'But you must promise to call me right away, when you get there.'

'Oh, of course, as soon as I find a phone.'

'I really wish you would get a cell phone.'

Alice mumbled something non-committal in response. Secretly, she was repelled by these annoying little devices that people became so enslaved to, like a dog on a leash. Seeing that his pathetic entreaties would not get him anywhere, Ronit let go of Alice and went and lay down on his side of the bed.

'Do you think it will be cold up there?' asked Alice.

'In Maine? In January? No, I wouldn't think so,' said Ronit.

'You don't think so?' Alice looked at him hard to see if he was being sincere. There was a smirk on his face.

'Oh, you're joking. I think I'll pack an extra sweater.'

And so it had gone, until they'd finally drifted off to sleep that night. In the morning, they parted, in front of the building, with a brisk kiss, him for work and her for Maine. Ronit set off for the office in despair, wondering if she would ever return, ever agree to marry him.

# 48

By three in the afternoon, with few stops, and no accidents, Alice drove by a sign reading 'Welcome to Swinchendon'. The main highway was many miles behind her now and she'd gained in confidence as the roads had grown smaller and more winding. As soon as she came to a parking lot – for a small, run-down-looking seafood restaurant – she pulled over and fished through her handbag for the directions she'd printed out for the two Jim Smiths. Arbitrarily choosing the one on 8 Stetson Lane, she set out, cheerfully whistling along with the opera, though not so very much in tune.

Stetson Lane, as the name suggested, was a very short street in a series of progressively more residential streets. The town seemed sparsely populated, and on a January afternoon daylight was already grey. No one moved about in the streets and Alice could feel the tug of a stiff sea breeze (or so she imagined it was) on the light Japanese car. She turned down Stetson Lane, and carefully looking at house numbers, she found number five, number seven; now eight should be next – on the other side, but here was only a burnt husk of a ranch or perhaps a trailer. The snow lay in drifts across the driveway, the tops of high grasses peeking out through the shimmering expanse of white.

It was a ruin. Perhaps this was not eight, thought Alice, willing herself to optimism as she felt tears forming in her eyes. She drove to the end of the street, which was near, and yielded nothing by way of houses. She turned the car around, nearly getting a wheel caught in the drift that marked the dead end of the street, and drove back slowly, pinning her hopes on the house immediately after the burnt one, whose address she had not noted earlier. It was number six. Eight was the burnt-out husk. In her imagination, she had played out a scenario in which the wrong house would easily help her discover the right one. She would approach; a kindly woman, perhaps in an apron, most likely baking bread (this was the kind of thing she imagined people in Maine to be doing), would greet her, invite her in for a cozy cup of tea and tell her, 'No, no, my husband is fisherman Jim Smith, out now with the lobster nets [did people fish for lobster in January? She wasn't sure] – you'll be wanting the other Jim Smith, the philosopher [Alice was not sure what profession to assign him, but philosopher was a nice combination of worthy but ascetic] living up the hill; a beautiful girl broke his heart long ago.' And Alice would agree to try a fresh slice of bread as it came out of the oven with a bit of home-made cheese, and then, comforted and warmed, she'd be on her way, with explicit instructions for finding the other Jim Smith, the correct one.

But now there was just this burnt shell and who knows what or who had burnt with it, but everything was gone. Alice bit her lip, feeling tears forming again. She stopped the car in the middle of the road – there was no one there anyway, save a large truck the next minute that just missed hitting her and honked loudly, which was bound for number seven. For a moment, she considered making inquiries at number seven, but it was bedecked with yellow ribbons, with bedraggled 'UNITED WE STAND' and 'THESE COLORS DON'T RUN' lawn signs peeking out of the snow. She winced, and with shaky fingers, picked up the directions for the other Jim Smith. She checked them carefully, then slowly headed down the lane again, and turned up the next street.

The other Jim Smith, the one whose entire home had not been charred to bits, lived at 25 Cherry Street, Apartment 3. Cherry Street proved to be the main street of the village and number twenty-five was a hardware store that also sold some items for tourists – antiques and such. To the left of the hardware store was a door, and along the side of the door were two buzzers marked 'Two' and 'Three', without any name tags. Perhaps in so small a town there was no need. Alice pressed the buzzer for number three and waited. When nothing happened after a minute or two, she pressed it again. Again, there was no response. She felt frustrated not just with the lack of response, but with the fact that she could not see where the apartment was, if anyone was there, the shape of the place. It was around four in the afternoon and dusk was falling. She thought she'd walk up and down the street a bit. Perhaps he was at work and would return shortly.

There was not much to the village. The hardware store, a tackle and fishing shop, a cafe, a post office, a firehouse, a small library. A few people were about, mostly at the cafe and the post office. In the other direction, down the street a way, there was only a small beauty parlour which actually looked crowded. She thought of inquiring there but shrank away when she looked inside and saw all the women cozily chatting and dyeing and drying. She'd never been to a beauty parlour and felt she'd seem an alien if she went in there. When she was small, Clare had cut her hair, and when she'd gotten older, she'd started to do it herself.

The only thing she'd eaten all day was the granola bar she'd stashed in her bag. She hadn't bothered to think about meals, because she'd imagined by now she'd have tucked into a large lunch with her newly found grandfather. Instead, she was alone and it was dark. The hardware store was still open, and she wondered if they might have something to eat. Candy bars, maybe. She could also ask about the tenants. She'd have to do something soon, anyway. The last motels she'd seen had been south of town near the highway.

She walked up the two steps to the shop and opened the door. This caused a cowbell to ring, which startled her. A round, middle-aged man was helping a customer at the counter. He called out that he'd be with her in a moment. She looked around. The store went back quite far, much farther than could be seen from the street. In the front were items of touristic interest, a rack of pamphlets advertising bed and breakfasts, fairs and the like, some of antiques – mostly nautically themed, T-shirts, snacks. She took a bed-and-breakfast pamphlet, though she wondered if such things were open in January. She also took a locally made energy cookie. Holding these tightly, she looked around.

She stopped to look at a display of paint chips, fanned out, nicely lit. Although she never came home with any paint that was not pale blue or green or at most periwinkle, she always liked to imagine each room wherever she lived in a bright colour. What would life be like if she could bring herself to paint her dining room a shimmering tangerine? Would her psychological outlook be different, she wondered? Maybe Ronit would like it? He was never fussy about the colours she chose.

As she stood and looked, she could hear, nearby, the rhythmic shaking of the paint-mixing machine. Then it stopped. She began to have an odd, prickling sensation in her skin. *I'm being watched*, she thought. Carefully, she looked to the left but saw no one. Then she turned her head to her right and saw, paint bucket in hand, seated on a stool, a tall, thin man, white hair, patrician nose, hollow cheeks, wearing a worn oxford shirt covered by a canvas apron with the name of the store written on it. He stared at her, as though she was not real, with no thought he might give offence, as though she were, it seemed, a ghost.

Alice smiled, slowly, so as not to alarm him. She walked towards him, took her glove from her right hand, and held her hand out to him.

'I'm so glad I've found you, at last,' she said.

# 49

The man seemed alarmed to see her move and hear her speak. In that half-light, half-shadow, as Alice had leaned over the paint chip display, he'd seen the face and figure he saw each night when he closed his eyes to sleep, and each morning as he awoke, her small, framed portrait awaiting him on the dresser.

He'd address her then, as he picked out his clothes, the styles not really any different from those days long ago, when they used to walk arm in arm along the cliff or down by the sea, sneaking away from a party, and he, a young man then, had found her to be everything – much more – than a human being. A cosmos, in which her voice, her smell, her grace was all he needed, what he needed more than air or water to survive. He knew for a fact that she was dead now. He'd gone to the funeral just to make sure. It had not bothered him to be shooed away; he knew he was not welcome or invited. When he'd returned after driving the full ten hours without stopping or trying not to stop, he'd gone to bed without food, expecting to cease to be that very night, and so there was no point in taking in nourishment.

Waking up the next morning, he was surprised, and maybe even disappointed, to find that his body was capable of soldiering on when she was no longer in the world. Since then, he'd begun to eat less and less, imagining that at his age, he would easily drift away soon enough. This had not yet happened, although those around him had not failed to notice that he seemed to be afflicted with some horrible wasting disease. Doctor's visits had been discreetly suggested, and when not heeded, the doctor himself had been sent to exam him on a ruse. He pretended he needed a new set of keys cut, which in point of fact, he did. But all he was able to get was that Jim Smith didn't have much of an appetite these days, so he'd suggested he come in for tests – a suggestion politely declined, as always.

And now, like a sage fasting in the desert, a vision had appeared to him, or perhaps the ghost herself had descended to deliver a message. The only thing was, the vision looked a bit off, when he thought about it, not quite Nanette. Too tall, the hair longer, lighter, the clothing more haphazard, and such an open gaze. The ghost put her hand in his, and the hand was warm, but angular. He stood and clasped it, staring at the white knuckles poking through the pale, greyish skin. It was the hand of a young woman, but it was also remarkably like his hand. *Flesh of my flesh*, he thought, and then he knew, maybe not in every detail, but he knew who she was, to some degree, and he lifted his eyes again and studied her face for further clues. He'd been wrong before. She was not just like Nanette, she was like him as well, or parts of him – his mother and sister, for example, were here too.

'But you are too young,' he said finally, 'too young to be my daughter.'

'Yes,' said Alice, beaming. 'That's right. I am your granddaughter.'

'My granddaughter,' he said thoughtfully. He'd known of the two girls, felt assured that they were his, though this had never been confirmed. But, more importantly, he'd never seen them grown, and rarely at close quarters. He'd thought of them at times, but every attempt to make some kind of claim on them had been firmly rejected, and, in the end, he himself had been dispatched, for Nanette was grimly determined to maintain her life as it had been decided long ago, raising her two daughters without scandal, and giving them the same official father as her boys.

'I am the daughter of your younger daughter, Clare. Nanette called her Trixie,' added Alice, after a moment, hoping to loosen his tongue.

'Clare. Trixie.' He thought about these names. He was quite sure he'd known it, though he didn't think he'd have been able to come up with it had anybody asked.

'The other one was?'

'Bix. The older one is Bix, short for Beatrix.'

'Have they known? Do they know?'

'Perhaps. I don't know. I haven't yet discussed it with them,' said Alice carefully, not wishing to turn him against them, at least not so soon. She could explain things later, when she knew him better. 'My name is Alice,' she added, now realizing she had not supplied that information.

'Alice,' he said, carefully, as though uttering a secret, sacred word. *Alice. Alice.* Still not convinced she was real, he wondered if it was possible he was hallucinating from inadequate nutrition in the past months; or if, perhaps, he'd died while mixing paint and an angel named Alice had come to lead him across to the other side, the way one reads of in life-after-death experiences.

To reassure himself, he reached out and touched her hair, which certainly felt like hair. He turned, still holding her hand, and tried the on switch of the paint mixer. The usual racket began immediately. When he pressed stop, it stopped. That seemed real, although of course one could not be sure whether paint mixers existed after death or not. He had always fantasized that in death, he would be reunited with his Nanette. It would be like some pre-Raphaelite painting, or something by Maxfield Parrish. All golden lighting, vivid colours, a Greco-Roman ruin: she and he, all dressed in white, hand in hand. There would be a cosmic hush, no need to talk, an eternal communion.

But perhaps it was actually as Mark Twain had speculated in *Captain Stormfield's Visit to Heaven*. Everything would just stay the same: no harps and so forth. He'd just end up incorporeal but still working at Danford & Sons Hardware Store, but in heaven.

Alice was familiar with the confusion she saw in his face, she thought, at least to some degree.

'You wonder if I'm real,' she offered. 'If I'm a ghost, or some such thing.'

'I do wonder that, yes,' he said, relieved to have the topic broached by someone else to avoid saying something that might be interpreted as demented if she were a human, or disrespectful, if she were an angel or a wraith.

'I am,' she said, with a smile. 'But I know how you feel. I've seen ghosts too. But I'm not one. I came to find you. I wanted to find you before you were a ghost yourself.'

'Just in time,' he said with a laugh.

Outside, a church bell chimed five.

'Closing time,' he said. 'Can I offer you tea, or something like that?' he asked, not sure what would be proper to say next.

'I'd love some,' said Alice.

And so, the two proceeded down the painting aisle, to the front, where the man at the counter was preparing for closing.

'I've got a guest, Tom,' said Jim Smith hesitantly. 'I wonder if I might leave early?'

Tom Danforth, his boss some thirty years, had never known Jim Smith to have a guest that was not someone he recognized. He glanced at the two of them, both beaming, almost giddy, and incorrectly surmised that Jim had gone and found himself some young thing on the internet, the way people do these days. *The old dog,* he thought to himself, and chuckled. A more discerning man would have noticed the physical similarities between the two of them, but Tom was not one.

'Get on with you, then,' he said with a wink and turned to lower the shades.

Jim Smith, oblivious to the innuendo, opened the door for Alice, and they stepped down into the frigid air of the street, now completely dark.

'You'll come to my apartment?' he asked nervously. 'I don't have much to offer. It's an old bachelor's pad, I'm afraid.'

'That would be lovely,' said Alice, who had no intention of letting Jim Smith out of her sight.

They walked outside to the apartment entrance, and Jim Smith unlocked the door, switched on a dim light, and led Alice up a bare wooden staircase. At the top landing there were two doors; he unlocked the one on the right.

Inside, he switched on another light, which illuminated a long, thin, windowless hallway.

'This leads to my apartment,' he explained.

The hallway was bare of ornamentation or carpeting but was lined to the ceiling on both sides with shelves of books. Alice followed him down to a small sitting room with a table, two chairs and a kitchenette. There was a sofa, a coffee table and more shelves of books here. On the wall hung a painted portrait of an elegant lady. The floor was covered by a Persian carpet, somewhat worn. All was neat. There was a door to one side that she assumed led to the bedroom. *I'll sleep on the sofa*, she thought. *He'll offer the bedroom, but I shall take the sofa.*

Jim Smith went to the stove and filled the kettle.

'I don't have much, I'm afraid,' he said. 'I think there are some crackers here.'

'Oh dear,' said Alice, looking down at her hand suddenly. 'I'm afraid I've stolen a cookie from the shop.'

'Well, then, we've got a cookie too.'

'After tea,' said Alice, carefully examining the portrait of the lady, 'I'll take you out to dinner.'

'Well, you needn't trouble yourself.'

'I don't think you eat enough,' said Alice, looking at him in profile as he placed a dish of crackers on the table. 'Now, you'll have to eat more.'

This *now* to which she had referred rattled him. His entire being had been focused on attenuating life, saying farewell and wishing for an end. *Now* had not entered the picture at all. But suddenly he was a man with a granddaughter – maybe more than one! Despite the emotion this brought into his heart, he was not altogether convinced that *now* could so easily replace *then* in his mind.

He placed teabags in two cracked cups, his mother's every day. The saucers seemed to be gone – he looked for them. He took the bag of sugar and poured some into a bowl. There was no milk, he knew. He put the sugar and two teaspoons on the table. When the water had boiled, he poured it into the cups and carried them slowly to the table, placing one on each side.

'My mother,' he said, as Alice was still gazing at the portrait.

'She's lovely.'

'Yes. She was, and very smart too. She knew her poetry.'

'Are these her books?'

'Some. My sisters took some as well. These are also mine.'

'You read a lot?'

'What else does one have?'

'And write?'

'On occasion.'

'Poems?'

'Yes, but long ones, or properly, one long one in particular.'

'Like the Iliad?'

'Something like that.' He smiled. 'There's no milk, I'm afraid.'

'No need,' said Alice. Then she added, 'I'm so happy, so very happy to be here.'

# 50

The rapport between the newly united grandfather and granddaughter was seamless. This was partly because the granddaughter willed it to be so, but also because the grandfather could never really be sure he wasn't dreaming. Days slipped by, Alice sleeping on the sofa, as she had decided to do, and Jim Smith, who had taken some days off work – something he'd only rarely done in the past decades, so how could they object – narrating to Alice the story of his love for Nanette. They took long walks by the shipyards and docks, along the cliffs, on the beach. They took a day trip to the place where Cece Butterworth had lived, now split into apartments – assisted living for the elderly – and took the cliff walk where he'd first declared his love for Nanette.

They dined at cafes, diners and restaurants, and Alice cooked for him, her usual experimental fare, making the best of a paucity of pots and pans and other implements. For once, Alice felt sated with information. Jim told her everything she wished to know. He read to her from his maritime epic. He translated odes by Horace for her; he shared with her his thoughts on the history of colonialism. Of this last, he had taken a particular interest due to his rival's trade in fabrics and other goods from India. Americans took over where the Raj left off, he explained.

Nanette had left him, or shut him out, for the sake of propriety, for social standing. This is what she had told him. This despite her conviction that her husband was a bigamist. But Jim confided to Alice, he always believed that nested in a concern for social standing was a fear of losing wealth. Some of it was naturally hers, but much of her fortune had been invested in her husband's firm at the time of their marriage. That had been the point of the match in the first place.

In the decades that had followed her disavowal of him, Jim Smith had taken up many topics of research and one was this: the neocolonial accumulation of wealth from decolonized places. Bigamy was not the only charge to be made against Grandfather, it seemed. He was also an exploiter.

'She wanted the money and the status, despite the fact that the money was dirty,' he said ruefully.

'Did you tell her all this?' asked Alice.

'I wrote her letters. I don't know if they were ever opened or read. But it didn't matter. What could I have offered her? An apartment above a hardware store in Maine? And consider this, my dear Alice. Could you ever possibly imagine her outside her domain? She was a queen, and I could not offer her that same station in life.'

Alice knew that this was true. There was a brittleness to Nanette, that perhaps had relaxed in the heat of her discovery of her husband's other family (she'd found letters from Violet, Jim explained), but gradually she stiffened again, and with the arrival of her daughters, she'd turned away. How could one raise these girls, the very image of her, without the standing to bring them out in society?

And what about his girls, Jim wanted to know. How had they turned out?

Alice cautiously explained Cece Butterworth's theory to him; that when she had turned back to tradition and appearances, away from him, she'd hardened, and Clare seemed to have suffered the most for it.

'Clare isn't well,' she told him. 'She drinks and behaves badly, and, well, she can be quite mean and destructive.'

'Ah,' said Jim. 'I will do my best to be a father to her, if she'll let me. I know it's late. And what about the other one? Beatrix?'

'Beatrix is like Nanette when it comes to appearances and tradition. I don't think she'll like the idea of having a new father appear in her life. But we can always try.'

'We can always try,' he agreed.

*

The other-worldly cast of Alice's stay in Swinchendon somehow made her forget to call Ronit to tell him she'd arrived and found success in her search. She hadn't called immediately, as promised, and Ronit had no way to reach her. Day by day, his anxiety for her well-being gave way to paranoia, anger and fear. Was she still alive? Had she crashed the car or been done away with by a murderous Jim Smith? Had she left him? And finally, how could she be so callous? He had all along entertained fears that his feelings for her were not reciprocated with equal ardour, and this long silence seemed to confirm them.

She'd taken his car and there was no clear way to get to a small coastal village such as Swinchendon by public transport. He thought of calling the police, but the idea of filing a report filled him with shame. What if he'd been jilted? What fun might the Boston police officers have with something like that – the Indian fellow who'd been abandoned by his WASP heiress. He couldn't face the derision.

Finally, fed up with waiting, he decided to rent a car and go to Swinchendon himself. He conducted internet searches, following in Alice's digital footsteps – all the same links had already been clicked on his computer – printed out maps leading him to the same pair of Jim Smiths and set out in a rented car. He wanted to drive fast – he'd loaded up his music player, not with jazz or classical music as was his usual custom on long drives, but with the rock music of his youth: Led Zeppelin, Peter Frampton, Boney M. Blaring these ballads and anthems in the rented compact vehicle he'd selected – almost identical to his own car – he'd driven, just a little above the speed limit, not a lot, for fear of being pulled over by those same White police officers to whom he had not wished to make a missing person's report.

By four in the afternoon, he'd made it to the charred remains of the home of Jim Smith number one, and by four-twenty, he was parked in front of the hardware store, his heart pounding with anxiety. He'd rung the doorbell, but got no answer, and then he'd entered the store, and asked where Jim Smith, or a woman – tall, thin, brown hair – might be.

The proprietor eyed him suspiciously. Not many persons of colour were seen in these parts. He thought from Ronit's precise diction that he might be an undercover officer or detective, and the thought crossed his mind that that young lady, Alice, who was now staying upstairs with Jim Smith, might be an impersonator, on the lam from the law. He heard about these scams to get social security cheques off seniors, and she was just the sort to gain a person's confidence easily. Especially the confidence of an elderly man who for all appearances seemed to have been on some kind of hunger strike. On the other hand, since the arrival of Alice, Jim's cheeks had glowed a bit brighter, and he'd looked a tad less gaunt.

All these thoughts swam through Mr Danforth's head not quickly but very, very slowly, and Ronit, professional listener that he was, stood and waited patiently for the man to speak. At last, he did.

'They've gone out for a walk, I'd expect. Saw them step out a while back. You wait here a spell, sir. You'll see them coming.'

Ronit, reassured that Alice was not dead, felt less fear now and more anger and paranoia. She still could have left him, after all.

'I'll just wait outside,' he said, and stepped out into the street, where he paced, back and forth, for about fifteen minutes, working himself up into a lather.

It was right about this point that he saw a couple at the other end of the street, walking slowly towards him. As they came into focus, he saw they were a tall, startlingly thin, white-haired man in a grey parka and blue jeans, walking arm in arm with a woman of similar build, in her thirties, a blue knit cap on her long, brown hair, her head leaning gently on the man's shoulder. The woman was Alice.

The two were engaged in a deep discussion and did not seem to see the agitated man ahead of them on the sidewalk. Alice, curiously, held a leash in her hand and at the end of it frolicked a medium-sized puppy.

They were only a few yards from him when Alice looked up and saw him.

'Oh, Ronit, there you are!' she said, breaking away from the older man. She rushed towards Ronit, pulling the puppy along with her. 'We were just talking about the wedding. And look! I got a puppy!'

# 51

If Ronit had had time to think about it, he would doubtless have interpreted these statements of Alice's in the darkest way possible, concluding that Alice was planning to leave him for this elderly gentleman and that they had already reached such a degree of domestic bliss with one another that they had adopted a puppy together. But Jim Smith, perfect gentleman that he was and always had been, strode forward and greeted him with a firm handshake, observing that he had heard much of a positive nature about him.

Ronit stood, bewildered, the words, *wedding* and *puppy* swirling in his head.

'Have you just driven up from Boston?' asked Jim Smith. 'You must be exhausted.'

'Let's get you some tea,' suggested Alice brightly. Delighted to see Ronit and completely unaware of his state of mind or the number of days that had glided by since she'd come to Maine, she chatted on merrily, leading Ronit up the stairs to the apartment, sprinkling the words *our* and *we* liberally throughout her explanations. The puppy, a cocker spaniel mix, had been given to her by the proprietress of the beauty salon in town and had already been named Nigel by his former mistress.

'When we move to the country full time, Nigel will be so happy,' she explained to Ronit, but it wasn't really an explanation, because he had no idea what she was talking about.

'Who is moving to the country?' he asked warily.

'Why – us! You and me, and Nigel.'

'But my work – why?'

'You can move your practice there – it will take time, but you'll find plenty of customers there; Grandpa Jim is sure of it.'

'Oh, yes,' said Jim, with a wry smile, 'plenty of customers in that town.'

'So, you are related then? That's been established?' asked Ronit, unable to find one point in the deluge of conversation that he could grasp hold of.

'Of course we are,' said Alice dismissively. 'Was that ever a question?'

'I thought it was.'

'I told you what a pessimist he was,' said Alice, smiling knowingly at Jim.

'Maybe you should give him some time to get used to everything,' observed Jim, noticing now for the first time the tension Ronit exuded from his spot on the couch.

Ronit smiled weakly. 'That would be nice,' he said. Alice looked at him thoughtfully.

'You do look tense,' she said. 'Are you all right?'

Ronit wanted to yell or cry, but he couldn't very well do that in front of this strange man in the face of all the relentless good cheer.

'You didn't call,' he said quietly, trying to keep his voice as even as possible. 'You didn't call for four days. I was worried. It was difficult to find you and I had to rent a car.'

Alice's face fell as he said these words. It had not until now occurred to her that she had done anything untoward. She hadn't noticed the days and imagined to herself that Ronit was just as happy as she, even though she hadn't told him a thing. The problem may have lain in the magical nature of her meeting with her grandfather. Added to this was Jim's lack of clarity about whether or not the meeting was taking place in waking life at all, so that things like making phone calls and explaining oneself had slipped her mind. Everyone was simply meant to know. Ronit would just know what had happened. His sudden arrival in Swinchendon seemed a confirmation of this.

Alice wanted to cry but she felt such an act would be ignoble. Her face ashen now, blinking slightly, she reached out and held his hand in hers.

'I am sorry,' she said. 'I didn't realize how much time had gone by. I wasn't thinking clearly.'

And this was how Ronit knew what she said was true and his anxiety and anger began to fall away. For Jim, who was standing only feet away tending to the tea kettle, this was the first real sign that he was indeed alive and awake. Ronit's arrival, his hurt feelings, Alice's newly sombre mood – these were all the sorts of things that happened to living people. Was he glad of this? He stood with the hot teapot in his hands and considered as he watched the young couple before him. The reunion in death with Nanette that he had been eagerly anticipating for many months was now postponed, but Alice would always be his angel whether he was living or dead.

'Do you take milk or sugar?' he asked suddenly, and Ronit started because Jim's behaviour throughout the conversation with Alice had been so unobtrusive, he had nearly forgotten he was there.

'Both, thank you,' he said. The puppy came and licked his hand. He wasn't sure he could get used to a dog, but there were many other things he was also being asked to get used to, so he decided not to place Nigel at the top of his list of worries.

Jim handed him his tea, and Alice hers, and sat down at the table to prepare his own.

'I was thinking of a spring wedding,' said Alice, brightening up as she noticed that Ronit looked less upset. 'That way your parents won't be too cold, and they'll have time to buy tickets. And I was thinking it could be a Hindu wedding on the terrace, or a Christian wedding in the church, but I don't so much want a church wedding, do you?'

And here was the wedding again, a topic long taboo between the two of them, one of the reasons he had panicked when Alice had disappeared, and this gave rise to the question of love, and whether she really felt any for him. Although he still worried about the sudden change, this was the thing, he decided, that he should embrace first. The puppy and the grandfather could wait until later.

'Whichever you like,' he said calmly. 'The terrace sounds nice, but it may not be structurally sound.'

'Yes, yes, we'll work on it,' said Alice. 'What do you think of May? Grandpa Jim's birthday is in early May. That might be nice. And he'll give me away, and maybe Biju can officiate …'

'Does he know how to do that?' asked Ronit, surprised.

'I think there are certificates online,' she said. 'It's easy, I've heard.'

'Well, there you go,' said Ronit. Go with the flow, he thought. Just let it happen. That will be the best way.

And so, the planning continued, the three of them soon to be bound together as family sat in the small apartment and cooked, ate, discussed. Eventually, with some wine, Jim shared details with Ronit about his maritime epic, and sections were even read aloud. They discussed psychiatry, gardening, Ronit's family, genealogy, stone masonry, colonialism, and more about gardening and maritime epics deep into the evening. Alice and Ronit took Nigel for a walk outside on the frosty, darkened street, Ronit hugged Alice tightly and kissed her and told her how much he loved her, and Alice apologized once again and looked at the stars, and Ronit gazed into her grey eyes looking up at the stars, and he felt he knew for certain now that though her attention would always be focused somewhere far away, she did love him and she wouldn't leave.

When they returned, they found that Jim had fixed up his bed for them, and the sofa for himself, and though they protested and did not wish to make an old man sleep on the couch, they finally agreed. And perhaps it was because of that romantic starry night and the room to themselves, that on a sunny day in May when they got married on the terrace at the house in Chichester, Alice's belly was fuller than usual, and her cheeks rounder and pinker than anyone had seen them.

# 52

Thus, it happened that Alice and Ronit were married and ended up living in Nanette's house in Chichester, along with Jim Smith, Cousin Biju and a growing number of little girls named Nanette, Geeta and Violet after the various grandmothers and great-grandmothers and not-quite-grandmothers.

Any given day might find Ronit at his small office in town where he did brisk business, and Biju and Grandpa Jim discussing Biju's new novel or Jim's epic, which was still in process. The two might be at the kitchen table, or mending a fence, or fixing a broken pane in the greenhouse but they were always talking wherever they went. As for Alice, she might be mowing the lawn with a push mower, a baby strapped to her front, her long, greying hair floating in the summer breeze, or sitting in the front hall, repairing an oriental carpet at one end while little girls wore it down on the other end with roller skates and building blocks, or in the case of small Violet, simply pulling carefully at one thread at a time as she tried to unravel it.

Alice's inheritance, it had turned out, was not quite up to the task of supporting so many annuities and keeping up a house of that size, so they had started a bed and breakfast, and were also fortunate that at least Ronit had a marketable skill. Biju and Jim both promised to contribute handsomely from their royalties once they started rolling in.

And what of Clare? Although she had reacted with a torrent of abuse when Alice had come alone and broken the news to her, she had eventually agreed to meet her father. Alice had sent Jim in alone to meet her at the Oasis and was astonished when she had encountered them walking happily arm in arm in the well-tended gardens about an hour later. Though she harboured no illusions that her mother needed only this to cure her, she continued to be surprised by Clare's calm and pleasant demeanour whenever she was around Jim. Alice now allowed her to visit the house occasionally, though she always put her up at the inn in town, an arrangement that Clare disparaged but stuck to, nonetheless.

And if Ronit ever wondered why it was that he was supporting a large, eccentric family in a tumbledown house in the country so far from his own home and family, he had only to pull into the driveway and open the car door to have his answer, for suddenly, out of bushes and doors and cellars would pop an assortment of small girls and puppies who would cover him all over in sloppy kisses and proudly show him a broken bird's egg or a bit of rock with moss. And if he walked through the house and looked out in back, and called to Alice, he'd eventually find her squatting in the garden, spreading compost, or on a ladder trying to knock a hornet's nest from the eaves, and she would turn to him with a faraway smile and say, 'Welcome home.'

# Acknowledgements

I owe much gratitude to my editor, Chirag Thakkar, who persuaded me to revisit this novel, begun several years ago, and share it with him. As always, many thanks to my agent, Kanishka Gupta, for his constant encouragement and support. To Camille Guthrie, an early reader of the manuscript and amazing cheerleader, thank you! Gratitude is also due to my husband and my child, who put up with all my literary shenanigans, and to the cats, two generations of whom have supported me during the writing of this novel.

# About the Author

Daisy Rockwell is an artist, writer and Hindi–Urdu translator living in Vermont. Her translations have garnered several notable honours, including the International Booker Prize for translating *Tomb of Sand*, the Warwick Prize for Women in Translation, the MLA Aldo and Jeanne Scaglione Prize for Translation of a Literary Work, and the Wisconsin Prize for Poetry in Translation. *Mixed Metaphors*, her collection of creative non-fiction and poems about the art of translation, is forthcoming from Bloomsbury India in spring 2026, and her memoir, *Our Friend, Art*, will follow from Pushkin Press the same year.